Roanoke County Public Library
Hollins Branch Library
6624 Peters Creek Road
Roanoke, VA 24019

W9-BPR-793

20 1197 0937552 9

NORMAN REEDUS

WITH FRANK BILL

THE RAVAGED

Copyright © 2022 by No. 5 Productions Ltd.
Published in 2022 by Blackstone Publishing
Cover and book design by Zena Kanes

All rights reserved. This book or any portion
thereof may not be reproduced or used in any manner
whatsoever without the express written permission
of the publisher except for the use of brief quotations
in a book review.

The characters and events in this book are fictitious.
Any similarity to real persons, living or dead, is coincidental
and not intended by the author.

Printed in the United States of America

First edition: 2022
ISBN 978-1-0941-6680-3
Fiction / General

Version 1

CIP data for this book is available
from the Library of Congress

Blackstone Publishing
31 Mistletoe Rd.
Ashland, OR 97520

www.BlackstonePublishing.com

To Mingus. I love you like the ocean.
—Norman Reedus

In memory of my uncle John H. "Jack" Bill, 1944–2021
—Frank Bill

HUNTER

One minute, Hunter is coming into work—he's what you call a gearhead, repairing and rebuilding motorcycles—the next, he's acquainting his boss, Ox, with the bike shop's oil-stained concrete, rattling the wrenches that hang from the pegboard walls in Ox's area, where pinup biker chicks in leather bikinis sprawl across custom Harleys and Indians. Entering the shop, Hunter had heard a yelp and a whimper from Ruby, Ox's ex-girlfriend's black-and-tan Walker hound, a dog Ox kept out of spite for her stepping out on him. Hunter had walked in just as Ox's steel-toed boot caught the hound in the ribs.

Next thing Hunter knows, Ox is on the floor, holding his jaw. He wipes blood from his cigarette-stained teeth, spits and coughs, struggles to find air, and tries to stand. "You rotten son of a bitch," he huffs, "you're done. Hear me? Done!"

Hunter lets him get up onto his knees, then serves the obese slob with a solid left boot to the chin, knocking at least one tooth into the leather bandanna knotted around his neck.

"No. *You're* done."

Before he can make good on his words, hands are pulling him from behind. He's still pumped with anger. Hunter jerks free and turns to a tall man with a Brillo-pad goatee and black dreadlocks, arms graffitied with skulls, pistons, eight balls, and serpents. Nothing more than a skeleton covered in skin, it's Slade, one of the other mechanics who work for Ox, holding his palms out to Hunter.

"Take a chill, brother. Just your old friend Slade."

Hunter eyes him, nods in acknowledgment, and pushes his long locks back from his face. "We're cool." Reaching down toward the floor, he takes Ruby by her studded black leather collar. Slade steps aside, and Hunter leads Ruby through the shop, past the grease- and fuel-scented parts of starters, plugs, motors, and exhaust pipes. Smells of Lucas Heavy Duty bearing grease and synthetic motor oil and WD-40 as they walk out the large bay door opening, across the parking area, to the passenger door of his primer-gray '68 Chevy pickup.

Back in the garage, Ox's voice rings up into the black sand-blasted rafters: "You're a piece of military-grade shit. You're done. Never work in this fuckin' town again. Hear me?"

Hunter hears him loud and clear, wants to go back to Ox's area and shut him down.

He had served two years in hell, a.k.a. Iraq, after acquiring a special skill on the GI Bill. That tour was money meant to pay for learning a trade, to reimburse him for the time he gave to Uncle Sam. Forty grand. Uncle Sam never paid. Hunter became a helicopter mechanic, gave his time to the Army Reserve—two weekends a month for two years. He landed a job at the Indianapolis airport, working on planes, only to be called up when the USA invaded Iraq. Four weeks of brush-up basic training in Jersey, then off to Iraq. Being flown out to repair Apaches, Bells, Pumas—you name it, he fixed it. Flying over the burial sites of locals who had died over the years, he saw mounds and mounds of graves, of unknown histories. They soon became a symbol of an unwinnable war, of Saddam's atrocities on the innocent. Other times, he would serve as a team leader, riding as fast as the Humvee could carry him and his team. Every bump and jar of the vehicle's frame made his butt clench tighter, rattled his nerves. Never knowing when they might hit an IED and go *boom!* kept him on high alert, nerves constantly frazzled, wondering whether he and his men would become like those mounds—casualties of an unending war.

Arriving in a town, he and his team of soldiers swept the clay-dirt-sand homes in search of insurgents and intel. With their lost expressions of hope, kids approached them, filthy faced, begging for help. They had torn clothing and busted bare feet. He never gave them candy—why rot their teeth out even faster than normal? So he offered them a tool for learning, always giving them pens and small pads of paper. He showed them how to write the nicknames the soldiers gave them. They loved it, pushing a stick of plastic over paper or skin and watching lines and shapes appear. He always carried several fresh packages of Paper Mate and Mead ballpoints. Those were Hunter's gift.

After giving his time to Uncle Sam, he came back to what he loved. Not the Indianapolis airport. Motorcycles. He told his father he was moving, and took a job at a small Harley dealership in North Carolina. Discovered he could make more on his own, so he began repairing motorcycles out of his garage. He started building them and riding more and more as he piled up more and more of the legal tender. Years passed and word of mouth traveled, and Ox offered him a job. He could do his own thing for more money, with wider recognition, more eyes seeing his work.

Working there for a decade or better, Hunter had come to

discover that Ox was a hothead with a thriving business. He let notoriety flood his brain and fatten his ego. It turned out that the more money he made, the more he turned into a self-centered jackass that shat on everyone and everything. He started to take others and their talents for granted, talking down and threatening everyone behind the scenes, never cutting any slack.

Add to that "animal abuser." Hunter always had a deep affinity for animals, especially hound dogs. Back in Indiana, when he was a kid, his father was always on the road, rolling in late on Saturday or Sunday, road worn and beat, then back on the road by Monday. Hunter spent many summers with his grandfather, who bred, raised, and hunted coonhounds.

Wanting to head home, he gathers his tools. His knuckles are scraped, wet with his and Ox's blood. Walking to his area, rattling the steel tool chest as he locks up all sixteen drawers, he stands like a specimen: round shoulders, wide back, tattoos etched up and down his athletic arms (his favorite being the rabbit on his right inner arm—an homage to his grandfather and the beagles they hunted rabbits with), muscles flexing as he wheels the black tool chest over the cold concrete floor, from the garage and out across the parking lot to his truck. Ruby colors the passenger's-side glass with her nose butter.

Lowering the tailgate, Hunter turns back to the garage's open bay door and yells, "Slade?"

Coming from the garage opening. Pulling a red rag from his hip pocket, he wipes something from his silver-ringed fingers, walks toward Hunter, and says, "You fucked him up good, brother."

"Why I'm leaving on my own terms, or it'll be Johnny Law taking me in on his."

"Guess you need a hand?"

Hunter tells him, "It'd be appreciated."

Stuffing the rag back into his pocket, Slade tells Hunter, "No problem. I got no beefs with you. Always had mad respect for you. Serving in Iraq. And you're a damn good mechanic. Just can't believe you're done." He bends down to grab the tool chest and brace it from the bottom.

Hunter does the same thing, and the men tilt the chest against the truck's tailgate. Hunter attaches a winch from the front of the bed, starts cranking it. Slade pushes. Red-faced and grunting, they muscle it flat into the truck bed. "Can't work for that heart-attack-waiting-to-happen no damn more. Not after this. He finds his feet, confronts me, it won't be in his favor. I'll finish what I started."

"I hear you. I'd join you, but I need the cheddar. Least you're taking Ruby. Good on you, brother."

"Got two rules my dad and granddad taught me: don't wrong a woman and don't mistreat an animal, no matter the circumstances."

Being a traveling salesman, Hunter's dad was on the road full-time. He was good. Could read people. Had a knack for judging character. Was always obsessed with how good he was at selling and at understanding others. Helping them when they were down on their luck. Hunter's mother had run off when he was three or four. Wandering soul, a stripper. Dad told him she wanted to be a model, wasn't ready to be a mother. He was left under the guidance of his grandfather Monday through Friday, and his father on the weekends. When his father came home, he would make time for Hunter—what little there was. Tried to teach him things, telling him stories from the road. Things that Hunter made little sense of. He was more interested in dogs and minibikes. Granddad bought him a Yamaha YZ80 to ride on the farm trails when he wasn't teaching him about breeding, training, and hunting hound dogs. Or sighting in a rifle.

Slade tells Hunter, "Fair enough." Offers his hand, and they shake. "Been an honor knowing you, brother. Don't be a stranger."

Pressing the clutch with his left foot, Hunter shifts into reverse, easing the clutch out and pressing the gas. Ruby sits lapping Hunter's shifting hand with her coarse pink tongue. "I know, girl," he says. "You deserve better than this. Shoulda done this long ago. My heart ain't been into it for a while." He rubs her silky ears. Shifts into first. Then second. Revs the 350 small-block. Hits third, then fourth gear. Then he's crossing over the clean blacktop streets of Rutherfordton, North Carolina, passing brick buildings, historical relics occupied by modern businesses: law office, bank, bar, and coffee shop all in one. Greasy-spoon diner. Hunter takes in the small-town beauty and early-morning aromas of breakfast through the rolled-down window. Ruby lifts her head, inhaling the waft of bacon, eggs, pancakes, biscuits and gravy. Smiling to himself, Hunter feels a warmth after saving Ruby from Ox's abuse. Hanging a right down a street that becomes a country road out of town, he feels the tires move from smooth blacktop to rougher, potholed county roadway.

Scents change from breakfast food to country air, trees, pollen, and new-mown grass. Navigating past a kid pushing a mower, mulching the bright green lawn of a chocolate-brown A-frame, he recalls his father, living in their small rural town in Indiana, teaching him how to mow their yard. They had a nice split-level brick home and a two-car garage that contained every tool imaginable—a nice perk of being a rep for Snap-on. It was one of his many traveling sales jobs when he stayed closer to home, when Granddad was suffering from dementia.

Tools, Bibles, encyclopedias, home alarms, and cable TV.

Hunter's father taught him to keep the height setting of the Briggs & Stratton mower on a three. *Keep from killing the grass— don't wanna mow it too short. Go back over spots you miss. Take a little pride in what you're doing.* He always took his time with Hunter, making sure he understood his instructions, never rushing him. Taught him how to sharpen the mower blade—start by removing the plug wire from the spark plug just in case the damn thing decided to fire on you, then prop the mower on the air-filter end, making sure it was low on fuel to keep it from spilling out and keep it from being top-heavy and tipping all the way over; use a stick of wood to block the blade from moving; using a half-inch socket, turn the retaining bolt counterclockwise, breaking it loose from the shaft; place the blade into the scratched and dented vise on the garage's nicked and stained workbench, add a bit of 3-In-One oil to a ten-inch mill bastard file, and use about forty to fifty strokes in the same direction until each end was a shiny razored silver. Then place the blade back onto the shaft, add some oil to the threads, block the blade in the opposite direction, and tighten the bolt back down just shy of a final turn. He had taught the boy how to change the oil by laying the mower on its side, removing the threaded plug from the bottom of the frame. Lowering it over an old dishpan to catch the oil. Screw the threaded plug back in once it was empty. Add back twelve ounces of thirty-weight oil. He changed the plug every couple of years. Kept the air filter clean by blowing it out with an air hose. Scraped the undercarriage free of wet grass that collected after every mowing. Keeping the mower from rusting and breaking down the metal frame as quickly. What he never realized then, but did now: his dad was teaching him responsibility. Improving his mechanical skills. Teaching him how to take care of something. Be self-sufficient. Same as he did now with his truck and his motorcycles.

He and his father talked only a handful of times a year these days. Not for lack of love. All they had kept was distance. One coast to the next. Divided by time zones. His father wanted a warmer climate on the West Coast. After his time overseas, Hunter had moved to North Carolina because of his buddy Nugget. They had been stationed together in Iraq. Became good friends with a love for motorcycles, small towns, hound dogs, and pumping iron. Hunter's visit turned into a change of zip code.

Turning down a dead-end road, home is a three-bedroom ranch, single-car garage, and well-kept yard of about five acres, plenty of shade from red maples. Along the back property line is farmland. Several hundred acres—plenty of manured air and unfiltered quiet.

The garage door is open. Inside, bike motors, exhaust pipes, chain-and-sprocket kits, master links, axle blocks, camshafts, crank-case covers, and guards lie scattered over workbenches. Wrenches hang from pegboard walls like those in the bike shop where he used to work.

The blacktop drive needs a fresh coat of sealer. Cracks created by the weight of trespass, time, and summer heat. Killing the engine. Opening the door. Out of the truck, Ruby follows, her nails ticking on the hard surface, tongue lapping on Hunter's red-stained fist. They cross green patches of yard, a combination of wild clover and red fescue grass. When the white aluminum storm door swings wide, Olivia comes out, her brunette locks all one length and paint-brushing her toned, sun-bronzed shoulders, where crazed gargoyle tattoos are lighting fires upon the demons that ride ink down her biceps and forearms, ending at her wrists. Braless in a wifebeater and loose pink sweatpants, on bare feet with chipped black toenail polish, she steps over the red brick sidewalk that leads to Hunter, who shakes his head.

"Baby, put on some clothes. You're getting me worked up too damn early in the day," he tells her as he wraps an arm around her waist and squeezes an ass as firm as a helium-filled balloon.

Mashing her lips to his, she takes a breath and says, "Your uncle David called."

Her shape is that of an angel. She tastes of cinnamon and coffee as Hunter tongues his lips and asks, "Hell he want? Haven't heard from him in a year or better."

"Didn't say. Just asked for Hunter. Told him you was working. He left a number, needs you to call him. A-sap." Glancing down at Ruby, Olivia changes the subject. "What's with the petite bitch?"

She breaks from Hunter's embrace, kneels to Ruby, who's all shaking ass and wagging tail and bubble-gum-colored tongue lapping Olivia's face.

Hesitating. Almost forgetting why he was home. Hunter tells her, "Name's Ruby. Purebred Treeing Walker. I caught Ox booting her in the ribs."

Hugging her and rubbing her ears, Olivia says, "Aww, that fat fuckin' degenerate. How could he mistreat such a pretty bitch?" As she is rubbing Ruby's sagging jowlss, it hits Olivia. "Wait. What the shit you doing back already?"

"Handed Ox his ass for mistreating Ruby."

Reaching for Hunter's busted-knuckle hand, she says, "Lost your fuckin' job for a *dog*?"

"Ain't just a dog. She's purebred. Worth every bit of a grand. Comes from a champion bloodline of coonhounds." Olivia rolls her blue eyes. Hunter tells her, "Look, animals don't deserve to be mistreated no more than a woman needs to be abused. You know my rules. So did Ox. They only know what we teach them." He hesitates. "The *dogs* know what we teach them—not the women."

Reaching back down, running Ruby's velvety hanging ears between her fingers, Olivia shakes her head, asks, "So now you're gonna be a goddamned coon hunter?"

"Look, I can get a job at the feed store. Go back to doing bike work on my own from here. Makes no difference to me. The whole Ox gig was wearing on me. Lost sight of why I's even working there. He was cutting into more and more of what I was earning any damn way. I got money put back. And you got your tattoo studio. We're good. I'm kinda at a crossroads."

He walks away from Olivia, up the sidewalk and into the house, Olivia and Ruby following behind.

"Where's the bitch gonna sleep?"

"With us. And she's housebroken. Just need to get her some kibble. Oh, and I need to call Itch and Nugget, get them to give me a hand unloading the toolbox. 'Bout broke my dick with Slade's wormy little ass and us two muscling that damn thing into the truck. Easier with a third set of hands."

Hunter's booted feet clomp over the scuffed pine floor to the marred black leather couch, where he drops down, grabs the cordless phone from the coffee table, where motorcycle magazines lie scattered. Picking up the phone, he asks Olivia, "Where's David's number? I don't got my cell on me."

"On the board in the kitchen. I'll read it off to you."

Hunter eyes Ruby, pats the leather space beside him. Ruby is all feet and uncoordinated happiness, but she curls up beside him, warms his thigh with her head. Exhales through her nose and makes slopping sounds with her tongue and loose jowls. Olivia yells David's phone number from the kitchen; Hunter thumbs the digits on the phone and presses Talk. Listens to the ring tone until someone picks up.

"Uncle David?"

"Hunter? It's about your dad."

Jokingly, Hunter asks, "What's the old man gone and done now?"

Since Hunter could remember, his father, Hank, had always found himself in these situations, immersed in someone else's problems, always at the wrong place at the right time, and he always helped them figure shit out. A Samaritan or savior in many ways.

"He's dead." Long pause. "I'm sorry."

"What happened?"

Hunter tells himself the old man has passed from the salesman existence on earth to the picket fences of life above.

"Mysterious house fire. Won't know anything until the fire marshal finishes his investigation. Coroner gets an autopsy. Why I called you. You're his beneficiary and executor of his will. How soon can you get to California?"

JACK

Blood forked from Jack's nostrils and crusted on his bulbous upper lip. Dancing at the four-way stop like a Yaqui shaman hallucinating on peyote, he felt the music flowing like a lullaby through his brain as he stomped the rubber tread of his heels into the baked orange dust of unpaved road. Nearby, standing in front of a run-down stucco bodega the same shade as their skin, two men in life-stained T-shirts and ragged dungarees fingered an armadillo-shell guitar and a panpipe, with a battered lard can between them for donations. From doors and alleyways, bodies slowly appeared, pausing to view this mad, crazy gringo.

Jack held his phone up into the sky, capturing his moment. Videoing himself. Not wanting to lose it as he had lost everything else.

The beatdown had been delivered by two men with flesh the color of a high-dollar medium-roast coffee bean. That was what went through Jack's mind when local number one, whose face was covered with acne scars and patches of steel-wool beard, asked if he had a smoke. Smiling, with his thumbs hooked beneath the straps of the worn black-gray Osprey pack that hugged his pudgy frame, Jack had said, "Sorry, young man, I do not smoke." That was when local number two mashed Jack's foot. Man number one stole his wind with a fist to the diaphragm, and Jack's knees had discovered the heated ground with a thud. Doubled over, salt-and-pepper locks stuck to the creases of his forehead, he'd reeled backward as his nose was introduced to man number two's right knee.

Still dancing. More locals came to view this crazed ritual, pointing and whispering among themselves, shaking their heads.

Replaying the actions in his mind, Jack remembered how his nose got smashed, how his blood tasted rich with iron. He remembered feeling like a child who has fallen from his bed. On all fours, dazed, huffing for air, he'd searched for a way to calm his breath, to center his panic.

Another hand had groped his right butt cheek, relieved him of the leather shape that was his wallet. And like that, he was left to view the pair of holey Chuck Taylors sprinting away.

In his peripheral vision, to the left and right, shapes were moving, approaching. All he could do was spit blood and cry. And he cried hard, bawled until it changed to loud laughter. Laughing at his weak, pathetic self.

He was discovering his center.

Backpacking through Argentina, hitchhiking from one fueling station to the next, devoid of conflict, of violence, in search of something more than what he once believed was an existence. Seeking the meaning of words spoken by his ailing mother. Getting mugged in a dirt street on the outskirts of Santiago de Chile. Rolled for two thousand, maybe three thousand, dollars. In America, it was enough to cover a middle-class household's monthly mortgage. Groceries, car payment and utilities, maybe a few movies and dinner out with the wife on a weekend. Here, in this desert outpost of a struggling country, that was several months of cushion. How many simple pleasures of life had Jack missed in his pursuit of the almighty dollar? Reflecting back on his life, more than he could count.

His Rolex watch, ID, insurance card, all his money—gone, except for his passport in his pack, and what he'd hidden in his left sock, which he must now spend on nourishment.

Yellow corn, ground between stones and roasted over coals. Woman's hands, callused and sun scorched, working the blade through peppers, onions, tomatoes, pushing back a strand of hair as she adds beans. Forearming sweat from her moist cheeks, she wraps the hash of vegetables and legumes up like a gift for the starved and scavenging, handing the fresh delicacy to Jack. The juices trickle down the stubbly beard, burning the scraped flesh, but the ripe taste triggers something he has not known since he was a kid: recognition of his own hunger. Of being fed. He has worked his life away so that he might never again know that feeling of want or need.

What he realizes in that moment is something he had forgotten: *appreciation.*

Before all this, the goal was money. Not to *struggle* like his mother, who had worked three jobs to keep a shingled roof over her and her boy's heads. To keep fresh food on the table and a clean house and a warm bed. And she had.

On the day she died, lying on coarse hospital sheets amid the smell of disinfectant and the beep of monitors, her blue-veined hand cold in his warm palm, she spoke the last words she ever would to Jack: "Run. Run and never look back."

He had wanted to laugh. *Run?* Run from *what?* After all he had amassed. A 6,500-square-foot house. Vacation home in Florida. Cars. A secure retirement. No want or need unfulfilled. But still he worked. Sixteen-hour days, sometimes eighteen.

That is what he remembered on all fours in the dust, watching those faded red Converse high-tops scampering away.

Jack had never understood what his mother's words meant. After all he'd worked for, buying her a new home, getting her the best of whatever she wanted. But all she ever wanted was happiness for her son. For Jack. And then, on his knees, hearing those feet recede into the distance, Jack realized that they needed the money more than he.

Working his way up from his knees to his feet, he'd felt the crack and pop of his joints, felt all the years of expensive dinners, felt the age. And he felt the heat of the day, intensifying the weight of his pack. Placing one foot in front of the other, limping at first until the hurt leveled out into a walk. Eyes gawked and followed his every step. Feeling the pain in his gut from the punch. From hunger. Ignoring the faces. Twenty-four hours had passed since he last ate. Hitchhiking to San Pedro de Atacama. Wandering in a dazed and famished state to the crossroads. Lifting his face to the sun's warmth. Images and sounds came in snapshots alternating between reflection and real time. The volume of reality was being turned up. Growing louder and louder. Stucco buildings the shade of smoked vanilla lined the dirt street. Men played music. His wallet stolen, his identity gone. All the actions came in a mad whirl.

The sun was turning Jack's pale sixty-five-year-old flesh the color of Irish red ale as he began to lift and test his creaking limbs. Right leg first, then the left. Pins and needles and a jolt of electricity coursing through his marrow. Sweat darkened his olive-drab fatigue pants and stained navy-blue "Life Is Good" T-shirt. Dust kicked up from his booted feet as he stomped in time with every clap of his damp, doughy hands, creating a rhythm that had nothing to do with the men who strummed their *charangos* like marionettes on strings, singing their Chilean folk music. No, all that echoed through Jack's mind was what his mother had said before accepting her own finality, her sclerotic lungs wheezing those words: *Run. Run and never look back.* Words he had never understood and always questioned.

All around him, people watching began to clap and stomp their feet. Jack pulled his phone from his pocket, held it high. The music he danced to wasn't from the street musicians; it was in his head. A backdrop to the echo of her words. But then, it wasn't just her words. It was the loss—of his daughter, his mother, then his wife—that had brought him here after everything he'd been through.

And now, covered in dust from his unplanned street dance, mouth full of vegetables and cornmeal bought with his last dollars, Jack reflects on how it all started. How it all haunts him. What he is in search of.

ANNE

Anne's head throbbed from the pain of memories—her mother's hard palm cutting the air and thudding her face, with the words *little cunt* attached to her whiskey-stained breath. Pale hands shook, remembering the time her father gripped her wrist at the circled burner glowing a skin-scalding orange, a fork pressed to it until it smoked, then branding her flesh until her eyes watered and she screamed, his beer breath spitting, *That'll remember you to be sure dishes is clean. Work all goddamned day and come home to this bullshit.*

Today came a blitzkrieg of words exchanged in anger: "Little bitch, skipping school again, gonna turn into a goddamned retard!"

"Better than a *drunk*!" Anne retorted. Her words sharp. She had learned that in this house, when you got hit, you hit back even harder with whatever was handy.

The Jim Beam bottle missed her head and exploded like a rotten tomato against the faded-blue kitchen wall. The cider-colored liquid sprayed the dishes piled along the scuffed Formica countertop, soaking the crumbs of PB&J sandwiches that had been eaten down to the crust, Lay's chips that had been crunched, Jack's pizzas that had been pilfered of their toppings, sticky cups of Mountain Dew that had been spilled. From the unwashed clothing that lay on the cracked tile flooring, Anne grabbed shirts, pants, socks, bras, and panties.

Anne was done. Had been planning for months to pack what little she had and run. Run as far as she could from this shithole that had been her home since birth. She and Trot, her best friend, had talked and talked. Wanting to jettison themselves from their shit lives, from her abusive domestication and Trot's longing to be understood. He had moved from El Paso, Texas, to Johnson City, Tennessee. Had been caught hopping trains off and on, had run with a group of dropouts who called themselves the Recon Rejects. Trot knew the ins and outs of freight hopping. How to hop one, when to hop one, and where to hop one. He knew where they would go: Louisiana, he'd said. There they would find a jungle where the hobos, dirty kids, and crust punks camped out. Earn their keep during the day: panhandling; flying a sign; dumpster diving; running trash cans for food, water cups, or clothing. Get accepted into a real family by people who understood them instead of abusing them with harsh words, trying to change who they were. No more dirty dishes, bloody fists, or flesh singed with eating utensils.

Hormones and rage feed her decision as she grabs her cell phone and charger and stuffs them, along with every garment she can, into the faded and dirt-smudged pink JanSport pack meant for schoolbooks, when she wasn't skipping. Her mother did not understand how this wasn't right, this way of living, only that her daughter had skipped school, not caring how the kids pointed and pranked and made Anne the butt of their jokes and puns about how she reeked of cigarette smoke and dressed in wrinkled clothing. But she was clean—always made sure to bathe, even if out of bath soap. If she had to, she would use dish or laundry detergent that dried and cracked her flesh. Always brushed her teeth. Some-times with baking soda when her mother was on one of her benders and her father was on the road running a delivery with the big eighteen-wheeler that kept everything afloat—food on the table, the rotted roof overhead, and booze flowing through their veins.

Anne had withdrawn from others. Words cut like serrated edges. They hurt but not nearly as much as her family's actions, their home, where she shared a single bedroom with two sisters. The other bedroom was her three brothers', and the living room and dining room were her mother's, where she collected ashtrays of cigarette butts, empty beer and whiskey bottles. The TV blar-ing with talk shows, cable movies, and forensic docuseries, window blinds pulled down. Sleeping off her hangover during daylight on the broken-down, cat-haired, cigarette-cherried brown vinyl couch, she was up by four every afternoon, starting with coffee, moving to bourbon, then chasing it with beer. Putting pizzas or boxed lasagna in the oven for her kids' supper every evening.

Petite and pale, with a mop of strawberry-colored tangles on her head, Anne wore rock concert T-shirts, tattered denim, hippie-handmade bracelets, and chipped fingernail polish on chewed nails. Some would label her socially awkward, but hey, who wasn't at seventeen, almost eighteen? Anne had had enough tough love. After the heated words and the near miss with the whis-key bottle, her mother had stepped out, cruised down the street and over to the liquor store at a shopping center, for a thirty-pack of Miller High Life, another ten-dollar bottle of Jim Beam, and a few packs of Camels.

Steve Earle's "Copperhead Road" blares through the closed door of her brothers' bedroom. Anne roots through her father's hickory-stained dresser, knowing that the smaller piece of protec-tion is somewhere buried beneath socks and boxers. Hefting its weight, she had forgotten how heavy the .38 revolver was. Her father had taken her and her sisters out to a trucking buddy's farm. Let them shoot aluminum cans from a picnic table while he and his buddy Toad sipped brews and smoked reefer. Grabbing the box of cartridges, she sinks them into her pack along with the gun.

Back in the kitchen, Anne pulls a Folger's can from the freezer. Takes from it a cold wad of twenties. Drops the roll in her JanSport pack.

"The fuck you doing with Dad's coffee can?" Mitch, her brother, startles her.

"Nothing. Mind your own."

His freckled skin is like uncooked bratwurst, clashing with cinnamon hair and a woolly-worm unibrow. Fifteen and a half with a naturally muscular build, he is bullheaded and cocky. "I don't think so. You're fucking stealing from Dad."

He starts coming at her, but they are separated by the table. "Fuck off!" she hollers. Flinging her pack over left shoulder, she grabs a bacon-greased plate and Frisbees it at his head. Missing him, it smashes on the tile floor, adding its shards to those of the Jim Beam bottle.

"You're so fucking dead!" he growls through gritted teeth. Anne turns to run; Mitch grabs at her, catches her pack, and spins her violently around. She spits in his face. Now Mitch is possessed. Gripping Anne's arms, he drives his forehead between her eyes. Her head and everything in it vibrates. Her eyes tear up. Released, she stumbles backward, vision blurry, head spinning. Her left hand stabilizes her against the counter. Mitch comes at her as an unfocused outline. Anne fumbles for a skillet handle, wraps her hand around it, and parts the air. Before Mitch knows what happened, Anne gashes his temple with a thud of cast iron.

Anne doesn't know what hits the ceramic floor tiles first: Mitch or the skillet. But next thing, Anne bangs her palm against the aluminum door to open it before she cuts to the side yard of dead grass. Her mother pulls up beneath the rusted carport. Running, Anne jumps over the charcoal grill that lay on its side. Ashes and half-burnt briquettes lay clumped like gray vomit. The car door slams. Chest heaving, she glances back at their home: siding stained the color of nicotine, missing shingles, rusted swing set, windows with torn screens. She had spent many hot summers, icy winters, and tornadic springs in that house. Anne just wanted a family—parents who didn't replace affection with abuse, who didn't drink and swear and scream and break shit as a means of bonding. And siblings who didn't accept this lower level of existence as normal. She is the eldest daughter, the one who wants something more. Then come her mother's screams from the house. Anne turns away, her feet digging into the ground. Hoping she didn't kill Mitch, the middle son, she zigzags from one neighbor's yard to the next. Screams become distant as she lengthens her stride, putting distance between the life she had always known and the one she wanted, whatever and wherever that was.

Anne's heart still pounds. She hopes that Mitch is breathing. Hopes his head hurts, though. The sun had dropped from the blue sky to hide behind the trees. Shaky, she pulls her pack off. Unzips it. Still walking, she reaches in for her cell, shrugs the pack back on. Several missed calls from her mother. Anne texts Trot.

Pack a bag. Meet at the shack. Blowout with mom. I might've killed Mitch. Ready to forget this town.

A dog barks somewhere. Voices converse from porches. Smells of food being grilled. Barbecued. People tilting back their evening swigs of booze. Sounds. Words. Muffled laughter, music playing, vehicles traveling from other streets, motors revving, everything rising in pitch and volume, vibrating Anne's eardrums. What if she has killed Mitch? She will go to jail. They will be hunting her down. It will be on the news. People will be looking for her. She will be a fugitive. An outlaw.

Then comes the pinch and clamp of teeth. The growl and tug. Jeans rip in the animal's slobbering mouth.

Her muscles and tendons exude sudden alarm. "Shit!" she yells, and starts to run. The weight of her life, crammed into her pack, slows her movement over the ground. She cuts over streets, through more yards. Shapes, sounds, and objects blur. The dog pants on her heels. Must be old, or she would have felt the teeth again by now. Anne huffs for air. Her heart punches and punches against the bones surrounding it. Running hard through a field. Finally, in the distance, the condemned lot. Boneyard of cars, all makes and models scattered over the acres. Rusting chain-link fence. Anne runs the perimeter to the back of the property, to what looks like a small barn, its wood grayed with age. The dog huffs and barks behind her as she leaps onto the fence. One foot planted in the wire, hands grasping the top course of rusted links, she swings her free leg up and over. The other leg follows suit, until something latches on—the dog. It had jumped and now has her ankle and a fold of her jeans locked between its jaws, its weight hanging and jerking. She would swear that ligaments and tendons were ripping apart like putty. The dog uses the fence, its paws climbing and bracing, its thick neck jerking. Tugging.

"Get off me, you bitch!" she commands. "Let GO!"

The dog is going to shred her leg. So she swings her other leg back over, comes down with all her weight and force, and drives her heel into the dog's jaw. With a yelp, it releases her leg. It takes everything she has to pull herself back up, swing one leg over the top of the fence, then the other. Weak and spent, she drops to the dirt on the opposite side. For a few seconds everything goes black.

Dazed, opening her eyes, she feels her world tilting, unbalanced.

Her leg aches. Reaching toward her ankle, she pulls back the torn denim. Her flesh is purple and red with bloody indentations from the snapping teeth.

The dog growls and barks, pawing and digging at the ground below the fence. Anne brandishes her middle finger at the dog. *Fuck you!* And thinks about the gun in her backpack. The hurt in her ankle where the bastard had clamped down on her. She stares at its smoky coat, black ticking and matching ears pointing up like spearheads. It is some kind of crazed cattle mutt, growling and whining, pawing at the dirt.

Kneeling down to unzip her pack, reaching in to feel the cold heft of the pistol, she pulls it out and points it at the dog's head, but she doesn't have the mettle to shoot the damn thing.

Inside the barn, old straw is spread everywhere. She tosses her pack down, sits on an old thin mattress. A few red and blue milk crates serve as chairs. Walls are covered in graffiti. Anarchy symbols. Black Flag. Slayer. Slipknot. Pot leaves. Clown heads. Penises. Boobs. She and other kids from school have been hanging here since she could remember. A hiding spot from their parents when shit went south. When one needed to drop out. Disappear. De-load.

Everything started to hit her. The adrenaline is beginning to slow, to dump. Fogging her mind. She mashes her eyes shut. Images of her brother lying on the kitchen floor. Blood ponding like spilled paint. Her mother cursing her, throwing that bottle at her. Packing up. Running away. Getting chased. Her leg starts to stiffen with hurt. A panic surges within her. She wants to scream.

Taking a deep breath, counting to ten, knowing Trot will be here soon, she exhales. They will talk it out, make their plan. Taking another breath, she wants to be anywhere that isn't Johnson City, Tennessee. But more than anything, she hopes Mitch is still breathing. She exhales again.

HUNTER

He had lost his purpose. Deep down, he knew that it was why he exploded on his boss. Rescuing Ruby had been the right thing to do, returning his sense of morality. He had gone overseas with the army, not so much to fight a war as to help people. Then he'd come home and eventually started working for Ox. Drudging day after day in that shop to meet deadlines. Rebuilding bikes. The job no longer mattered. The nine-to-five had become a grind, lost its flavor. Not that he had ever acquired a taste for it. There was nothing to gain in doing the bidding of others on his own time.

He feels the weight of the toolbox against his callused palm. And the weight of his uncle telling him his father had died in a house fire. Add "mysterious" to that caption, and the wheels in his brainpan begin to crank. Both things create a burn—one in his knees and lower back, the other in his conscience. Itch on one side, Nugget guiding the center, they slide the massive bulk to the concrete amid the clank and clatter of wrenches, sockets, and breaker bars and roll it into Hunter's garage.

He hadn't heard from his father in months. They were never what one would refer to as "close." They talked. Stayed in contact, but visits were a rare thing. He couldn't remember the last time they were face-to-face. Now the news of his passing weighed Hunter down.

Nugget asks, "When's the last time you spoke to your ole man?"

Nugget keeps his head shaved slick beneath the biker ball cap with a flaming death's-head and bold letters that spell RIDE TILL DEATH. With a black-and-chrome goatee, a neck like a grizzly bear's, and arms like two twenty-five-pound hams stenciled in ink, he cuts an unconventional figure in his Misfits T-shirt with a big white skull, Dickies jeans, and biker boots.

"Been months."

"That's a kick in the dick, brother," Itch tells him.

Like Nugget, Itch is massively built, though shorter. He has a black-stubbled head, thick beard the color of bourbon, big shoulders and chest, tatted arms, and a fondness for the metal band Pantera. He is always sporting a T-shirt with their logo. Today he wears faded Levi's jeans and solid-black DC skate shoes, preferring comfort over the tough-guy appeal of boots.

Wheeling the toolbox to the far wall, away from where Hunter's nearly three thousand pounds of Olympic weights, squat rack and bench, pulldown station, and reverse hyper take up space, they push the box between two workbenches—two-by-four legs and a half-inch plywood surface, splotches of paint, grease, and oil. Motorcycle stickers all over the place, with American flag Punisher skeletons, skeletons riding bikes with such captions as "Forever on Two Wheels," "Dark Side Rider," "When in Doubt, Throttle Out," and "Ride or Die."

Bike parts laid out for a custom job, a rebuild, the reconstructing of a Buell S1 Lightning. Same as his first bike. Somewhere, there was an order to all this, some sense to be made—Hunter just didn't know what it was. Attacking his boss. Rescuing Ruby. Losing his father. Rebuilding this bike. And, now, having to travel to California.

"When you fixing to leave?" Nugget asks.

"Soon as I can get packed. Get my phone, Google maps. Just need some clothes; then I'll take my time, get there when I get there."

"You ain't going alone," Itch tells Hunter. "Nugget and me is going with."

"Best get your asses home, then, get packed. Ain't waiting around."

"Roger that, brother," Itch says.

"Don't forget your roll and tent for camping."

Hunter hears Itch's and Nugget's 1978 shovelhead Harleys roar to life, tear down Hunter's drive, and burn through the valley, their straight pipes warning everyone on the country back road that they were coming through. Walking out of the garage, toward the house, the sun heating things up through the trees, Hunter recalls how he had saved his money working at a downtown gas station with a single-bay garage, a Union 76, pumping gas, fixing flats, replacing wipers and taillights, until he had enough money to buy that orange-and-black Buell S1. Proud was how he had felt. As his father had told him he would. *You work and save, buy it on your own, you'll appreciate it more.* Had a V-twin four-stroke, pushrod-actuated overhead valve, self-adjusting hydraulic lifters with two valves per cylinder. Electric start. Five-speed. Kevlar belt. Rear suspension single shock, spring preload. Compression and preload damping. Top speed 128.9 miles per hour. Rode the tread right off the tires on that son of a bitch. Then his buddy Money Thompson got thrown in the can—pulled over one night after leaving the 76 station late. They had sat in the auto bay after closing. Shooting the shit and loading up the brass bat of Money's one-hitter with some primo skunk bud. He always kept the wooden box under his driver's seat. Had a burned-out taillight Hunter had offered to replace at the station. "Don't worry about it," Money had told him. "Another time." Money was too stoned for his own good. Eyes frosted by glaze and burning red hot, he could hardly place one foot in front of the other. Should have listened. Next thing Hunter knows, he's at home, crashed in his warm bed, when his phone is ringing with a collect call from the local hoosegow, wanting to know if he'll accept the charges. Money got pulled over for the taillight. Was asked to step from the car when Barney Fife's flashlight registered his heavy, filmed eyes. A quick search beneath the front seat was enough for a paraphernalia charge, and the diced-up green dope inside was another tiny charge for possession.

Money, untrue to his birth name, had none. Parents were deadbeats who would rather let him rot in jail than bail him out.

Go to Hunter hocking his Buell for bail money.

Go to Hunter never getting paid back by his buddy Money. It seemed the name was more aspirational than accurate—the fucker was always broke.

Go to Hunter never getting his bike back.

But his father always told him, you never turn your back on someone in need. Friend or stranger. Walking toward the house, Hunter remembered how his father had always talked of giving hitchhikers a lift. Of helping people who had broken down on the road, helping them change a tire, giving them a lift to get gas if they had run out. Some folks called it being a good Samaritan. His dad called it being a person.

His father, Hank, always came home with stories. One Friday evening, he brought home a 1911 .45 Colt handgun. Told Hunter about a man down on his luck. Broke. The wife had packed up, taken the kids, moved back home to stay with her folks. He was out of gas, way off the beaten path down in southern Missouri. Hank carried a spare gas can in his trunk, gave the man a lift to a pump-pay-and-eat mart. Hank paid for everything. The husband told Hank he'd lost his job. Next went his identity and self-worth. He had decided he was done with life. Was going to drive to an undisclosed area, a state park, or some pull-off out in the middle of nowhere and eat a bullet. Those Reagan years were tough at first. Lines with government cheese. Unemployment rates were like the murder rates in Detroit, Michigan, or Gary, Indiana—off the charts.

Hunter's father got the man some supper. Lifted some of the gloom. Brought some color back to his complexion. Bought him some groceries for the road, some gas for his car. And when Hank dropped him off, he gave the man all the money he had left in his wallet. Told him he wanted to buy the gun he'd planned to off himself with. Then gave him a phone number to call for a job, said tell them Hank Offutt had told him to call, that they'd have work for him. After that, he told the man he needed to get his house in order. Get his wife and kids back and don't give up. There was always hope. Always another mission, a new life waiting—you just had to go out and find it. Hank told him how his wife had run out on him several years after Hunter was born. Some kind of free-spirit hippie bullshit. How, with his father's help, he had raised Hunter while working on the road as a salesman. It wasn't easy, but he was a father with a son, and he had responsibilities.

Hunter hadn't thought much about it then, but now he reflected on how he'd helped Money out, the way his father had helped out a guy down on his luck, who was going to kill himself. His father had maybe saved that man's life, had maybe taught Hunter something without his realizing it—something he never acknowledged then but understood now. Giving up something of value to help another. How damn many lessons had his father maybe tried to teach him as a kid and he never realized it?

In the house, Olivia sat on the couch reading a *Tattoo* magazine, her brunette locks pushed over her ears, one hand balancing the magazine, the other rubbing Ruby's head.

"Get the toolbox unloaded?"

"Unloaded and wheeled into the garage."

"Didn't block any of the weights, did you? Don't need the extra workout of moving that heavy son of a bitch."

"All good and outta our way."

"Cool beans." Olivia paused, then told Hunter, "Go do whatever it is you gotta do. I'll be here with Ruby when you get back. I can see you need time, that it's weighing on you."

"Itch and Nugget say they're gonna ride along."

Smiling, Olivia said, "They're true to you."

"Always have been." Staring at Olivia, he smiled. Walked over and kissed her on top of her head. "Enough of the soap opera bullshit. Best get packed if I wanna get some miles in before nightfall."

Walking from the living room to the hallway, stepping down the hardwood to the bedroom, the only thing that brought Hunter peace of mind was being on his bike out on the open road. Air peeling his skin. Sunlight lifting his mood. Alone with his thoughts. At one with his surroundings.

Pulling his vintage military olive-drab backpack from the closet, he grabbed some T-shirts, jeans. Underwear from his oak dresser. Took a .45 Colt and a box of shells from his gun cabinet in the corner. Same gun his father bought from that guy all those years ago. A gift before Hunter left for the war. Dad felt it held some kind of luck. For Hunter, it was one of the few items he had from his father. It had sentimental value and also gave personal protection. You never knew what you might encounter when riding cross-country.

Slinging the pack over his shoulder, he grabbed a road atlas and compass from his office, just in case he needed it. Hunter was old school. Coiled his phone charger. His phone pressed into his pocket along with his matte-black Benchmade Infidel double-edged knife. Though he still had three grand in his wallet from work that he'd never deposited, he needed to stop by an ATM for some extra travel cash.

He bent down and kissed Olivia, patted Ruby on the head, told Olivia, "No idea how long I'll be gone."

"Your father died. I don't expect you to punch a damn clock. I just expect you to come back."

"I will."

Stepping out the door, Hunter walked down to his knucklehead motorcycle. With an onyx hand-painted Sportster gas tank, a rigid Big Twin setup, chrome ape-hanger handlebars, and tall sissy bar in the rear, with a 93ci S&S engine and a five-speed Indian transmission case. Hunter loaded his pack onto the sissy bar; grabbed his sleeping bag, small tent, and from the garage his bass-tube-looking black barrel bag with a few tools, spark plugs, and flat repair kit, just in case, and tied it all down. Then he latched on his flat-black skull half helmet, kick-started the bike, inhaled deep, gave the bike some gas, and roared down his driveway, knowing his next mission.

JACK

He can't stay here, in this woman's mud-brick home with a straw roof, just outside San Pedro de Atacama.

Outside, orange dust funnels up into the clear blue, obscuring the view of sunbaked mountains and salt flats. It reminds Jack of something from a Sergio Leone Western.

Inside the house, behind the electric-azure-blue door, wanting to leave, Jack starts to get up from the table carved from a hefty slab of tree. Slickplaned with rounded corners, nails set and filled. The chair he sits in is similar, built by hand, not mass-produced in some soulless factory. Sanded smooth, stained, and sealed.

The woman sits across from him, her liver-spotted hand pressing down on his thigh. Her touch is a working woman's—strong and callused, knowing. "Stay," she tells him.

Silver streaks the thick black hair hanging to her neckline. Her lips, smooth and dry, look penciled on as if from a portrait of Frida Kahlo. The woman's complexion is a pecan shade, as if toasted by the high-desert sun, and her face frames eyes that glitter black and bottomless and seem to read his soul.

"Ma'am, I cannot accept your offer of kindness," he tells her.

She laughs. "I welcomed you into my home. And here you sit. *Un gringo loco.*" She gives him an appraising look. "*Cálmese, señor.* You need rest. To talk. Forget. Let go of your *demonios.* Then you can leave. After some good drink. Some food. Relaxation."

Money. It was all he contemplated, all he had ever worked for. And right now he had nothing. No medium of exchange. No currency of any kind. Couldn't get a hostel. Couldn't argue. It would be dark soon. Too late to hitchhike. To walk out from wherever this was and into the Atacama Desert, which would soon turn cold. He might not even get a lift. Or he might get in with the wrong people and get beaten and mugged for being dumb, attacked and maybe eaten by a cougar. Come morning, maybe he could find a Western Union, get money wired. He could at least pay her for her troubles.

He says, "First thing tomorrow, I will walk into town and I will get money wired to me. *Dinero. Telegrama.* Then I can compensate you for your generosity. That is the only way I will stay here."

She shakes her head emphatically. "*No quiero su dinero.*" She pauses, then goes on in a softer voice. "You broke down. I watch. You dancing to the music. Not to the *guitarrista* or the flute of *bambú*, but to your own music." She taps a wizened finger against her temple.

She had watched Jack's actions—his breakdown, his dancing at the crossroads. As if in a trance, he had begun to shuffle step. And that was when she hurried up to him—gripping his arm, stopping him—and offered him shelter for the night. A place to relax. Regroup. She told him to follow her. And he had, but now, as everything was settling in, sitting on the hard chair in her kitchen, he wonders whether he made the right call. Above the long bench where his backpack lay, hung wood-framed pictures of her family, of her and her husband, possibly her son, grandson. Everyone smiling on some holiday, festival, birthday. Appearing peaceful. Content. It feels almost like being back home and fifteen years old, being comforted by his own mother.

Pushing a damp lock of hair back from the age lines etched into his forehead, he sticks out his hand just as he would to a business client. "*Señora*," he says, "I appreciate you helping me and offering me a place to sleep tonight. My name is Jack Dudgeon."

Smiling, she tells him, "I am Fabiola. I make ponchos and throws, and sometimes I do pottery to sell to the *turistas*. It is as my ancestors did for ages." She stands up and walks over to a counter, where bottles line the sill below a small window. "Who have you lost?" she says. "It is staining your being. You wear it like the clothing that covers your flesh. Death does this to a person."

Astonished, Jack says, "Fabiola, you are reading me like a stock report. I . . ." His eyes tear up. "I have lost so much in the past five years."

Uncorking a bottle, Fabiola grabs two clay cups from a door-less cabinet and pours a dark liquid into each. She says, "I know death. I, too, have lost much. Let me tell you, all we got is time."

As she shuffles back toward Jack, the filled cups in her hands, he demands, "Why are you being so kind to me?"

Holding a cup out for Jack, she says, "Drink. It will ease your torment while we talk."

He takes the clay cup from her. Fabiola sits back down, opposite him at the table. Eyes tunneling into him. "My husband, my son, and my grandson all worked the Chuquicamata copper mine. Made a good living. Long hours." Pausing for effect, she presses the middle finger and thumb of her right hand together. *Snap.* "Taken from me like that. *Muertos. Una explosión.* The mine collapse on top of them."

Jack takes a swallow and somehow keeps from grimacing. He has tasted some great Chilean red wines before. This isn't one of them. "That is horrible," he says. "I'm really sorry for your loss."

"Time is all we have on this earth, Jack. Never take it for granted. Up to you how it is spent. You can wake up angry at the world every day and blame yourself, blame others, drown in self-pity. Or you can do things that make joy. Help others. Only so many breaths, heartbeats, morning views of the sun to be had." She holds up the clay cup. "This is what you need. Let you *see* your pain. Sort your troubles. Open your mind. You need to feel. To realize." And she takes another sip.

Realize what? Jack wonders. *Feeling*—he gets that, as a sort of rootless tingling stirs inside him. And he tells Fabiola, "I lost my mother nearly five years ago. Just before she passed, she told me to run. Run and never look back. I couldn't make sense of it at the time. Skip to a few years later, and my wife became terminal. She fought hard. She was a very strong woman. But in the end, pancreatic cancer was stronger. All I've ever known is hard work, loss, and how to earn a lot of money. *Mucho dinero.* But here's the thing: A few months ago, I found myself coming home to an empty house. All that I had worked to amass no longer mattered. I was, and still am, alone. So here I sit before you, not knowing where my life has gone. Everything has passed me by."

"*Evaporado,*" Fabiola tells him.

Taking another sip of the dark maroon liquid, he watches with idle curiosity as the baked-earth walls begin to expand and contract, as if he were inside a living, breathing organism. And he tells Fabiola, "Yes, it has evaporated."

"Mothers always know," she tells him. "When I met Esteban

at the Fiesta de San Pedro y San Pablo when I was fourteen—a festival in honor of the town's patron saint—my mother told me, 'He will bring you pain someday, but he will be a good provider.' My mother, she always had that sixth sense. Esteban asked me to dance. I accepted. He asked me to marry him. Again I accepted. We wanted a child. Had a boy. Before he was eighteen, he gave us a grandson, and next thing I know, I have three generations of men. It was beautiful."

Listening to Fabiola reminds Jack of his own love. Sarah, his high school sweetheart. Long blond locks and piercing emerald eyes. Soft, creamy skin. He is lost in the memory of her, can even detect her flowery-fresh smell. He notices that the stone floor is beading up with sweat. Some distant corner of his mind finds this odd, and it occurs to him that he is babbling incoherently. Fabiola and whatever she gave him to drink have loosened emotions and memories, fragmented images and sounds and thoughts and words he has not discussed or even thought to speak of, with anyone, ever. He has kept them bottled and sealed like small-batch Kentucky bourbon.

"When my wife passed, it caught me by surprise. I watched her fight so hard for months, and I watched days drop from the calendar. I found her the best hospital, the best doctors. The best care money could buy. All the years we had together, ended by a rampant division of cells in her body. That's how the doctors explained it to me." Jack stops to compose himself. Then he tells Fabiola, "And every time a roadblock came up, my Sarah, she'd forge her own route and fight harder. Then her fight was over, and I wasn't prepared for that day." Wiping tears from his cheek and snorting mucus, Jack says, "We have a son. His name is Duncan. It kills me, but he's an off-again, on-again addict. And of all the professions to earn a degree in, he becomes an *electrician*. He's way too smart for that. I mean, I went to an Ivy League school. Not Duncan. Nope, he went to a community trade school. Became a journeyman. But he has issues with addiction. And then there's our daughter, Megan. She was adopted. But she committed suicide. Things just weren't right in her head. She had some loose wires—lot of awful things mashed up there that Sarah and I didn't know about. She . . . she did some horrible things that could have shed a bad light on my family."

Jack feels the lightness of his cup. Craves more. Fabiola sees him looking into the empty vessel and grabs it. Goes back to the counter, picks up the bottle, fills Jack's cup. Brings it back and hands it to him.

He nods. "Thank you, Fabiola, you're too kind." He sips more of the sweet taste that has created a world of illustrations in his brain, shards of forgotten truths. And with the walls heaving and the floor taking on a wet sheen almost like heated tar, he thinks of those boys. Their faces. So young. Seeing his daughter in court. He tells Fabiola, "You know, I paid big money to keep my daughter out of the papers. Keep what she did away from the news. I went out and found her a place that would hospitalize her and care for the sickness she had. But as I said, she was adopted. She wasn't my blood. And you can't control the outcome of something you never created. People who aren't your own have different ways about them, unknown to you. That's what my mother tried to warn me about before the adoption went through. See, how this happened was, Sarah had lost our second child. And she couldn't do it again. She could not go through all that. But those kids, Megan had babysat them. They trusted her. And who wouldn't? She was such a beautiful girl. She could have had a wonderful life. But something wasn't right up there. And a person never knows the *why* when they decide to do what she did. You just never know what that child's bloodline was. My mother was right. Megan could have had mass murderers or rapists or psychos in her real family's tree. Like everything in life, it was a gamble. Turns out, it wasn't right."

"What wasn't right?"

Talking aloud. Outside the boundaries of himself. Tingling in his fingertips. He feels the vastness of galaxies inside him. His words loud and deep, the bass tones rattling his bones loud enough to hear.

"The big problem was not being around enough—always at the office or traveling on business."

"*Who* wasn't around?"

"I. Me. I wasn't really around. I mean, I was there when I wasn't traveling. And in the courtroom, I was there for everything, but I was always busy. Buried myself in my work. Reading reports, facts, and figures. Had documents to review. But my wife, she dealt with that. She dealt with Megan. I paid the court costs. But I was working, always working. It's all I knew to do."

Sipping her wine, Fabiola tells Jack, "*Mi marido*—my husband—he wasn't around much. Always he work at the mine. Long hours. Early to bed on Sunday night to get to work on Monday morning. Unless there was overtime. He took it. Always. Sleep in his truck between shifts. Not come home. Always told me, it's not safe, but it's a good living. Before leaving, he would say, 'remember the insurance and the *pensión* that goes to you if I do not return.'"

Jack feels the sudden weight of grief, thinking of how much he worked. How much he missed. He is realizing just how closely he followed his mother's example. She held down three jobs to raise him, working morning to night, then working half the night too, day after day. But she never seemed to miss anything. If he needed her, got hurt or sick at school, she was there. Baseball games, graduation, she was there.

"Time, Jack—it's all we got. It's how you spend it. I never took it for granted. The holidays. The birthdays. My men. I think about those things. Brings a smile to my face. Waking up every day, knowing I have each of them in my heart, in my actions, in my mind. What I do now, I help others."

Jack wonders, who has he ever helped? His business created jobs, turned into a huge franchise. He revolutionized pharmacies. Came up with the drive-through, added groceries and one-hour photos. Sold those ideas off and came up with new ones. He donated to other organizations. That was a tax write-off. In the end, it was all about making money. Scratching each other's back. Doing favors. He never met the people the donations helped. Never knew the faces. The names.

Why? Why is he realizing all this now? After these years. Is it a reckoning?

"It took near twenty-four hours before I learn of their death—of the mine blowing up," Fabiola tells Jack, who is staring at the floor. The stones have grown slicker, almost molten. The walls continue to heave and sigh. On the wall above the bench, Fabiola's family has bloodshot eyes. Tears run down their faces and drip onto the bench. Jack's fat, soft palms are damp. And he closes his eyes. Squeezing them tight to keep them in their sockets.

Seeing the wine open passages within Jack, Fabiola tells him, "My brother-in-law come here to tell me of the explosion. The mine owners, the supervisors, never told nobody nothing. They waited. Racing around to figure out how to handle the situation. Then a radio station picked up on the news."

Taking another sip of wine, Jack tells Fabiola, "Growing up, during my teenage years, every day after school I washed dishes at a diner in town. My mother worked three jobs. She worked at a bakery in the mornings. Then a diner during lunchtime. It was the same diner I washed dishes for. Then she bartended at night. She always kept all her loose change from the tips she earned in an oversized glass pickle jar at the front door until she filled it up. Then she had it counted at the bank and she'd take us out for supper. 'My boy,' she called me. I was her favorite. She'd take us out for hamburgers, french fries, and vanilla floats. That is where my work ethic derived from."

"And your father—he was absent?"

"My father went crazy after his brother died in a car accident. Driving downhill, the brakes went out on my uncle's old Plymouth—slammed into a limestone wall. My father worked in a mill in Ohio. And he began to drink a lot. My mother started to call him 'Adolf' because he would come home in these fits of rage after work and he would rant about the unions. Talking about the working man getting screwed and how bad the conditions were where he worked. He'd take all his anger at the world out on us. Then one evening, he threatened my mother with a pistol. But only once. That's all it took—one time. My mother packed my brothers and me up the next morning after my father left for work, and we left Ohio for Kentucky. She was a good mother. Didn't take any shit from anyone. She raised and mothered us, worked and provided everything we needed. She never asked my father for a dime, not one cent, and she never allowed him any contact with us."

Laying his empty cup on the table, Jack is shivering and shaking, wanting to scream, gritting his teeth. Wanting to break down. His limbs have drawn tight. An aching begins in the soles of his feet, travels all the way to his jaw. His right hand pulses with pain as he rocks back and forth in his chair. Is he having a heart attack? Fabiola sets her cup on the table, reaches for Jack's hand. Looking at her, he doesn't see Fabiola. What he sees is divine—someone he has not laid eyes on for years. His mother. Her face. Her smile. Hands touching his, she tells him, "It's okay. Let it out, Jack. Let it all out."

And he does.

ANNE

Hands grip her shoulders, shake her body awake. Lids part. Eyes open. Anne feels as if she hasn't slept in weeks. The adrenaline dump left her body in a fatigued state. Her blurry field of vision contains an outline with Nick Cave locks slicked back, flaming red-rimmed glasses that glow next to the phone light by his face.

"Anne?"

Anne's groggy brain hurts, her neck is tight and stiff, and her ankle aches with every beat of her heart. Feeling like a punching bag in Mike Tyson's training camp, she says, "Trot?"

"No, it's Santa fuckin' Clause. Fuck yes, it's Trot. We gotta git." Trot stands, looming over her.

"Fuck you. Get that light outta my face." Balling her fists into her eyes, she yawns and asks, "What about the dog?"

Kicking her feet with the side of his boot, Trot says, "Dog? What fucking dog? Come on, up off your ass, greenhorn."

Pulling her legs in, Anne says, "What the fuck, man? Give a girl her space. Damn dog chased and attacked me."

"Well, there's no call of the wild waiting for us, so hurry the fuck up. 'Cause we do have a ride to the outskirts in Bristol."

"Bristol?"

"Yeah. Train don't stop around here much. We gotta motor. Ride won't wait all night."

Working her way to her feet, Trot smiling. "What's with the black eyes?"

"Black eyes?"

"Yeah, on top of everything else you told me, your eyes are black and there's some crusty blood rimming your nostrils."

Recalling the rage. Mitch coming at her. Spinning her around. Headbutting her. The skillet. Body dropping to the floor. The blood puddling around his outline. "Mitch," Anne says, remembering the scuffle. "Fuck!"

"Yeah, in your text you did mention you killed Mitch."

"He caught me lifting Dad's money. Headbutted me. It was intense."

On her feet, Anne wrestles with her pack. Her ankle is sore, but she can walk on it. Trot steps behind her, helps her get her arms through the straps, turns her around. Hugging her, he says, "He'll be fine. Can't worry about that now. We got brighter futures ahead of us."

Walking out of the shack, Trot says, "Must've broke your nose. Sounds like he deserved a little cast iron upside the head. Always was a fucking hothead."

Making her way to the outline of a vehicle, hearing a putter and miss of the engine, smell of fuel and exhaust fumes heavy on the air. Anne's fingertips are ice cold and painful to the touch. Index and middle fingers gently trace her features. "Shit!"

Walking beside Anne, Trot asks her, "Really think you killed him?"

"He attacked me. I hit him in the temple with a number eight skillet. Dropped like he was paralyzed or some shit. It was so insane. Didn't know what else to do—I just ran."

"Self-defense. What he gets for fucking invading your personal space."

Walking in the dark toward the bass beat thumping so loud it rattles the license plate, dirt and pea gravel sloshing like coleslaw beneath their feet. Stopping at the car, opening the door, they get Slayer's "Angel of Death" blaring from the stereo. The kid behind the wheel of the Ford Probe with a crinkled right fender and duct-taped trunk is named Pistol. He dropped out of school at age sixteen. Is now twenty-one, still doing the same dumb shit he did at sixteen. Hanging out with the younger crowd. Scoring them booze. Selling them weed or hash. Trying to get his single-eyed snake wet when he could, trying to be Scott Weiland cool. He wasn't ugly or obese. Just odd with hair like the lead singer of Green Day before they won a Grammy—uneven strands shifting in all directions. He had this shy but friendly demeanor. Blue eyes and an athletic build. He wears a faded Rancid T-shirt, black jeans, and matching Vans slip-on shoes.

Anne takes off her pack, sinks down into the back seat. Trot slams the door, which rattles as if it might fall off its hinges. Pistol turns the music down while Trot gets in the front seat, and eyes Anne in the rearview. "Hell happened to your face? You look fucked up." He shifts into drive.

"Spat with my brother."

"Siblings. They're the worst."

The Probe's headlights cut through the pudding-thick night. Houses swish by. Pistol takes the highway out of Johnson City to an old back road. Glancing at Trot and then making eye contact with Anne in the rearview, Pistol tells them, "Could've crashed at my place till morning if needed. Got a comfy cushioned couch, spare bed, air mattress. Cabinet full of booze. Plenty of weed."

Trot tells him, "We're good, dude. Told you, we's hopping a train."

"Some Huck Finn shit—I get it. Rad!"

Trot stares out the window while Anne sits chewing what length she had left on her chipped nails—wordless, each waiting for the other to reply.

Anne meets Pistol's glancing eyes in the rearview, fake laughs. "Yeah. Huck Finn, only it ain't no damn boat we're hopping." Pausing, she spat a piece of nail onto the back the passenger's seat. "It's a fuckin' train."

"I feel you, little lady, I feel you. More like some Dean Moriarty shit."

"Dean More-what shit?"

"*On the Road*, by Jack Kerouac—the Beats. Where he travels 'cross the country with his friends. Great fucking book. Should stop at the first bookshop you find and buy a copy."

"I'll get right on that."

Trading suburban landscapes for country landscapes and farmhouses and pastures, twenty minutes later Pistol pulls to a turn out off the side of Pleasant Grove Road. Shifts into park. Reaches over and shakes Trot's hand, who slides him two twenty-dollar bills.

"Safe travels, brother."

"Appreciate it, Pistol."

Unlatching the door, Trot steps out into the cool night air. Anne pushes the seat forward, grabs her pack, feeling Pistol's eyes undressing her. She steps from the car, looks in at Pistol. He tells her, "Don't forget that book."

Not caring for the way he keeps eyeing her, she tells him, "Why don't you go feel someone else up with your eyes, you fuckin' creep."

Embarrassed, Pistol shifts into drive. Holds up his hand, flies the middle finger. "Screw you."

He speeds off down the road, leaving Trot and Anne standing out in the darkness of crickets chirping and dogs barking.

"Did you *have* to be such a bitch?"

Overhead, the sky is clear, with Orion and the Big Dipper and an airplane blinking. "Fucker was making me sick, molesting me with his eyes. Talking about some damn Jack Kerouac—probably some kinda cock book or something. You got some weird friends."

A full moon guides their steps away from the road to the woods, where they walk through some brush, then stop. Trot tells her, "He's an acquaintance, just making conversation. Everyone you meet ain't like your family. Pistol's a good dude. First person I met when I moved here."

"Might be nice to you, but he ain't wanting to get with you. How old is he? Twenty?"

"Ain't my type. He's twenty-one."

"That explains it all: twenty-one and hanging out with two seventeen-year-olds. He should be into the bar scene, not the teenage scene."

Stepping out of the brush, Trot pointed to the other side of the darkness, where the railroad tracks gleamed in the moonlight. "There's the tracks."

"Great. Now what?"

"We wait. You can take the first hour nap. I'll take the second."

Sitting on the hard ground, crunch of dry leaves, legs stretched out, head resting on her pack, Anne looks around at the shadows of trees and what she hopes are dead limbs and not snakes forming dark curves on the ground. Thinking of Mitch. The sound of that pan cracking against his skull. She could still hear it, feel it in her bones. The loud thud that rattled his eyes. Eyes rolled up to stare at the back of his brain. Dropping to the floor, blood spilled. What if she really has killed him?

Trying to think whether he had ever been nice to her, she digs deeper, trying to remember a time when *anyone* in her family had ever been nice to one another. When her mother didn't drink and her father hadn't threatened her. When her siblings had ever known affection for one another or their parents. There were no more celebrations for birthdays or holidays. Those had faded long ago. Everything is wrapped around booze, soaked in it. Threats. Screaming and hurting. She often wonders what her mother and father were like before they had her and her sibs. Had they been abusive to each other? What was their affection like back when it was just the two of them? Was her mother always an alcoholic? And before Anne knows it, her body is free-falling, traveling downward on a plunge, riding a roller coaster. She is dropping hard until Trot wakes her. It seemed like only a split second, and night began to dissipate and fade. The evaporation of darkness, replaced by daybreak. Everything is lifeless and gray. No sunshine, just overcast and gloom. Her face heavy with dew.

"Wake up," Trot tells her, "We gotta get moving."

Eyes heavy, crust in the corners like tiny crumbs of bread, her body fights the exhaustion and stiffness that saturates her young being. Her movements feel rigid and artificial. In the distance, the train's horn raises their senses, summoning its approach. Their stomachs knot with anticipation, the morning hunger replaced by nerves. Metal clack against metal, picking up speed. "We gotta be quick," Trot told her as they rush from the brushy area where they had lain.

Out of breath already, Trot tells Anne, "Least we won't see no bulls out here."

"Bulls?" Anne questioned.

"Railroad cops. They always do their rounds on the yard."

Running and half limping through the weeds, dew soaking the

legs of their jeans, feet smashing down on the trash strewn about the area: soda bottles, beer cans, cigarette packs, and candy wrappers. Seeing all this garbage reminds her of home, of what she is running from, leaving behind. And fear of the unknown sinks away, in its place a smirk. Because refuse is familiar. In fact, it is all she has ever known.

Anne's heart is skipping beats, pounding like that of a marathon runner in the last miles of the race. Feeling pressure ball up in her throat. Running down through a ditch with her gimp leg, the earth dropping, pack on her back weighing her down, then hitting the graveled edge of the right-of-way, feet digging hard, the pop of the grooved steel wheels meeting the rounded I-beam, crossing the break of the high-quality alloy tracks, hands reaching for the metal ladder. Closing in. Running harder. Burning thighs and hips. Fingers reaching. That tentative smirk slowly softening into a hesitant smile. Though she worries about losing her grip. Her footing. She would slip. The wheels would be unforgiving, parting skin and bone like butter and ending her uncertain future before it even began. At the same time, the fear feeds another side of her brain, which yearns for the adventurous unknown.

Bubble-lettered graffiti, bold and shadowed by color, decorates the dull railcars. Feet digging, hands reaching in, pushing from the balls of her feet, she feels the extension of tendon and muscle. Hands grabbing, Anne pulls herself to the ladder, forearms and biceps flexed, every fiber in her body engaged. Taking each step up onto the rough platform, her thighs, calves, and hips burn, her whole body shakes. The ankle throbs. The smile is no longer hesitant as she feels a glimmer of hope for what is down the tracks. To come next. Whatever it is has to be better than what she has left behind.

Trot comes up right behind her, his glasses steamy and halfway down the bridge of his nose. They are both gasping for breath, lungs greedy for fresh air. The sound in their ears is volcanic. Loud. An eruption of decibels. Trot smiles at her, the same hope-filled smile that she feels on her own lips, as he points, yelling, "In there. Get in there."

Pulling her pack free, her frame still shaken and numb with the rush of nerves. Sweat dampens her shirt. Face covered with droplets. Feeling like a melting candle. Stuffing her pack into the circular opening. Squeezing in behind the pack. Inside, it's dusty, with particles in the air. Smells of metal, urine, and rot. Several plastic bottles lie inside—remnants from earlier passengers. Potato chip bags. Standing up, Trot yells, "This is a grainer car. Used to haul grain, corn, wheat, sand, or clay. Got lucky. Even has a porch. Ones without are called suicide rides. Them that don't have solid metal on the porch. Fuckin' dangerous."

Moving back into a corner, Anne wishes she had a pair of earplugs. The loud rattle of travel. They sit on their packs. Anne yells, "How many trains you hop back in Texas?"

"Plenty. Told you I ran with a group of riders known as the Recon Rejects. Learned about hopping the rails from them. Had planned to finally catch out and not come back. See the USA. But my folks moved me before I got enough money saved and my shit packed to run."

Until now, since he and Anne had become friends. Two misfits with family issues, only they wouldn't call it a family. Now he can run away with Anne, see America, see whatever he wanted, be among like-minded people, find a family of their choosing.

In her head, Anne keeps a grocery list of unknowns. Top of the list: where the train is headed. Hoping it was going south. Alabama. Louisiana. Mississippi. But the other worry is, what if they get caught? What her mother and father will do. Her stealing the money they had stashed for booze, food, bills, or whatever else they might blow it on. The pistol, their security against break-ins and bad actors. So many unknowns. The kind of people they might encounter. When and where to hop freights. How long it will take to get from one destination to another. Where they might find food once they run out of money. Where they will sleep.

Glancing into another opening, to her left. Another section to sit in, identical to the one where they are holed up. Anne sees feet. *What the shit?* Her teeth chatter with the vibration. Attached to the feet are bone-thin legs attired in camo tights. On the feet are scuffed Doc Martens boots. An unconscious fear shoots through Anne and numbs her with alarm. Here is another human being, but she has no clue who that human being is. She and Trot are not alone.

HUNTER

Hunter's mind drifts comfortably, lulled by the loud, throaty rumble of engines and the press of warm air against his face and his leathers. The long stretches of smooth blacktop shift and curve, only to grow straight again. The solitude frees his memories: a cold morning out in the woods, leaves crackling under his boot's instep as his father, home from the road on an early Saturday morning, beckoned him forward. Peering up into the collage of limbs and leaves in the early-morning light, his father breached the silence with words. "See 'em? They're just like the people I see every day on the road. Look far enough ahead to the other trees, you'll see where they're headed—maybe back to their nests. Those are the huge mounds they've built from twigs and leaves. Or they're headed for their provisions—acorns or walnuts scattered on the ground. You just gotta look for the trees that grow those nuts. Like people, they're easy to read."

Leaning into a curve, Hunter thinks about his father's words, thinks about Itch, meeting up with him and Nugget after Hunter stopped at the ATM back in their hometown. Withdrawing an extra grand to go along with the three he'd already packed. Itch mentioned he needed to stop in Middlesboro, Kentucky. Had some business to reconcile. Hunter thinking of those squirrels, of what his father told him. Itch is dealing marijuana again. Hunter knows this. Hell, Nugget knows this. So why didn't Itch come out and tell Hunter or Nugget? He is either picking up more to sell or paying the guy he sold for. It isn't a thing to keep secret among friends. If you couldn't trust your friends, who could you trust?

Somewhere around the area, Itch is headed to his tree to "gather his nuts"—Hunter's father's term for stocking provisions. Hunter chuckles to himself. The old man is speaking to him from the grave. Over the years, Hunter had never given much thought to anything his father tried to tell him when he was growing up. But now it's as if his father's lessons are everywhere, waiting to be reflected on and realized.

Something that worries Hunter, something he doesn't like, is the idea of traveling across the country with Itch if he is transporting weed. If that were the case—three bikers, out of state—it conjures an image of outlaws, which none of them are. Just three gearhead buddies who like bikes, ink, and powerlifting, and enjoy tossing a few beers back and grilling some steaks; they are the type of guys who don't wear watches. Which fueled their decision to meet at the Sagebrush Steakhouse for a tender cut of beef and maybe a few hoppy brews. Itch had told Hunter and Nugget to go ahead; he would meet them at the steakhouse once he got his business done.

Hunter's mind rolls with tidbits of facts—something the road produced within him—as they cross over from North Carolina, the Tar Heel State, and into Tennessee, the Volunteer State. Eventually, they hit Kentucky, the Bluegrass State.

Taking in the surrounding wilderness the hue of an unripe avocado. Loblolly pines, beech, birch, magnolia, and black oak.

Hunter thinks about his father, who had been pretty much absent from his childhood Monday through Friday, but then present on Saturday and Sunday. He thinks of the long walks they would take, learning about the different trees that made up the woods around them. He thinks of his father's love for the road. Maybe, being a salesman was something in the blood—something his dad had passed on to him. But for Hunter, the road is most satisfying when he travels by motorcycle. He had gone by car and even on foot, but biking is best. He prefers the long road trips, the scenery, passing through the small towns. When he can, he takes the country roads, seeing the rural areas. The mom-and-pop eateries and gas stations. Older homes and farms. There is something about seeing the lives of others out there, how they live. Their day-to-day culture. There is a freedom in just being able to get up and ride, never answering to anyone. But you need your bike. He thought of Chinese monks, given a single rice bowl and told to not lose it, because it was a symbol of life itself. Well, Hunter's motorcycle is his bowl, his symbol of freedom, of life.

Itch is to meet someone in a rural area outside the town, then motor over to the steakhouse. They had discussed camping for the night at the Cumberland Gap Park. Or they might get in some more miles before dark—cruise over to Daniel Boone National Forest, maybe make it to Louisville or even cross the bridge into Indiana to camp. If they make it to Indiana, Hunter can look up his old friend Dog, a spelunker he hasn't seen or spoken with in years. Then they can make their way to Illinois the next day.

Throttling their bikes down, they rumble into the steakhouse parking lot. They park in what they hope is a line of sight from the bar so they can keep an eye on their bikes. Boots stepping off highway pegs and onto gravel. Unbuckling their half helmets. Hunter looks over at Nugget. "What the hell's up with Itch?"

"He's been strange of late."

"I mean, it's not like we don't know he peddles weed. Got nothing against it. But try and hide it, calling it his 'problems to reconcile,' his 'affairs'? Come on, man, kinda jive-ass turkeys he think we are?" Hunter chuckles.

"Right. We're all friends here, like family. Think maybe it's his lady?"

"*Like?* I believe we *are* family. And yeah, she's a feisty gal."

Carrying their helmets into the bar. The atmosphere meets them as the door opens: loud conversations; sets of eyes checking them out; men, women, and kids; smells of grilled meats and vegetables. They walk over the smoke-colored floor, past booths, to the bar, a long rectangle of clear-coated white oak. Pulling out three chairs, laying their helmets and then their leather coats in the third one, piling them up. Nugget's and Hunter's arms are a road map of ink. Hunter could feel the eyes from neighboring tables staring holes through them. Buzz-cut Nugget, with biceps like grapefruits, is the larger of the two large men, whereas Hunter is leaner and has hair. He rubs his chin stubble and looks around the room. On a stool to his left sits a stocky lump of a man, thick in the middle, with thick black-framed glasses like the old-school Clark Kent and a thick box-cut head of hair. He sips a sweating glass of bourbon with a single monstrous ice cube. Making eye contact with Hunter, he nods, gives a down-on-his-luck grin. Hunter feels the questions that will lead into an autobiography of woe, when the man asks, "Out for a ride, or just traveling through?"

"Traveling through. Making a stop for some food and maybe a beer or two." Hunter offers his hand. "Hunter."

The guy's impressive gut hangs out over his blue jeans, balanced on a metal belt buckle that looks built for the job. He sticks out his hand. "Johnny."

"You from around here?"

"Yeah. Used to work down at the Coca-Cola plant. Got

shit-canned." Lifting his drink, he says, "Why I'm here. Nursing my wounds." Takes a sip.

Strong scent of bourbon. *Gotta be on his third drink*, Hunter thinks as he slides onto his stool. "Lost your job. That's gotta hurt. Come to think of it, guess we're in the same boat—I lost mine this morning."

"Union?"

"Naw. Handed my boss his ass for taking his personal failings out on his dog."

"Sounds like the fuckhead deserved a good ass-handing. Kinda dog?"

"Yes, he did. And it's a Walker hound. I took her home with me. Left her with my girlfriend. You?"

"Damn, them's some good dogs." Taking a sip, Johnny says, "Wish I coulda punched my boss. Working sixteen-hour days, no double time on the weekends. Took a sick day, and they gave me my walking papers. Can you believe that?"

"No shit?" For all Hunter knew, the guy was a horrible worker. Called in all the time. There was always more to the story.

"No shit. Management's about as useful as tits on a boar hog. Don't give two fucks about a man and his family; only work, work, work. Twenty years," Johnny says, fingertip stabbing the bar top. "Twenty damn years I been loyally busting my ass for them."

"They got a bottom line." The guy is really down on the management. Hunter is glad he never really dealt with big organizations—only the higher-ups in the army and only for a short stint.

"Better bet your ass they got a bottom line. And I get that," Johnny tells him, spreading his arms out, palms facing up. "But you best be on board with it, or else—"

"Or else it's the unemployment line." This Johnny guy had

been sitting on this bar stool and simmering, and now he looked just about ready to boil over. Dying to chew the fat with another soul. Starving for a release of his troubles.

"Nail on the head," Johnny says to Hunter. He takes another sip of his bourbon.

A young woman with peroxide locks and a flaming-red T-shirt approaches Hunter and Nugget, laying down two menus. Hunter sees her as the kind who is attractive to guys who drink every day. She has that party-girl vibe going on as she asks sweetly, "What I can get you gentlemen to drink today?"

Wanting something with a bit of hop. "I'll take a Sierra Nevada." Hunter says.

"Same for me," Nugget says. "And we got another guy coming."

"No problem, hon. Will he be drinking?"

"Yeah, just not sure what."

"No worries. I'll get your beers; you-all look over the menu. My name's Lisa if y'all got any questions or need anything. This on one or two checks?"

Hunter says, "I got it."

Nugget says, "Nah, man, come on, I can get it."

"So can I." Hunter opens his menu. "You getting a ribeye?"

Johnny, eavesdropping, tells Hunter, "They got a damn good ribeye."

Nugget says, "That's me, the hand-cut ribeye."

Johnny says, "That's a damn good choice. Probably their best steak."

Hunter tries not to get irritated by Johnny's whiskey-scented interruption. The poor fuck just got sacked from his job. Hunter closes his menu and lays it on the bar. Lisa returns with two frosty glasses. "Two ice-cold pale ales for you guys. Wanna order now, or wait on your friend? Or maybe an appetizer?"

"No appetizer. Give us ten minutes; then we'll order."

Nodding, Lisa tells Hunter, "Will do, hon."

Hunter took a swallow of beer and said, "Appreciate it."

"Ya know, you'd think after twenty years, I'd be able to miss a day," Johnny mumbles as if he and Hunter were still deep in conversation. "I mean, I earned them days. They're mine to miss."

Nugget seems to be holding back a shit-eating grin. He rolls his eyes as Hunter says, "Twenty years—that's quite a bit of time under your belt."

"No shit. None of them fuckers give a cow's cock. Family owned, even. Company's been here in this area for about a hundred and ten years, like five generations of family has owned the damn place. Passing it down the line. 'Course, the only family they care for is their own."

Trying to inject a bit of reason, Hunter tells Johnny, "Thing with management, it's not always the decision of the guy who fired you—coulda come from above him." Chain of command. Hunter knows it and understands it. He also knows that shit rolls downhill.

"True, but they all got families. My kid was sick, wife was working. Figured I got the days, I'll take off instead of her."

"That sucks. Last minute, huh?" And yet, here the guy sits, lost his job, getting hammered on whiskey, wasting money instead of being at home with his family.

"Pretty much."

"Probably couldn't get coverage." Call in at the last minute, got production to meet, a quota, gotta remove the weak link. Probably not the first time he missed at the last minute.

"Probably not," Johnny says, his tone simmering down a notch.

"This a busy season for you all?"

"Oh, yeah, been busting our asses. I got what they call 'kangaroo court' next week. Where I meet with the managers and a vice president or some other honcho, argue my side. *Maybe* get my job back."

"That's a plus. Then, there's still hope?"

"There is. But—"

"But it's still a pain in the ass." Hunter sips his beer. You never know how important something is, until it gets taken away.

Outside the steakhouse, the muffled rumble of a shovelhead Harley. Hunter and Nugget turn around to see Itch wheeling in, parking beside their bikes.

Johnny says, "I'm guessing he's with you guys."

Nugget says, "Gotta watch this Johnny guy—can't nothing slide by him."

Smirking, Johnny says, "Them sure are some nice bikes."

"Thanks," Hunter tells him. "That's what I do for a living. Repair and build bikes."

Itch enters the steakhouse and Nugget waves him over to the bar. Moving their jackets and helmets, spreading the leather over the backs of their chairs, laying their helmets on the floor between them, Itch sits. Nugget slides him a menu. "Hand-cut ribeye is what we're eyeing."

"Get your affairs in order?" Hunter asks.

"Maybe don't say it that way," Itch replies. "Makes it sound like I'm planning to be dead."

Lisa comes back and asks, "Can I get you a beer?"

"I'll have whatever they're drinking."

"'Kay. 'Nother pale ale. You-all ready to order too?"

"Yeah. I think everyone wants the ribeye." Hunter looks down at Itch and Nugget, who nod their heads in agreement. "Medium. No salad. Baked potatoes with butter."

"Any A-One?"

"No, ma'am," all three say in unison.

"Got it. I'll get that other beer," Lisa says to Hunter as she takes the menus.

Johnny finishes his bourbon at last. Slides down from his seat, sticks out his hand to Hunter. "Nice to meet you, Hunter."

Turning to Johnny, Hunter asks the question whose answer he already knows. He shakes Johnny's hand. "Headed out?"

"Yeah, best be getting home. Wife was expecting me hours ago."

Hunter suddenly thinks of the guy who broke down and wanted to commit suicide. It was damn near suicide letting this poor schmo drive home. He knows what his father would do. "Sure you should be driving?"

"I'm fine. Really. I got this."

"How many you had?"

"Four."

"Why don't you let me call you a ride home."

"Really, I'm—"

"Give me a number." Hunter stands up, towering over Johnny. He already has his cell out of his front pocket. No way in hell is he letting Johnny get behind the wheel after four glasses of bourbon. He needs some guidance. "Just lost your job. No sense in adding to a long losing streak."

Johnny seems to shrink a little, as if defeated by the truth of Hunter's words. "You're probably right." He says a number, and Hunter thumbs the digits into his phone. A female voice answers. Speaking to Johnny's wife. Explaining who he is and that her husband had a few drinks and probably shouldn't be driving. Hunter tells her where he is. She tells Hunter she is on her way and not to let him leave, that Johnny already has two DWI's, and thanks him.

Hunter tells Johnny, "Get yourself a coffee. Your wife's on her way."

Sheepish and slump-shouldered, Johnny sits back down at the bar, waves Lisa over, and orders a black coffee.

Nugget asks Itch, "So what gives, dude? You gonna tell us what's up?"

"What's up with what?"

"This 'affairs in order' shit, 'problems to reconcile'. We all know what you're up to."

Lisa brings back a steaming mug of coffee to Johnny. Behind her, a server with crazy brown hair obstructing his field of vision comes out from the kitchen with three plates—one in each hand, a third riding on his right forearm. He sets the plates in front of them, and Lisa returns with silverware wrapped in white napkins. "Can I get you guys anything else?"

"Water," Nugget say, and Itch and Hunter echo his request.

"Three waters coming up."

Picking up forks and steak knives, the three fall silent and focus on the task at hand.

"Damn good," Hunter said. Looks over at Johnny and says, "Good recommendation."

Johnny raises his cup of coffee. "Glad you like it," he says, and takes another sip.

As the three hungry travelers slice and chew and swallow and slice some more, Johnny turns around in his seat, looking at something in the parking lot. Turning to Hunter, he says, "I think there's some guys outside in the lot loading up one of your-all's bikes."

Itch turns around and springs to his feet. "Motherfucker," he mumbles around a bite of ribeye and baked potato. "That's my damn bike!"

Crossing from the bar, they speed-walk through the dining area and out the door. Outside, Itch's motorcycle stands in the bed of a faded and rusted Dodge Ram, cinched down with straps and come-alongs. Rubber chirps on the blacktop, and the pickup speeds away with two bearded guys in the rear gleefully waving the middle finger at Itch.

Hunter had come out just behind Itch. Still chewing his food, he says, "Thought your business was squared away."

JACK

Pulling his hand from his mouth, his mother clasping his digits in hers the way mothers do, telling him, *Jack, all that time away was time lost.*

What did she mean?

Jack squeezes his eyes shut. Inhales deep.

This isn't real, he tells himself. He opens his eyes again.

In that blink of an eye, in that exhalation of breath, everything changes. He is no longer sitting in Fabiola's home.

He is living in that memory that haunts him, that is too familiar. He is back in the hospital, his mother lying in a bed. Thin and quivering. Smell of isopropyl alcohol. The skin of her face translucent over the bones that construct her cheeks, chin, jaw, forehead. Stretched and connected. Pink tissue beneath. Hair from her head pressed back like a bathing cap. Arms lifted. Sag of flesh, loose folds. Hands webbed with veins and shaped by years upon years of labor, gripping Jack's hand, a hand wet with his own blood. Indentations of teeth as if bitten by another human being. Parched lips part and speak. "Jack, look what you've gone and done to yourself."

Her words echo as if he were in a canyon. His hand swells and throbs in rhythm with his heartbeat. It feels damp and warm.

And Jack asks, "What have I done, Mother?" Weak, smiling with a lost stare.

Vanilla-framed monitors all at once start a continuous, irritating loud beep, piercing his eardrums. Jerking his hand from her grip, backing away from the bed, from his mother. Palming his ears. Blocking out the noise. Feeling as if his eardrums are going to burst. He wants to scream but can't. Something isn't right. Looking up at the mint-colored wall where a flat-screen TV is mounted, an episode of *Matlock* playing, but there is no volume. Only the redline tone, the continuous beep. Removing his hands from his ears, reaching for the remote attached to his mother's bed, he thumbs the button to ring the nurse. Nothing. Turning around. Stepping over the waxed tile floor to the door. The handle is hot. It won't turn—stuck. He can't leave. He pounds his fists on the hard slab of door. Screams, "Nurse? Nurse! I demand this door be opened immediately. Nurse?" Then the knob begins to turn. The door opens. Jack steps through the opening, into a bathroom. A wooden vanity in the distance. Mirror over a salt-blue sink. It is the bathroom from the home he grew up in. Approaching the sink, in the mirror Jack's features are covered in whiskers. He's a young man again. Running his hands over his cheeks. Feeling the growth there. He never grew a beard before, was always clean shaven. He must shave. On the sink sits a can of shaving cream. A straight razor. Reaching down to turn on the hot water, cupping his hands, catching the water, he splashes his face to relax the whiskers. Steam rises from the liquid. Fogs the mirror. Distorts his reflection. Reaching for the shaving cream, he fills his hand with a dollop of white fluff, smooths it onto his face. Picks up the razor and begins long, even strokes along his jawline and chin. Rinsing off the razor under the flow of hot water. Continuing to shave his neck until the razor doesn't glide. It nicks the skin of his throat. Blood starts to ooze, then gush down his neckline.

He drops the razor, can't get the blood to stop. Reaching for a box of tissues that sits off to the side, he hears a door creak open, looks to his right, into a living room. He's in his old house. Long brown vinyl couch beside the door. Large pickle jar on the orange-carpeted floor beside the couch. The jar is full of silver coins—spare change from the tips his mother earns at the greasy-spoon diner where she waits tables. Watching the door open. In walks a clean-cut man, his hair slicked and parted on the side, white T-shirt and khaki pants, work boots. He kneels down and picks up the jar. Cradles it to his chest as if he has caught a football. Turns and runs.

Jack hollers, "Dad? What do you think you are doing? Dad, come back here! You cannot take the money Mom has earned." Jack runs after his father, into a small concrete shed with a shiny tin roof. Jack follows him, winded and limping. Inside, his father stops, lifts the jar over his head. Gasping for air, Jack screams, "DON'T! Mom's worked too hard for that money!" But his father laughs, smashes the jar on the floor. Glass and coins scatter. Looking down, the coins have turned into faces of people from Jack's life. His mother-in-law and father-in-law. His wife. His mother. His father. His son. His daughter. The kids his daughter babysat and abused. The judge who presided over his daughter's court case. The doctors who wanted to help his daughter. The doctors who cared for his mother. His wife. Faces of clients. Business associates. All these faces from Jack's life. What does it mean?

Jack grabs for his father, who fights him off with fists and palms.

He punches Jack with a straight right. Jack has zero defensive skills. Jack has no skill set. When it comes to anything physical, he's just a soft pudge of male incompetence. He knows numbers, not fighting. His body has no equilibrium. It's as though he's drunk. A newborn learning to walk. Stumbling and staggering. The ground feels alien to his feet. He doesn't want to tread or fall on any of the faces.

Running to a corner, his father grabs a red metal gas can. Jack finds his balance. Steps away, evades the faces, pursues his father, who comes at Jack, telling him, "You're a weak little man!" Swings the gas can at Jack's head. Uncoordinated, Jack raises his hands, half shielding himself from the blow, which knocks him down. The floor is cold and marble hard. Jack fights to stand up, but it's like swimming in molasses. He can barely work his way to his feet, let alone stand. Like the kids who mugged him and ran away, his father runs, and Jack looks on, helpless, watching him dash away from the shed, which has somehow grown almost to the size of a concert hall.

Fighting the stiffness and quaking of his muscles, Jack stands, trying not to step on any of the faces that have inched toward him on the slick stone floor. The mouths of the faces are speaking, but at first it's all chatter, as if they were speaking in tongues. Then he can make out his father in-law telling him, "You fucked me, Jack, you really fucked me." His mother-in-law just shakes her head. Says, "We expected so much better of you, Jack." He presses his hands over his ears. Warmth floods the side of his face. Blood drips from the gash made by the gas can. Running from the shed. Out in the distance, his father removes the can's cap, starts sloshing the liquid onto the side of a house. It's the house he was raised in, the house he ran from only moments ago. His father enters the house. Jack follows. Inside, the thick whiff of fumes. His father is dousing everything inside: couch, TV, pictures, walls—everything his mother has worked to provide for herself and Jack. Coming at him, his father swings the can again. A repeat of before. Jack is slow to react. Gets knocked down again. His father then pulls a lighter from his pocket. Thumbs the rough Hot Wheel–size striker. Sparks up a flame, drops the Zippo onto the floor, and everything ignites in bright orange heat. Fighting to get his feet under him, Jack finally gives it up and crawls on all fours. Coughing and gagging. Reaching the wall, ripping curtains from the window, he levers himself up by the sill, swings the drape, trying to beat out the flames. But they have taken over the room. Covering his face with his forearm, he's spitting smoke. Runs from the burning house. Backing away as citrus flames climb into a sky that is a mound of cotton-candy glow, when a weighty arm reaches over Jack's shoulder. It's his father, laughing. His face is dusky with soot. He has a cigarette between his lips, coal on the end a bright orange-red, and he pulls it from his lips, blows smoke. Fixes Jack with eyes that glow hotter than his cigarette and says, "Can't run away from your demons, son. Eventually, you gotta face them or burn that shit to the fucking ground." Jack returns the hard stare to his father, who laughs again. Jack tries to pull away from the embrace, but his father's arm is locked around his neck and shoulders. The cigarette dangles from his lip as he tells Jack, "Don't try to be strong, Jack. You're a weak man. You were always weak. No amount of money will ever change that, son."

His father takes his cigarette from his lips and lifts it to Jack's left eye. Jack struggles to get free, but he's too weak. He feels the heat of the smoldering coal. Is his father really going to stub it out on his eyeball?

Jack wakes up panting and coated in sweat. Sitting up, he twists a fist against his eye. Looking around in the dead silence of an unknown room, eyes blinking the blurry haze away, he focuses, follows the mud walls to Fabiola, standing in the doorway and sipping coffee from a clay cup.

"That musta been some dream. You been in here talking and yelling in your sleep."

Jack's body aches, joints inflamed, his shirt damp, feet resting on the tiles. Feeling the cool stone beneath the arches of his Smartwool-socked feet. Off to the side of the bed lay his Merrell hiking boots, coated with orange dirt. His heart still rushing behind the bones of his chest. He can not say for certain what was real. Maybe he is still dreaming. "Why didn't you wake me up?" he asks. "I was having a terrible dream."

Smiling, Fabiola tells him, "Not my place to wake you. In my family, we are taught that our dreams hold meaning."

Running a trembling hand through his gray locks—Jack's nervous tick; he is lucky he still has any hair—he slows his breath. "How did I get into this room from the kitchen and into this bed?" he asks. "I have no recollection of walking in here last night."

"That's what you did. You walked." Fabiola chuckles. "You were in a relaxed but odd way. Kept calling me 'Mother.'"

He has no memory of walking to this room, getting into this bed. It is nothing more than a rectangular wooden frame about sixteen inches off the floor, with a cushion and sheets and a blanket and pillow. The air in the room is fresh. Breathing in deep through his nose, expanding his lungs. Out a square window, he can see hints of a clear blue sky. Eyeing Fabiola, he recalls the wine. How it released this kaleidoscope of emotions and remembered images. The wine was like a shovel in a cemetery, digging deep into the soil of his existence, resurrecting the dead of his past.

He asks her, "What was in that wine you gave me?"

Sipping her coffee, Fabiola swallowed and told him, "*Shori*. In Ecuador, they call it *natem*. Maybe you have heard it called *ayahuasca*."

"Hallucinogenic wine. You fed me *drugs*?"

"Yes. It's a family recipe."

"But you're telling me that you drugged me? In the States, we call that getting a roofie. That is dangerous and illegal."

"No, Jack, I helped you open your mind."

"Feeding a crime victim drugs is called 'help'?"

"You have *demonios*, Jack. That's why you're here. You're running from them."

Pressing his hands to his face, he says to Fabiola, "I had dreams of my mother and my father. It was the craziest thing I've ever encountered."

"Your father? You told me your mother left him."

"I did? I don't remember. But yes, my mother did leave my father. Even though it was a dream, it sure felt real. That's the first time I've seen him since my mother left him all those years ago. In the dream, I was back in the hospital. At first, my mother was dying all over again, and then things got strange. I couldn't leave the hospital room. The door was stuck, but then I got it open and I was back in our old house. I was a young man again. And I walked into our bathroom and I needed to shave, and before I knew it, I was having a confrontation with my father. He stole my mother's jar of change. I chased him to a shed, where he grabbed a can of gasoline, and then he burned down the house that I grew up in."

"Our dreams are trying to tell us things about ourselves."

Jack wants to believe that. But all his life, he's worked in a corporate environment. Built companies up. Made them huge profits. He isn't into the spiritual side of being. Not into anything magical or make-believe. Or Buddhism or Taoism. Hell, he is barely a Christian. He is having a hard time swallowing any of this. But then, he had packed a bag and flown to South America, so there must be something calling him. Landed at an airport and started hitchhiking. Didn't even tell anyone he was leaving.

"Look, I'm not a spiritual man," he says. "Not really even

religious, for that matter. For the sake of me buying into what you're suggesting, let's say I believed even a hint of what you're trying to tell me. What is my dream telling me that I don't already know?"

"Sounds like you maybe never dealt with your *mamá*'s passing. Or her leaving your father. Maybe the fire is a way of removing something. But then you chase him. Like you're after something. What are you chasing, Jack? Did your father or mother speak to you?"

"My father did speak to me, but it was a lot of crazy nonsense. Like I told you, I haven't seen that man since my mother left him. I don't even know if he's alive. *Muerto*, maybe." He feels sluggish, as if his mind were covered with a thick film. Before Fabiola can say anything else, he asks, "Could I maybe get a cup of coffee, assuming that's what you're drinking?"

"Of course, Jack."

Splashing water onto his face from the kitchen sink, Jack blots off with a towel. Feels the doughy flesh under his windburned chin and jaws, the white hairs that had sprouted along his eyebrows, the shadow of frosty stubble, and the dimness of his blue eyes. In business, he can do anything, but now, stripped of his family, with no money, he realizes he has nothing. No formidable skills. Nothing he can do with his hands. He isn't athletic or mechanical, never was. Laying the towel on the sink, turning around, walking to the kitchen table, where a clay cup sat with steam rising from it. Reaching for it, he says, "This is only coffee, correct?"

Fabiola nods. "*Sí. Sólo café.*"

Raising it to his parched lips, he sips. It warms his mouth, his insides, its sharp, fresh taste enlivening his senses. "Thank you," he says.

Seated across the little square table, Fabiola raises her hand. "No need to thank me. You're my guest." She regards him in silence for a moment. "You know, I dreamed my husband's, son's, and grandson's death the night before. It's a cruel thing to admit, having that intuition, that premonition, but it's true."

Jack is at a loss for words. How is he to register this confession of witchery? Better yet, how is he even to accept it as fact? But he is in her home, so he shows respect. "I cannot imagine the weight of that," he says. "I imagine that it is a heavy burden to admit, to carry." He sips the coffee and says, "Back in America, in the world I come from, this is all crazy talk. Nonsense. I mean, all this is a lot of mumbo jumbo. It's a huge amount of information for me to gather and translate, and it's really hard for me to accept any of this as real. But I've lost so much. And you're correct, I have not dealt with any of it. I don't mean to come across as disrespectful, but I don't know what any of this means, I've never really had to sit down and realize that everything I once had in life is now my past—a past I was never really present for. I was always working. I *buried* myself in my work. And that's why I loaded up a backpack and bought a plane ticket."

"You ran away from a world that you controlled. Because you couldn't control what you had lost."

Jack sits reflecting on Fabiola's words. "You're correct. Maybe I need to employ you to council me and the people I work with." Jack laughs at how Fabiola is such a simple person, yet she is so spot-on. And he realizes it at that moment. But all this—his situation, his meltdown, the dream—is still hard to accept. "Regardless, you have to know that for me, in my world, this is a lot of crazy talk. I come from a world where things have to be concrete. I need facts. If I can't see it or touch it, if I can't hold the product, I can't quantify it."

"What more do you need than the *here* and the *now*?" Fabiola lets those words sit with Jack, then says, "What if I told you that the night before I saw you, I dreamed of a man? A tortured soul. Crazed and dancing to his own lunacy in the streets of San Pedro? Would you say I am crazy?"

ANNE

Clang and rattle of steel on steel. Wheels clatter over rail joints, Anne and Trot feeling every bump, sway, and vibration. Elbowing Trot and directing his attention to the round opening at her left, to the scuffed Doc Martens worn by *someone* in the opposite compartment. Anne spreads her feet and bends into a squat, and a second later she is looking into the eyes of a young black girl. She seems too young to be riding a freight train on her own. Her head is covered by a military olive-drab bandanna. She is holding a rolled-up blue sleeping bag against her stomach. Behind the sleeping bag, she wears a Jack Daniel's T-shirt that once was black, now faded a dingy gray. Her full lips break into a smile, and she comes forward, stepping and working her way through the opening until she is standing before Anne and Trot. Putting out her hand, she almost shouts, "Name's Cinnamon."

Oh, what the hell, Anne thinks. *She's making herself at home, might as well meet her halfway.* She reaches out and shakes the hand. It is as soft and warm as the girl's features. And she tells Cinnamon, "I'm Anne. He's Trot."

Cinnamon shakes hands with Trot and asks, "How long you-all been catching out?"

Anne's head tilts sideways. "Catching out?"

Cinnamon laughs. Her teeth are Tic Tac white. "Train hopping. You must be a greenhorn."

Anne tells her, "My first train. Yeah, a *greenhorn*. Situation at home was a total shit show."

Out here, she realizes, they have their own language, their own "speak." And Cinnamon tells her, "Hear you loud and clear, girl." Shakes her head up and down. "What about you, thin man? What's your history?"

Trot's gaze never rises from the rough metal floor of the hopper car, and he speaks as if reciting a passage of scripture or an alibi. "Started hopping trains when I lived in Texas. Ran with a group called the Recon Rejects. The folks got tired of warning me. Caught me the last time I ventured home, moved me to Tennessee with them. Same as Anne—got a shit sentence at home. My way didn't line up with what Mommy and Daddy had planned for their son."

"Gotta be careful out here," Cinnamon says. "You got lucky hopping this grainer. It don't always happen that way. Get a grainer with no porch, it's not solid, just a skeletal crossbar. It's what you call—"

"Yeah. A suicide ride," Trot interrupts.

Cinnamon smiles. "Right, a suicide ride. Gotta ditch that bitch. I see you know your cars."

Cinnamon seems to be feeling them out while offering up her wisdom of the rails. Anne would need a notebook to keep track of all the dos and don'ts of hopping freights.

"I know a bit," Trot says. "Any idea where we're headed?"

"If luck is with me and my research is correct, Alabama. Birmingham. But we need to scoot before it stops in the yard."

"Bulls?" Trot asks.

"Oh, yeah," Cinnamon tells them. "Rail pigs. But there's a jungle I hang at down in Alabama. Group of crust kids. Kinda run by a skeez calls himself Dredd."

"Dredd?" Anne says.

"Yeah, like in the comic book, Judge Dredd. Something he grew up reading. Huge fanatic. Dude is a total perv, though. Used to teach college."

"How long you been riding?" Anne asks.

"Since I was sixteen. I'm twenty-five now."

"Nine years."

"Yeah, run away from home. Mother was no-account. Father got touchy when I got older—'developed female qualities,' as he spoke it. I had a boyfriend, couple years older. Started riding with him. Then we got separated, but I kept going. Was addicted, you know. No ties, no strings. Nothing holding me down."

"That's awful about your father."

"Yeah, it's a real letdown when you realize that family you see in the movies and the family you's born into don't live on the same block. That's some make-believe Disney bullshit."

"You got that right," says Anne. "My home didn't have no Peter Pan or Wendy. I was constantly at odds with my brothers and sisters. They seemed to think how we lived was the accepted norm. Where'd you call home?"

"Bluefield, West Virginia. Not much to talk about. Rural folk. Hard living. You?"

"Right around where we hopped this train—Johnson City, Tennessee. Mother's a drunk. Father drinks, but he's more into the abuse that delivers his point when you do something wrong. Big on the old fist upside the head or a heated kitchen utensil to teach a lesson." Anne pulls up the sleeve of her sweatshirt and shows off some of her father's fork-and-stovetop handiwork.

"Branded you good," Cinnamon says, shaking her head. "That's cruel. Real battle scar. How about you, thin man? How's your parents?"

"Not abusive," Trot says, puckering his lips, "They just never accepted my interest in the same sex. Couldn't get that their young man liked other young men, like being queer was a choice. They saw it more as a terroristic threat to their cozy little lives. Tried sending me to counseling. Private schools. Public schools. Christian Summer Camps. Group therapy. You name a supposed cure for being gay, they tried it on me. It was easier than just accepting what I was."

"That sucks five kinds of ways," Cinnamon says as she sits down. A big brown North Face pack cushions her back from the grainer wall.

Everyone's bones are rattled from the train travel, but the tension begins to ease with the passing of words, and the sense that no one here poses a threat to anyone else.

"How much you know about freight hopping?" Cinnamon asks Anne.

"Only what Trot's told me, which ain't much."

Cinnamon says, "This train here is run by Norfolk Southern. They run the tracks through half the Midwest, North, South, and East. Then it switches over to Union Pacific—they go west and north and south. They's certain cars you want and some you don't when you're catching out or, uh, hopping freight."

"Grainers are best, least in my experience," Trot says. "It's what we looked for back in Texas. Or boxcars."

"Grainers with the double barrel like this one are a sweet ride. Boxcars are good. Gotta be careful, you hop one. Sometimes, they carry vehicles inside, could crush your ass. Also, the doors—good idea to jamb the track with a railroad spike, cause that son of a bitch shuts on you, you're trapped till someone in the yard opens it a day or a month later. If you're still alive, you're caught."

Trot doesn't say anything, lets Cinnamon have the stage. Then he says, "I hear they'll beat you silly and then call a bull, and he beats your ass too."

"Some of those yard dogs are cool," the girl says. "If you cool with them, they might let you go. Shit, some will even be friendly, let you know where the train's headed, and if it's not your direction, they'll let you know a train that's coming in and headed your way. Some even give you a bull's schedule so you know when it's safe to hop on from the yard. Others will turn your ass in. Toss you in the clink. Get a hefty fine."

"How about tankers?" Trot asks. "I hear they're a no-go."

"Got that right. No room to ride. Gotta watch the junk cars, too. They can be dangerous as fuck. Some loaded with scrap steel that'll shift and crush you. Get some loaded with coal. I had some friends riding in an open-top gondola. They was sleeping inside when it was empty, didn't wake up when it stopped, got loaded with rock. Crushed their asses."

"Shit! That's horrible!" Anne says.

"It is, but having the variety of cars means more places to hide when traveling, you just gotta pay attention, be on your toes."

"And you learned all this in nine years?"

"I've rode a lot of trains in them nine years. Met a lot of different folks out here, each carrying different knowledge from their travels and encounters. Some good, some not so. You gotta know your shit, pay attention. Ain't no joke. I've met people that wanna follow me, pay me money to do things."

"What kinda things?" Anne asks.

"Sexual things. Being a girl out here is dangerous. Ain't gonna lie. Best get you a blade. Keep it sharp and available. You'll also meet people that'll watch your back; you just gotta return the favor. They's people you will meet that will be like a real family. Lot of freedom, but it comes at a cost of your livelihood. Out here, payment is your attention or your life."

"You ride any intermodal?" Trot asks.

"Yeah, they're the fast track. Get you to where you're headed in a hurry. They get hotshotted, don't have to stop anywhere."

"What's 'hotshotted'?" Anne asks.

"When they don't have to stop in the yard, got clearance to blow right on through rail yards. They're double-stacked containers. Good, steady ride. Loaded with lighter freight, usually consumer goods." Pulling a water bottle from her side, Cinnamon removes the cap, takes a sip. Swallows. "Y'all want any?"

Anne waves her hand. "I'm good, but thanks." She's feeling comfortable, then remembers about her brother. About whether she might have killed him, or just left him for dead.

Cinnamon lays her head back. "Feels good to meet new people. Just came from up around Roanoke. Got a whore's bath. First one I had in while. Out here, it's good to stay dirty. Build up a good stench. Keeps the predators at bay. Take their focus off your *female* attributes. Less your sexuality is exposed, the better, until you find someone you can mesh with. And trust me, you will. But being dirty will save your skin."

Anne and Trot sit back, listening to the steel grind over the track. Anne asks, "How long you think we got before we're in Alabama?"

"Many factors to that question. Depends on how often we slow down for curves, track switching, if something breaks down. If there's a shift change, they gotta stop somewhere and let another crew meet them to take over. Hopefully, it's only a few hours. We can knock off some rest and just chill until then."

"How do we know when we need to jump off?"

"Trust me, I'll know. It's my stomping ground. Just sit back, find your calm place, and enjoy the countryside."

Leaning her head against the wall of the grainer's compartment, she feels the metal's vibration in her skull. Eyes closed, backpack cushioning her spine, she sinks into the soft ebb of the adrenaline. Her limbs feel heavy, weighted. Her entire self is sliding, free-falling, hitting warm water. The calm starts in her toes, traveling up her shins, knees, thighs, through viscera, rib cage, chest, shoulders, and down her arms until all she can see in her mind's eye is her brother, sprawled facedown on the kitchen floor.

Next thing Anne knows, her neck is aching. Her legs are full of thumbtacks instead of blood, poking around beneath the skin, pricking her marrow. Her limbs have lost the rigid support of bone; they are asleep, hanging from her like heavy vines. Eyelids part, and her blurred view comes to focus on Trot and Cinnamon over her, one arm shaking her to wake up while an index finger to the lips shushes her. Anne reads Cinnamon's lips. "We all zombied out, missed our jump. We're in the rail yard. Gotta motor outta here without getting caught."

Following Cinnamon and Trot out of the circular hole, into the daylight, jumping from the steel porch to the gravel, brutish voices coming loud behind them.

"Hey! Hey, what the fuck do you-all think you're doing?"

Cinnamon yells, "Run!"

HUNTER

"It's called collateral," Hunter tells Itch. Straddling the worn leather seat of his knucklehead. Pressing his crazy locks behind his ears, he straps his flat-black Street & Steel half helmet under his chin. "The shit were you thinking? Shorting a guy you're selling weed for. You think he'd just let it go?"

"I thought they took it pretty damn good," Itch tells Hunter, standing like a stranger between him and Nugget. "Figured they'd take it out of my salary for selling their shit, that I'd get everything straight when we got back from Cali." Fixing his half helmet, sliding on his shades and leather jacket. "Who am I riding shotgun with?"

"You mean riding *bitch*? Sure as shit ain't me," Nugget tells him.

"Thought they took it pretty good? And you think somebody who grows weed in Kentucky for a living just lets people *do* that?" Hunter asks, sliding on a pair of black leather gloves with skulls decorating the knuckles. He fires up his motorcycle.

Yelling over the engine, Itch says, "Well, when you put it like that, I s'pose not. But I ain't like everybody else."

"You got that right," Hunter tells him. "Get your bony ass and half-baked brain on the back, but remember, no fucking foreplay."

Itch slides onto the back and tenderly wraps his beefy arms around Hunter's chest.

Hunter says, "Cut the shit." Pauses and asks, "Why would you pull some shit like that? That's like me building a custom bike for a customer for an agreed price and they decide to only pay me half after all the time and money I put into it. Thinking they'll pay the rest in their own sweet-ass time."

"Like I said, I's thinking I'd get the rest of the money when we got back from our trip."

Beside Hunter, Nugget shakes his head. He runs a hand over his smooth skull, then pulls on a pair of leather gloves. Laughing, he talks over the rumble of the bikes. "It's like Hunter told you: they took your bike as collateral. Now we gotta go and get it back. Fix your fuck-up. How much you owe them to get it out of hock?"

Itch holds up three fingers.

"Three hundred?" Nugget yells. "That ain't so bad."

Itch twists his head vigorously from left to right. "No. I's three grand shy."

Nugget and Hunter yell as one, "Three fucking *grand*?"

"Yeah. I—"

"Stop!" Hunter demands. Holding up a gloved hand to stop any more words from falling out of Itch's mouth. "I don't wanna know why. Seriously, I don't wanna know."

Nugget yells, "I'm sure it's got to do with a fair-skinned, shit-stompin' maiden named Dani."

Dani. About five feet five inches. Toned and covered with more ink than the Sunday comics. Raven locks of hair all the way to a truly memorable ass. She doesn't take any shit from man or beast. And if she wants what Itch has, she'll just take it—leave him with the responsibility or else resolve to fix any problems that might arise from her actions. And she loves to fill her lungs with a long, luxurious drag of that wacky tobacky.

"We've wasted enough damn time," Hunter yells over the two rumbling Harley engines. "Let's get this debt settled before dark. I'd like to make it to Indiana."

Wheeling the knuckle backward, pointing the front tire toward the highway, they roll out of the lot and onto the pavement.

Miles and miles down the road, immersed in the thick green of trees and ditch-weed hemp, he drinks in the smells of pine pollen and lupine blossoms that line the long driveway of patched gravel and potholed dirt. Opening up to a menagerie of white and tan goats, chickens, and stray hounds trotting about and barking as if to convince someone they're earning their keep. The landscape is littered with broken-down swing sets, vehicles in varying states of decay and disrepair. A young woman with long brunette locks and impressive breasts is slouched comfortably in a rusted lawn chair. A sweating five-gallon bucket of ice and longneck beers sits beside her in easy reach. She wears a Pabst Blue Ribbon bikini, white on sunburn pink. Next to her sits a pale-skinned, potbellied male whose hair looks to have been bleached out with lemon juice. His do is all business on top and a party in the back—a full-on mullet—set off strangely with wraparound gangster-chic shades. To complete the ensemble, he wears a snakeskin-patterned Speedo and cowboy boots with a riding heel. Standing up from a wooden rocking chair that has seen better days, he waits for the boss lady to stand upright and approach her visitors.

Before the bikes are parked and throttled down, the three guys who took Itch's bike emerge from a barn with an open front. A large motor hangs by a rusty log chain slung over a double six-by-six roof joist. A huge circle of grease and oil blackens the earth beneath the engine. All three men appear squirrelly and underfed. Their jeans are filthy with dirt, crankcase oil, and bearing grease. Heads buzzed down to a thin fuzz, beards decidedly not. Arms and necks stenciled with bad ink.

Hunter mumbles, "What the shit did you get us into, Itch?"

Two hounds with chocolate-and-white coats spiked up by mud and chicken shit muster the boldness to come bawling and nipping at Hunter's and Nugget's bike tires.

Nugget shakes his head. "Think somebody needs to feed these mutts."

Sizing up his surroundings, Hunter takes in two weathered and dented trailers sitting off in the distance. With cardboarded windows and rotted decks painted by mint-green mold, they sit apart from an old farmhouse with flaking paint and a barnacled roof. All this is surrounded by maybe a square mile of mixed woods.

Planting her bare feet on the soil, the woman stands up on strong, shapely legs. The gallons of beer aside, she appears athletic. The skinny-fat man in the marble bag does not. He follows behind, all bony legs and arms, as she approaches Hunter, Itch, and Nugget. The man works a toothpick in a mouth beyond the help of modern dentistry. The woman, leading the way with a PBR longneck in her hand, stops a few feet from Hunter. Lifting the beer to her lips, she takes a long pull and swallows. Looks at Itch. Shakes her head with a shit-eating grin. "You best be here with my goddamned money, or we got jack shit to talk about, Itch. You and your little gang of scooter trash'll be passing slang with my three boys and their colleagues Smith and Wesson."

Confident, Hunter doesn't let Itch talk, tells the lady, "Why we're here—to clear up Itch's payment, what he owes you. Get his bike back and get on down the line."

Eyes stab like bayonets into Hunter's sight and out the back of his skull. "Don't recall talking to you." Pausing, she makes a face as if she maybe ate some spoiled brussels sprouts. "Sorry, who the fuck are you? I didn't get your name. Oh, wait, that's because I wasn't fucking talking to you!"

This chick is napalm. "Name's Hunter, friend of Itch's." Swinging his leg over his bike, he steps toward her, offers a gloved hand. "And you are . . . ?"

Green eyes lined by thick, sweaty eyeliner glance from Hunter's hand to his crotch, then her stare carves back through him. Smirking, she takes Hunter's hand, shakes it. "I'm Malone. Ms. Marylin Malone. And this steaming-hot hunk of horseshit behind me is Oscar, my multitalented fiancé."

Nodding, Hunter tells Ms. Malone, "Got Itch's debt covered." Reaches into his hip pocket. Malone's men mirror him, reaching behind their backs and hauling out large-caliber handguns. Hammers click, and Malone says, "The hell you think you're doing, reaching behind your back like that, Mr. Hunter?"

"Easy." Hunter holds his left palm up as his right hand gingerly lifts out his chained leather wallet. Holds it up for everyone to see. "Like I said, got Itch's payment covered. Just going in my wallet to get your money."

Oscar laughs. "You 'bout got your ass lit up like a Roman candle, son."

Hunter unsnaps his wallet. The three men in his peripheral vision keep their pistols trained on him. Not the Taliban this time, but maybe not so different.

Malone tells Hunter, "Just keep it slow and simple there, Mr. Hunter."

"No need to go tribal. See?" Hunter says, pulling a wad of bills from his wallet. "It's all Benjamin Franklin."

Hunter counts out thirty of them. Slowly. Presses the wad of bills to Malone's open palm. She takes the wad of cash, hands it over her shoulder to Oscar. "Be a dear and make sure the number's correct this time, Oscar. Don't wanna take any chances this go-around, seeing as Mr. Itch didn't bother to mention that he was shorter'n a mosquito's peter when last we crossed paths."

Sliding his wallet back into his hip pocket. There is the feeling of discomfort that comes from having three pistols pointed at you. Hunter thinks of the 1911 Colt .45 tucked in his ruck. But it would do him little good at this juncture, with three good ol' boys already sighting him up. Hunter feels a bit blindsided to find that Malone wears the pants in this operation. He had assumed that Itch was dealing with a male. A dude. Itch never mentioned otherwise. Regardless, it's pretty visible that she's a bigger swingin' dick than any of the men she surrounds herself with. She's the alpha broad. Hunter is sure of that. And he's pretty sure Oscar can't get a grip on the numbers, is maybe allergic to basic arithmetic, or maybe missed school the week they were learning how to count. He fiddles with the loose cash, has dropped several bills and picked them back up, as if they were burning his fingers. Hunter thinks about offering to recount it for him.

"You know, maybe I should just say fuck it! Start with you, Itch, right in your fucking head. Then Mr. Hunter and this other slab of chuck roast—sorry hon, what was your name? I didn't catch it seeing as you weren't rude enough to offer it."

Not rising to the bait, Nugget says, "Nugget."

"Nugget, like the McDonald's Chicken Mc-type. I bet your family is proud of that moniker. Pleased to meet you, Mr. Nugget. Like I's saying, after I shoot you, Mr. Hunter, I'll shoot Mr. Nugget just for having the poor judgment to even be associated with Itch, just for tagging along. Have my boys take your asses out in my woods and find you a nice quiet plot of untrespassed soil." Malone's eyes bore right through Itch. Her guys come closer, looking jumpier than before. Nerves are taut and getting twitchy, waiting on a response.

Hunter's *"Oh, shit"* radar starts blipping. He flashes to his father and how he was good at talking a bad situation into a good situation—had that gift of gab when shit wasn't going so well. Hunter says, "Ms. Malone, I can see you're dealing with a real shit sandwich, Itch skipping out and shorting you. And ol' Oscar back there don't seem to know his numbers too good—been fiddling with three grand like maybe it's a foreign language he can't comprehend. I can count it out for you, right here or wherever, have your guys watch. Regardless, I get it. The stress. Why I quit my job. Tired of dealing with less talented fucks."

"And what was this that you did for a living?"

"Repaired and built and rebuilt motorcycles. Choppers. Harleys. You name it, I can fix or refabricate it. My boss was a total dickweed. And average with bikes. He just happened to be the guy with the reach, the connections, and the capital."

"Well, this is my business," Malone replied. "And when product goes out, cash must come back in. Got a daughter's college tuition to pony up for. Employees to pay. Hell, ol' Itch here must think I'm running a rental service, in which payments can be deferred. He just give us an envelope of cash like he always has, thinks things is all good, and cuts out. Turns out, he shorted me. Never done that before. Always been a square dude."

"I *am* a square dude," Itch says, and Hunter cuts in.

"He is a square dude. I think he got in a bit over his shoulders. Got a lady with a bad burn for primo bud on the home front, and she's a strong-minded woman like yourself."

"Mr. Hunter, I have two girls. One in high school, one in college. Both from the same weasel of a man that's buried over on that hillside, right under a rosebush. Thing is, I'm thirty-seven years young, and I don't put up with any malcontents. Man works for me, I give him product, he sells the product, returns what he earned in order to get compensated. And I give enough freebies of my product to those I employ to not be shorted."

Hunter searches for something to latch on to. Sometimes flattery helps. "You don't look like you're a day over thirty."

"Thank you, Mr. Hunter. It's referred to as *good genes*—taken from my mama's end of the pool. Regardless, our issue isn't what age I look. I'm not some two-bit redneck, to be walked on and then roll over and piss on my belly. I'm a lady who believes respect is earned, not given, and I believe in second chances but never a third. I conduct my business in the same manner." Malone inhales deep and exhales hard. Wearing a gruff face of lost patience, she asks, "Oscar, did Mr. Hunter give us a suitcase of Franklins, or just three fucking grand?"

Oscar stammers, "No-no, dear, no suitcase. It's three grand."

"What's the holdup, then? Paint dries faster than you can count. We're not even talking first-grade math here, Osc. This is just *counting*."

Fiddling with the cash, Oscar tells Malone, "No, honey. Just used to using that machine that counts it for us, is all. Trying to take my time, make sure it's all here."

"Well?"

"We're good, honey, we're good."

Malone waves a hand at her men, tells them, "You can put your hardware back up, boys. One of you make nice and bring Mr. Itch his bike." She takes another swig of her beer. The men lower their pistols. One of them goes into the barn. Comes back wheeling Itch's chromed-out shovelhead motorcycle with neon-jade flames down the tank. Coming from the rear of Hunter's motorcycle, Itch approaches Malone's guy, takes the weight of his bike from him. Straddles it. And Hunter asks, "Everyone square?"

Malone's eyes pierce a chill through Hunter, and she tells him, "At this juncture, we're square as a newly built home. You seem to be a good friend." Looking to Itch, she tells him, "Get your bitch lined out at home, 'cause that was your second chance. There won't be a next time"—pausing, looking back at Hunter and Nugget—"for any of you."

JACK

Her words echo in Jack's brain. *I dreamed of a man. A tortured soul. Crazed and dancing in the streets to his own lunacy.* Excusing himself now. Needing to piss. At his age, he is lucky he hadn't pissed the bed. Getting up from the kitchen table, he walks to the bathroom. Jack is broken and weak. He unzips his pants, relieves himself, flushes, and turns on the faucet. His soft, uncalloused hands cup cold water, lather up, rinse. He splashes his face again, wanting to wash away whatever reality he had wandered into. There is the acrid smell of old sweat, of himself. Perspiration and dirt collected in transit, from his dream. And Jack feels beaten and worn, powerless. His hips, knees, and elbows are aching and bruised from the pummeling. He stands in Fabiola's bathroom, taking in his surroundings: sink, toilet, chipped claw-foot tub. There is no large, spacious area, no marbled shower stall. No Jacuzzi tub, no bidet, no mirrored walls, and no sauna room. Here he stands, feeling a deep burn in his bones and gristle, a back spasm like a dagger, and something akin to judgment being cast upon him. He takes in his splotched face, pouches dark as an eggplant beneath his eyes. Deeply lost internally and searching for his center, he had found this woman, Fabiola, for a reason. An answer to an unknown query, but she is as crazed as he. He couldn't sit at the table any longer, couldn't be in the same room as Fabiola and her crazy talk about dreams. It was like being stuck in a modern-day episode of *The Twilight Zone.*

Overcome by emotion, he remembers his father calling him "useless" when he was a kid. Jack grits his teeth, recalling the endless put-downs telling him he would never amount to shit. And that only incited him to become something, to make good grades, get into a good college, and earn a living that created a cushion for life. He never saw what was happening around him unless it involved work, unless it involved growth for earning more money. Board meetings, pie charts, Excel spreadsheets, market reports, think tanks—these were his everyday lingo of life for all those years. What he never realized then was the slow crumbling of lives—the dominoes that lined up around him, that would tip and fall, one into the next. He never planned for the sickness, the death, the fear. This unraveling is haunting him.

Dry air warms the home as daylight brings heat. Drying sweat has left a faint white dusting of salt on his skin. There is no smell of wood smoke, no fumes. Only his unbathed body—something he's unaccustomed to. Till now, he seldom went more than twelve hours without a bath. He fights back tears. He fights back at how weak he feels after being stripped of all the things in his life that made him *him.*

Maybe Fabiola was right: he isn't accustomed to things he can't control.

Back in the kitchen, Fabiola sits at the table, looks in his eyes. She's hard, unlike Jack. She smiles. Jack wonders if this is what simple folk do to pass the time: sit and stare at one another until a thought crosses their mind to start a conversation. Running her palm over the table, Fabiola tells him, "My husband crafted this table with his own two hands."

Jack's own two hands have never built anything. Almost never held a hammer. A screwdriver. He hasn't mowed his own lawn or changed a tire. Hasn't known labor since he was a kid. And even back then he wasn't skilled at any of it. He paid people to do such things for him. Inside, he is going crazy with questions. It may be that Fabiola is crazy too. Maybe she is rubbing off on him. He thinks something is off about her. Saying she saw him in a dream. Maybe this is what *loss* does to a person. Regardless of social status, of money. It drives everyone to the brink. Over the edge. It breaks them. And Jack tries like hell to be polite, to gather his wits, get his bearings. Trying to be polite, he asks her, "Where did he acquire the lumber to build the table?"

"He ordered it. Then sawed and planed and smoothed it himself. He had a shop out back of the house."

Running his palm over the table. Jack feels as if someone had beat his skull with a shovel. The coffee seemed to help at first. Now, well, Jack is having second thoughts.

"Where did your husband hone such a craft, a skill?"

"His father. He wanted him to be a *carpintero*, or what you Americans call a woodworker."

Jack's father never taught him anything. From the brief moments Jack was allowed to be around him, to be his son, he recalls a vile, unhappy man. Cursing and belittling his mother and him. With such a lacking fatherly example, it's no wonder that Jack never really taught his own kids anything. He was always working. Any time he spent with them, he spent thinking about work. The teaching and sharing he left to his wife, Sarah.

Unable to take it any longer, at the mercy of all these thoughts and memories, Jack wants out of here. He has to get moving. And he tells her, "I really appreciate all your kindness, Fabiola—especially your taking me in and offering me a place to sleep, listening to my ramblings. But I need to get back on the road. I need to move forward."

"I've packed you some bread and cheese. It's all I have. And I've filled your bottles with water."

In placing someone else's needs before her own, she is like Sarah. Jack tells her, "I deeply appreciate that. You are way too considerate. You really should not give me all your food."

"You will be hungry. You will need it more than I."

Fabiola brings Jack his boots. Watches him put them on. Tie them.

Shaking her hand. It's rough and hard, unlike Jack's. He offers her a feeble smile and a baby-soft hand. Fabiola smiles back. Wishes him a safe journey and waves to him as he steps out the door.

The heat of the day beats down on Jack like Dempsey pounding on Jess Willard. Placing one foot in front of the next, the pack already tugging on his shoulders, bottles of water slosh behind him, and the phantom axe keeps digging into his lower back, a little deeper with every mile of progress.

The map says twenty hours by foot to Calama, but a little over an hour by vehicle. Taking in the mountainous outcrops and clumps of clay and rock in the wide and treeless expanse, Jack thinks this must be what it's like on Mars. With each step, he listens for a vehicle. A truck or semi. He hitched to San Pedro from Argentina. There was no shortage of vehicles, of people offering the kindness of a lift. Today, he won't be so fortunate.

Out here, there is nothing but space and time to reflect. With barely a hint of life, it is the serest, most inhospitable place he has ever seen. Out of habit, he looks to his wrist for the time. Nothing but a pale stripe to show where his watch once resided. A gift from Sarah, now gone forever, leaving behind only a bad memory. His tongue feels dry and foreign in his mouth. He thought about Fabiola—her kindness and her insistence that he believe in her dreams. That his are trying to tell him something about himself. Did she take him for a fool? Jack never believed anything outside the realm of science. He tried to explain this to her. If it wasn't something of physical form, something he could apprehend through scientific methods, he had no use for it. But out here, maybe things are different. The people and their customs. Their culture. Their beliefs that were millennia in the making. Here, life is hard, but not nearly so maddeningly complex.

Jack's heels are rubbing in spots and have started to burn. To take his mind off the hurt, he reflects on what brought him here, to this moment. After losing Sarah, he realized he had nothing left, that life had passed him by. So he decided to travel, to pull up stakes and fly to South America. With the same skills he had learned in business, he researched the different countries he would be crossing. Reading up on Chile, Argentina, Peru, Bolivia, and Colombia, taking in histories of the people and the regions, adding to what he knew about this area he is now traversing: San Pedro de Atacama. Yes, it is the driest desert on earth, and yet people have lived within it dating back some ten thousand years. The people here were once ruled by the Inca Empire. Then the Spanish arrived, and the Incas fell. War came. Independence. And the creation of the Bolivian and Peruvian territories. Then, in the eighteenth century, came the War of the Pacific, and a division and self-identity among the Peruvians, Bolivians, and Chileans. Chile claimed the Atacama region and its indigenous people. During the nineteenth century, the Atacameños were employed to mine silver nitrate and copper.

Then, in the twentieth century, the silver industry collapsed and created an economic crisis. And life in the Atacama got even harder.

Hours have passed, and Jack has a problem. Not a single vehicle has driven by, and the burning sensation on the ball of his right foot is getting worse. But even though everything hurts, he can't take his eyes off the beauty of the skyline—brilliant blue above, against it the earth tones and glowing orange of the mountains, aproned with dazzling white mineral deposits. Breathtaking, but there is no shelter from the unrelenting sun. No hiding from the heat. And for all the material wealth he has accumulated, none of it can do him a damn bit of good. He wants to stop and sit, but that won't get him anywhere. He needs a ride, a rest area, or a gas station—even a scraggly thornbush to provide a little shade. He wonders whether the heat is making him delirious. Tears sting his eyes as he thinks of Sarah. Meeting in high school. Him washing dishes in a diner. Studying with her. Sharing their dreams. She wanted to be a lawyer—something not too many women did back then. Dating all the way into college. Coming home in the summers. Working for Sarah's father at his family-owned insurance company. It was there that Jack saw a way to make a lot of money fast. His future father-in-law wouldn't be too happy about it afterward, but by then it wouldn't matter. Jack would already have his ticket up the corporate ladder.

Studying the market, Jack learned how he could achieve economies of scale. Earn the biggest return. So unlike now, slogging down an empty desert highway at the ends of the earth, broke in more ways than one. Broke of money. Broke of spirit. But in the beginning, for Jack it was all about money. When a man comes from nothing, he is hungry to create something. Jack was always about creating something more, doing something no one else had done. He used Sarah's father's company to run a scheme. Was it crooked?

Not if he didn't get caught. He used it all summer after college. Building his bank account to buy into American Pharmacy. A business he would parlay into something much bigger. His scheme was simple. When customers made their insurance payments to his father in-law's company, he took their cash and invested it in stocks. Got a return. Made their payment, and whatever return he made from the market, he reinvested. His net worth kept piling up. He kept gambling their payments. Then he cashed out.

His business plan for American Pharmacy was also simple: go beyond the pharmacy; create a drive-through; add groceries; expand the makeup, shampoo, snacks, and other consumer goods. Create a one-size-fits-all solution in the puzzle of American consumers' lives. Twenty-four-hour photo development. And before long, he had restructured and helped open stores all over the United States. And his ideas were catching on in other retail sectors, eventually combining retail with pharmacies, groceries, oil changes, and lawn and garden. A one-stop shop to pull trade from both the supermarket and the department store. Creating superstores. The only remaining task was to outsource labor. Hello, China and Mexico! Hello, profits.

All the years he'd spent building and networking, promoting his ideas, was time spent away from a family that was growing without him. A son who had attended a trade school, for God's sake! A fucking trade school to become a journeymen electrician, only to lean on the crutch of drugs. Inevitably, the crutch grew to become an addiction.

Sarah would lose their second child and want to adopt, only to see that child grow into something unlike anything she or Jack could have imagined.

They adopted Megan as a small child. She was vibrant, cute, and smart. Had come from a broken home—an alcoholic father and mother who didn't want a child. Meanwhile, Jack was out dining on Kobe beefsteaks and expensive whiskey. Getting little sleep. Following expense reports, business trends. Staying ahead of the game. Sarah was giving up her dreams of becoming a lawyer to be a good mother. Jack never paid attention to the trends in his own family. How his adopted daughter's earlier abuse had damaged something deep inside her. So many things he missed. Warning signs that would lead to Megan hanging in her cell after the trial. And to his son rebelling by turning down a topflight business school for a trade school, then becoming addicted to cocaine, meth, and booze. And his wife was becoming tired more often, and Jack thinking it was from everything she had to deal with. Then his mother's age just sort of sneaked up on him. The strong, fearless woman who had raised him, going into that hospital to die and telling Jack to "run, run away from it all." Processing it all, he realizes he never really knew his children—he only paid for them, for their habits, their luxuries.

His shoulders are already sore from the pack straps, and his feet sting and burn with every step. What he would give to sit in a vehicle with an air conditioner! Even a beat-up truck and a rolled-down window. Anything other than walking under a brutal sun. He had decided on South America because he told himself he needed to get away from everything. Everyone. A change of scenery. Well, this certainly qualifies. He looks out at the barren landscape. An excursion to clear his mind, rebuild his soul. To run, run away from it all. To figure things out and, just perhaps, discover something within himself. But he has no good idea what that might be.

Fabiola's words ring loud and clear in his head. *You ran away from a world that you controlled. Because you couldn't control what you had lost.* And that's when Jack hears the sound of tires on hard dirt, and the Doppler swoosh of a vehicle passing from behind.

ANNE

Voices come from all directions, bouncing through the silent maze of boxcars, tankers, grainers, and flatcars, mixed and matched, coupled in rows on several tracks. Crunch of ballast stone beneath their feet. Anne is a ball of anxious worry as Cinnamon yells, "This way! Hurry!"

Searching for a grainer to hide beneath, because the wide V-spaced compartments have enough space for multiple bodies to wait while the foot traffic passes, watching the hustle of angry men, their feet clomping up and down the row of cars, and then crossing over to the next track. Cinnamon, Anne, and Trot slowly uncrouch and look up and down the line, ready to dodge the yard workers. Staying hidden. Listening to steel toes kicking up rock, the beer-bellied men winded and panting. The ring of cell phones, the static of radios.

One whiskered man in a camouflage ball cap and faded bib overalls looks to another man with thick muttonchop side-whiskers and faded bibs and mutters, "Where the hell'd they go?"

Hunched forward with palms resting on his knees, chest heaving, Muttonchops lifts an arm and points. "Seen 'em over that way."

"How many, you think?" asks Camo Cap.

In a tone of uncertainty, Muttonchops says, "Four, maybe five—not real certain."

Kneeling and waiting, watching the two men from a distance, then pulling back, Cinnamon holds up a fist to halt, then an index and middle finger letting everyone know there are two men. Then she points in the direction they need to flee. Watching the two men turn away, half limping, half walking in the opposite direction, Anne feels frightened enough that she might vomit. Maneuvering through the rail yard illegally. The thought of being caught, taken to jail. Sent back home to face what she left behind. All these thoughts are roiling in her gut. Cinnamon waves at her and Trot to follow her. Crossing to the next track. Maneuvering under another grainer car. Smells of diesel and creosote. Staying hidden. Waiting. They listen, hearing only their own gasps as they try to catch their breath, slow the adrenaline.

Cinnamon peeks out. Looks left then right, sees nothing. Not a single shape. "Move," she tells Anne and Trot. Crouch-walking to another track, sliding beneath another car, their packs snagging and bumping, getting caught on the undercarriage of the cars each time they bend down to maneuver.

Waiting again, this time Cinnamon tells Anne, "Take a peek, real slow. You need to learn the ropes of evading the yard bulls."

Peeking out. Looking both ways, her whole body vibrating with nerves. Thrown into a situation she's never been in before, not even knowing where she is, going on instinct. Not seeing any motion, she looks straight across, searching for a break, for the next car to hide beneath. Closing her eyes, she focuses through the surging adrenaline. *Get your shit together, girl*, she tells herself.

This is what you wanted. Takes a deep breath, opens her eyes, leans her head back in just as legs come from nowhere on the far side of the next track. Yard workers walking up the row. Stopping. Kneeling to search down the row. She fights the urge to bolt from cover and run. Not wanting to get caught, sent to jail. Have everything end before it even begins. She wants to face her life head-on. See this through.

She sees the single track enter off in the distance, splitting into multiple tracks on the left, then the right. Some empty, others with long rows of coupled freight cars. Beyond them, beyond all the steel of rails and locomotives and chain-link fence, are the welcoming woods, soft and green and vibrant.

Anne feels closed in, hunted by predators in the wilderness of the rail yard. If she were to envision an industrial hell world, it would look a lot like this.

Still sucking wind, trying to slow her breath, she feels her jitters turning to outright panic. She asks, "How do we get out of here?"

Cinnamon says, "Breathe. We're close. Got a few more rows of cars and track to manage, then a stretch of bare ground to cover before the fence. Then it's the woods. That's what we want. But they's gonna be a bull positioned somewhere, trust me. They know to funnel us where they want us to go."

Trot asks, "How we get by them?"

"We wait as long as it takes. Then we cover ground. Watch. See where they go, and remember who we seen. Sometimes, there's more than one. So when I give the word, we break for the woods and you-all follow me. The jungle ain't far."

Anne feels queasier than ever. Is this a test? To see if, when shit goes sideways, she and Trot will hold up or crumble under the pressure? Or might Cinnamon leave her and Trot as bait for the wolves so she can make her way to the jungle?

Slinking from track to track. Watching legs in grimy cover-alls walk up and down the rows, pause to look beneath a car, then move on. More waiting. Anne's heart is thumping loud enough to wake the dead. She tries to imagine an unknown future, in which she meets and surrounds herself with others like her. They are the misunderstood, the mistreated, who had a gap in their home life and who want only love, family, connection. Maybe this will be her chance for that family. If she survives this. If she doesn't get caught. And then she sees Mitch, lying on the kitchen floor. All that blood. Stealing the money. Cops looking for her. *No. Pull your shit together!* Not a useful train of thought. Placing her hands over her ears. Bending her head foreword. *Quit obsessing,* she tells herself. Trot's hand squeezes her knee. Whispers reassurance. "We're gonna make it."

Anne's head lifts. Her eyes meet his. She musters a tentative smile.

Cinnamon's head jerks back. Anne says, "What's wrong?"

"White pickup parked twenty feet away. Looks to be a bull. Probably keeping watch. We gotta wait a little longer. When he drives away, we make a run for it. Not a moment sooner."

After a few very long minutes, they hear the pop of gravel under tires as the white truck backs up and rolls away. Cinnamon makes eye contact with Anne and Trot. Smiles and says, "Y'all ready?"

Anne gulps and says, "We are."

"Let's move," Cinnamon commands.

Coming from beneath the metal compartment, moving over the empty tracks until they hit another row of railcars. Hearts are pounding, they work their way down the last line of boxcars. They hunker down and duck walk beneath. Thighs burning, they come out the other side and are looking at the chain-link fence, a mere twenty feet away. Beyond it, the woods. Freedom.

From nowhere, a deep voice yells, "They're down here!"

Turning, they see the muttonchops man leaning against the next car, a tanker, huffing air.

"Now or never," Cinnamon says. "Follow me. The break in the fence is down here, just past the pole. Come on!"

Running down the fence line, Anne's dog-bitten leg is throbbing. The yard bull is coming at them. Though he's not fast, he's constant.

"Stop!" He yells.

Anne keeps running, through the pain.

Trot yells, "Where is it?"

"Farther down," Cinnamon says, waving her arm.

Pointing at a large pinkish rock, she says, "There!"

Hands grab the stone and roll it away from the fence, pull back the stiff panel of galvanized chain-link. Trot goes first, snagging his pack on the clipped wire ends. "Shit!" He yells.

Anne's fingers work frantically to get the pack free. Then, shoving it through the gap, she holds the wire up for Cinnamon. Clomp of boots and heavy panting from the winded yard bull. "Damn you kids. Don't get paid enough for this bullshit." Growing louder, closer behind Anne as she unhooks Cinnamon's sleeping bag from the wire. Shoving her and her gear through.

"Shit, shit, *shit!*" Anne mutters aloud.

Trot is holding the wire back for her while Cinnamon tries to pull her through. Leg throbbing, she wriggles her head and shoulders under, then can't go farther. She feels her pack being jerked backward. She tugs forward. "Get the fuck off me!" she growls.

Muttonchops snags his forearm on the sharp wire. Releasing Anne's pack, he snarls, "Little cunt!"

Her waist and butt have wriggled under, and she is using her elbows to dig and drag herself through. She's spent, swimming in slow motion, moving through taffy, trying to pull her feet through.

Her pursuer manages to work his way back down onto all fours and grabs her injured leg. A jolt of fire sears up from her ankle to her hip.

"Fucker!" She screams. Rolls over onto her butt. She sees a face scrunched up in anger as he tugs her back toward him. She cocks her other leg and kicks hard. Trail-runner shoe sole meets face, and she feels the give of nose cartilage and bone. The man's hands go to his nose, which is fountaining blood as his mouth spews profane threats.

Cinnamon and Trot grab Anne's arms and drag her up off her ass, onto her feet. Cinnamon yells, "Sorry, not today, yardman." And they run.

Into the woods, Anne half limping and half running. Dodging trees and being raked by brush and briars. Through a swarm of gnats. An evergreen branch slaps her face. Moving through dense undergrowth until Cinnamon is satisfied the pursuers have given up the chase. She slows to a walk. Everyone catching their breath.

Cinnamon laughs. "Wow! What a fucking rush."

Anne can no longer contain the stress—or whatever is in her belly—and she pukes. Planting her palms on her thighs, bends forward, heaving and coughing until she's dry.

Hands, warm and comforting, gently rubbing her back, giving her a clean bandanna to wipe her mouth. There is affection, a tenderness of emotion that Anne has never felt from another person, male or female.

"You okay?" Cinnamon asks with a look of genuine concern.

Anne straightens, smiles, her lips filmed by ick. And she laughs. "I think so. But you ain't lying. I thought that whiskered tub of guts had me."

Trot laughs too, saying, "Damn, that was too close."

They walk for what seems a long time. Then sounds of voices grow in the distance. Cinnamon tells them, "Just a little ways."

The sound grows louder and more distinct. Bicycles are strewn about the little clearing in the woods. Leaning against a big oak tree, others lying on one side, some with wheels, some without. A headless doll, buckets. Wads of trash and a dirt path curving and leading to an orange-and-gray tent on the left. A blue-and-gray tent on the right. Beyond these, several lawn chairs. Then everything opens to a clearing with tarps spread out over poles and tree limbs to create a shelter. Young men and women sit around in lawn and camp chairs or on the ground. Grimy faces and matted hair. Greasy. Dreadlocked. Twisted and braided. It's a combination of styles, with "ungroomed" the prevalent theme. Some are smoking. Mouths chewing. Shooting the shit. Eyes reading books. And when some of those eyes look up and see Cinnamon, bodies rise and come forward with arms spread wide. Offering warm, heartfelt hugs.

"Cinnamon!"

"Where-all have you been? Dredd's been wondering about you."

"Was up north. West Virginia."

"You've brought guests?"

"Meet Anne and Trot."

A young woman comes forward with warm hugs for Anne and Trot. Her blond hair, brown at the roots, is braided with beads on the ends. A leather dog collar around her neck. Fingers like twigs. She's milky-fleshed, wearing a Ramones T-shirt. Torn black knee-high socks and a raggedy scarf-like skirt. "I'm Canary. A friend of Cinnamon's is a friend of mine. Welcome to the jungle."

Anne is overwhelmed with emotion. She tells Canary, "Nice to meet you."

"Let's mingle, let you get acquainted and make yourselves at home," Cinnamon says, pulling them away from Canary.

Home. This grubby, cluttery little clearing in the woods is the first place that ever felt like home. Her mind tingles with the thought. Just arrived among strangers, and she has already been hugged—offered more warmth from another human being than she encountered in her entire seventeen years with her blood kin.

Walking past more tents. Chairs. Rocks placed in a circle for a fire pit that is still smoldering. They step over scattered trash, trampled and mashed underfoot. And there it is: the smell of food—soup or stew, maybe. They follow their noses to a row of tents set up with vestibules and entry areas and spaced out like neighbors with yards. Some are orange, others green, blue, brown. Tarps stretch over tree limbs to wooden pallet walls bounding a large area like a kitchen and living room all in one. Milk crates abound, some for sitting, others stacked and used as bookshelves. Suitcases and backpacks lie about. Empty food cans litter a table built from scrap two-by-fours and a door. The ground is thick with beer bottles. Clothing hangs from a rope stretched between saplings. On a pink plush couch with no feet, two thin-faced teens sit reading.

From one of the tents, a man appears. He is older than the others in the encampment. Windblown hair parted on the side, matted and wavy, some of it braided. Tattoos on his cheek, silver hoop through his nose. His hands thick with crud. Stretched and stained T-shirt. He eyes Cinnamon and yells, "You're back! Been gone too long, my dear. Still lovely, as always."

Arms spread wide, she and Dredd embrace. She says, "Travel sometimes takes us back to our roots, only to return us to our real home."

"And you've brought friends," he says. "Introduce me."

"This is Anne and Trot. They caught out from Tennessee."

"Welcome," Dredd tells them. "Make yourselves at home. Everyone is accepted here. We all chip in and earn our way. We're one big family."

"Billy the Kid has some rabbit stew over on the fire. Help yourselves."

Making eye contact with Cinnamon, Anne says, "I'm fine right now."

What Anne wants is rest. To sleep. But her body is rushing with excitement. Seeing the faces of people her age. Thinking of how she came here and what it took. Her home, her life—it suddenly seems a million miles away. Like a separate existence, another incarnation. She feels as if she has stepped into a time warp. An alternate universe.

Cinnamon walks over to the table. Trot follows. They grab used paper bowls and head toward a young man stirring a pot on a metal oven rack over glowing orange coals.

Anne starts to follow, when Dredd grabs her arms. He says, "Let's talk."

A bit startled, not knowing what to say, Anne nods her head. "Oh, okay."

Pulling her over to the edge of the clearing, Dredd sits her down on a fallen log. His wild blond mane is shot through with gray. The silver circle through his nose reminds her of a bull's nose ring. He's thin. She looks down at the crud-caked fingernails resting on her knee. They migrate to her thigh. His T-shirt hangs lank from his bony shoulders. His eyes look as if he had on liner, but it's just dirt from not bathing. He smells like onions and old sweat.

"Your name is Anne?"

"Yes."

"You're very lovely. We'll have to create you a moniker."

Anne says, "Thanks. What do you mean by a 'moniker'?"

"Your freight-hopping name." He pauses, then starts peppering her with questions. "Tennessee was home?"

"Yeah."

"Why'd you run away?" He speaks as if he were speed dating. A rush of sentences.

"It was a shitbox. Mom's a drunk. Dad was abusive. And school was loaded with dedicated half-wit assholes."

His hands constantly shift. Touching her arm, her leg, as if she were an instrument he was tuning.

"I hear that a lot. Everyone here has a storied past. Running from something. From someone. Leaving something behind. But here you'll find no judgment. We're all about family. Freedom. We're a mix of hippies and what folks call millennials. We are the revolution. We follow the DIY way of life."

"DIY?"

"Do it yourself."

He reaches up, fingers the strap of Anne's backpack. "You can take your pack off. Get comfortable. Make yourself at home."

Sliding her arms through the straps, she lays the pack on the ground between her feet. "How long's this place been here?" she asks.

"Quite a while. We catch out not far from here. Get a lot of traffic coming and going, see new faces and old."

"Yeah, we came from the yard. Fell asleep. Had a wild encounter."

"I bet. Those yard guys are overfed and underexercised. Cinnamon's smart. She can maneuver. She's killed, you know."

"That she can. Took good care of us." Anne hesitates. "*Killed?*"

"Yeah, ask her about it sometime. I'm rambling—not my place to tell you." Dredd pauses, reaches over, rubs Anne's cheek. "You got black eyes. Your folks get cross with you?"

Feeling uncomfortable at his touch, she senses something forced and slimy about Dredd. She had forgotten about her eyes. "My brother. We had a fight before I left."

"Siblings. Older?"

"Yes."

"Well, there's no attitudes around here."

Is this guy for real? Anne muses. He is kind. Warm. But fidgety. Too touchy. Too hands-on for her. Her upbringing has made her cautious of people. She keeps a barrier up. A shield.

"Cool," Anne tells him.

"Do you like to read?"

"Depends. Wasn't much time for books in my house." Escape was the mall—that and booze at the shack where she met Trot.

"We gotta fix that. Get you caught up on Kerouac. Tully. Bukowski. They're the greats. They have a way with words. Back then it was so free. Unique and new. Real freedom in their day. All they had was time. How about comics?"

"What about comics?"

"You ever read them?"

"No."

Anne's emotions, overwhelmed at first by the newness, are slowly shifting from feeling welcomed and warm to a sense of pause and caution. Feeling like an object, a rare piece of meat. And not knowing what is in store for her.

Dredd points to the youngsters on the couch. "They all read. No television to poison their thoughts, guiding them to an agenda of fear. No 'buy this,' 'gotta have that,' slaving for the man at a job you don't want." Pausing, he points to the stacks on the ground, next to a softly billowing partition that looks like parachute material. "Those are just a few of the books we have. All bought from libraries. Brought here by folks who travel all across the country."

Touching her thigh, he gently rubs it. His breath is warm on her face. His hand is searching, working toward her hip and abs. Anne tightens with revulsion. Looking around, she doesn't see Cinnamon or Trot. Wonders where they've disappeared, when a hand warms her shoulder. She turns around, looks up.

"Come on, I got my tent pitched. You can rest. Trot's already sawing a forest's worth of logs."

Relieved, Anne grabs her pack, stands up.

"Aw, we were just getting to know each other," Dredd says.

"I'm sure you were," Cinnamon tells him. "But she's had a long, crazy journey."

"Nice to meet you," Anne tells Dredd.

"We'll talk again soon, Anne. Rest up."

Out of eye- and earshot, Cinnamon wraps her arm around Anne's shoulders and says, "Sorry, didn't mean to vanish on you. I'm guessing you got his spew about books, freedom, and the like."

Chuckling, Anne says, "Oh, yeah."

"Always keep another person around when in his presence. My fault—wasn't thinking. He ain't what he presents himself to be. All that talk is bait."

"Bait for what?"

"Nothing good."

HUNTER

Long, curving stretches of US 25E provide scenic, wooded solitude, with the quiet rumble of three Harley engines for a soundtrack. Gliding over new blacktop, it feels like flying low to the ground. Then, all too soon, they merge onto Interstate 75 North, which they have to share with commuter traffic, vacationers, and tractor-trailers moving everything from loads of pipe to live chickens. Traffic is thick all the way to their exit in Berea, where they pull into Walnut Meadow RV Park to camp for the night. With its green-roofed office, worn wood siding, and six-by-six pillars in the front, the office reminds Hunter of a run-down gas station from the late seventies or early eighties.

After paying the cute pigtailed attendant in a washed-out black Lucas Oil T-shirt, they follow a gravel lane that splits off into different clusters of campsites. It takes them to a flat area with a few shade trees, the nearest neighbor a gold and tan RV opposite them.

They throttle their bikes down, come to a stop, heel their kickstands. In the abrupt calm, they can hear shouting kids and raucous birdsong along with the crack and pop of their engines and exhaust pipes cooling.

No one seems ready to disrupt the mood of quiet. Itch eyes Hunter and Nugget, then finally speaks his first words since getting his bike back. "Really appreciate you guys helping me out."

"Anything for a brother," Hunter says, bumping fists.

"Yeah," Nugget says. "Just don't do no more dumb shit, all right?"

"Right. I know." Itch pauses. "Anyone want cold water and some jerky?"

"You buying?"

"Of course! Think I'd ask the guys who helped me out to pay for it?" Itch chuckles. "Get settled in. I think there's a Shell station up the road. I'll run up and grab us some."

"Ten-four, good buddy," Nugget tells him.

Itch's bike rumbles away as Hunter and Nugget remove their helmets.

"He's about the craziest son of a bitch I know," Nugget mutters.

"Would you expect him to be any other way?"

"Nah, I s'pose not."

They unstrap their mats and sleeping bags from the rears of their bikes, rolling everything out onto the manicured grass, where Hunter smooths his marshmallow-looking mummy bag. After shucking off his leather jacket, he wads it up and sticks it behind his head as he flops down on the bag. Ankles crossed, fingers laced behind his head, he hears the soft crunch of gravel from a black Silverado pulling an old-school twenty-eight-foot Airstream.

Across the way, in front of the long, glossy gold-and-tan RV, a father and son lay shapes on a picnic table.

Hunter hears a snort and gag from Nugget, who has sprawled out on his sleeping pad and begun snoring, all in the space of about ten seconds. Continuing to watch the father and son, who stand over a circle of stones, Hunter notices the quartered splits of firewood, piled according to no particular scheme. The father kneeling down, trying to light what looks like wads of paper beneath the wood. The sight takes Hunter back to another campground, when he was around fourteen and his father took him fishing one Saturday. They had unloaded everything from his father's 1978 short-bed Ford Ranger with a topper and had set up their two-man tent, an old olive-drab pyramid, piled up splits of wood from the campground office, then gathered a double handful of twigs and pine straw. Once they got the twigs crackling, they stacked larger sticks on the flames, in a log-cabin structure. After the larger sticks caught, they stacked on the small quartered logs. Meanwhile, from the neighboring campsite of another father and son came a constant stream of complaining. Hank had told young Hunter in a low tone, "Can read it all over that guy's every action."

"What's that?"

"Man's got some skills, but he's never taken his son camping before."

Hunter and his father walked over. The father and son had on white Fruit of the Loom T-shirts and cutoff jean shorts. Opening a big nylon drawstring bag, the father shook out a new tent. The directions were spread out on a barn-red picnic table where a tackle box and fishing rods also lay.

The father muttered, "This damn shit can't never be easy."

Hank told the father, "Look like you could use an extra set of hands."

Looking up from the instructions, the guy said, "You'd think after all the shit I seen and done over the years, I'd be able to outsmart a fucking tent. You ever set one of these up?"

"I have. Just get one of the poles extended and locked in, and we'll start working it through the sleeves."

The father, a short, fit-looking man, said, "Roger that. I just gotta find them first."

"They're in the parachute-looking pouch there about a foot and a half long."

Hank pointed, and the dad's eyes lit up. "Ah, I see. If it was a snake, it woulda' bit me." Untying the pouch, he handed one of the little bundles of wands to Hank, who shook it loose and watched the elastic shock cord pull the wands together into a single tent pole. Hunter and the guy's son spread the tent out on the ground and staked down the corners while Hank and the father assembled the other two fiberglass poles. The father said to Hank, "Thanks for walking over."

Hank told him, "Don't mention it."

As Hank worked a pole through the sleeves from one side of the tent to the other, he told the father, "We'll do this with all of them. They'll cross over the top, create a frame of support—surprisingly strong, even in a windstorm."

"Makes sense," the dad replied. "Did something similar years ago in boot camp. But we was a company of soldiers. Had less complications to worry about—just the DI, really."

Hank said, "Sorry to interrupt your camping. Never introduced myself." He stuck out his hand. "I'm Hank, and this is my son, Hunter."

The father smiled, shook his hand. "I encourage the interruption. Name's Sid, and this is my boy, Travis. I really appreciate the gesture. My dad never did anything with me when I's growing up, and I thought I should start taking Travis camping and fishing. Get him out of the house. Thought it'd be good for both of us. I work so damn much, ain't enough hours in the day."

"I hear that. Nothing wrong with exposing your boy to the

outdoors. Better late than never is what I say. Let's get the other poles in, and you'll be set."

As they threaded the other two tent poles through their sleeves, Hank said, "So you from around the area?"

"Yeah, I'm a car mechanic down at Kitterman's garage. You?"

"Sales. I'm on the road all week, travel all over the country. I try to get some time in with Hunter when I can."

"That's good. So, a real outdoorsman, I'm guessing?"

"Not as much as I'd like, but mostly, yeah. My father owns a farm not far from here. You ever hunt?"

Punching the pole into the end grommet, Sid said, "When I was a kid, my grandfather hunted everything that walked, crawled, or flew. That's next on the list. You'd think, if I served my country and worked on cars, I'd be better at stuff like this."

"You probably are, but you weren't born a soldier or a mechanic, either. I'm sure you had to learn those skill sets."

Sid told Hank, "Never thought of it that way, but you're right. I did have to learn everything. My granddaddy was a mechanic. I learned a lot from him growing up. Then, when I joined the Army out of high school, Corps of Engineers, got shipped off to Vietnam for the war."

"A vet?"

"Yeah. I was over there for two years. Dozed down a lot of jungle. Built base camps and laid steel for C-130 runways. Came back stateside, did another year, and when I got out, I moved back here and found a job working on cars."

"I wanted to join the military, but it wasn't in the cards for me," said Hank. There was a lull in the conversation as the two men threw the rain fly over the newly constructed tent. "At any rate, I'll let you and Travis get back to it. You need anything, don't hesitate to give me or Hunter a shout."

Sid and Hank shook hands again, "I really appreciate that."

Hunter's father had a way with people. He just knew how to talk to them. How to relate to whatever problem they were wrestling with at that moment. Always seemed to be at the right place at the right time. Always knew how to help. There was no second-guessing the situation. He just reacted. That next day, they all went fishing. Hank and Sid became good friends, kept in contact.

Now, twenty years later, watching the father struggle, Hunter gets to his feet, starts walking, crossing over the grass, then the loose gravel of the driveway, and back onto the grass. He approaches the father, who looks up at him.

"Need a hand?" Hunter asks him.

Dubious eyes take in the long hair, the biker garb, and all that ink. Apparently deciding that this stranger is no threat, the father says, "Unless you got a gallon of gas, might not be any use at all."

Studio tan, frosted blond hair, muscular—looks like a gym rat that tripped and spilled a jug of bleach on his head. Hunter kneels down, removes the thickest hunks of wood, grabs some twigs and pine needles. "Trick is, you just need to start small, build up to bigger pieces. Got any more paper?"

"Umm, y-yeah, sure." The father grabs a newspaper off the picnic table. Hands it to Hunter, who begins ripping and wadding up pages and dropping them in the center of the stone circle. Then he starts crisscrossing small sticks and twigs over the wads of paper until he's built a teepee. Grabs the pack of matches. Scratches one. The paper flames orange up into the twigs. He starts laying larger sticks over the burning twigs. "Do this for a few; then add a larger stick. We'll get it."

"Man, I tried to get that shit going. It just wouldn't fucking burn for me."

"We'll get it. Just takes a little finagling."

"Patience, more like. I just don't got much of that anymore."

On the picnic table are paper plates with a bag of marshmallows, a box of graham crackers, and Hershey bars. "Making s'mores?" Hunter asks.

The guy chuckles. "Well, hell, we just might get to, now that you came along. I appreciate the help. Wasn't sure if you was coming over to help, or to hand me my ass 'cause of something I did in a bar years ago when I was too drunk to remember."

The man offers his hand. "Wendell."

He doesn't introduce his son. Gripping Hunter's hand, he's trying to show his strength.

"Hunter."

"Dude, I really appreciate the help."

Releasing the man's hand, Hunter looks to the skinny kid with long dark bangs and green eyes. "And you are?"

"Devon." He's wearing a Slipknot T-shirt.

Hunter shakes Devon's hand. "Cool shirt."

And Wendell asks, "Stupid question: You lift?"

"Yeah, my buddies and I spot each other back where we live."

"Thought so. You got that swollen look about you," Wendell says, puffing up his chest while pulling on the collar of his shirt. It's like a nervous tic. "Where y'all from?"

"North Carolina."

"Out for a long ride?"

"You might say. Traveling to California. My father passed away. Taking our time, taking in the countryside. Figure it'll take us a week or better to get there."

"Damn. Sorry to hear that, man."

From behind comes the rumble of Itch's Harley. "Appreciate it, dude. Hate to run off, but my buddy's back. You and Devon have a good evening. Need anything, give us a shout."

"Appreciate it, man," Wendell says.

Walking back to the campsite, Hunter sees Itch turning off the fuel petcock on his motorcycle. Pulling some white plastic grocery sacks from his leather saddle bags, he says, "Grabbed us a six-pack of Zombie Dust beer, some candied almonds, Mingua beef jerky, Grippo's chips, and a little water to keep us hydrated." Looking at Hunter, he asks, "Everything cool?"

"Yeah, just giving some campers a little help with their fire."

Laying his mat on the ground, then his sleeping bag. Now everyone is laid back, chewing jerky, sipping suds, and crunching chips. "What's his story?" Itch asks.

"Told you, couldn't get his campfire lit. Thought I'd be a good scout, offer some help."

"Well now, ain't you sweet."

"More'n you'll ever know." Hunter chuckles. "Guess we'll head to Indiana at first light. That work for you guys?"

"Sounds like a plan."

To muttered complaints, Hunter rousts his two wingmen in the thin gray predawn light. After packing up and tying their bedrolls down, they wash up at the sink in the bathhouse and head out. Getting off the interstate, they pass horse farms with rail fences, huge barns, and green rolling pastures.

They round Louisville and cross over the Ohio River, leaving the Bluegrass State for the Hoosier State. Hanging a left onto 135 to old 64, they exit down into Milltown, Indiana, and through a hard-bitten neighborhood of mobile homes, sad houses, and yards full of unmowed weeds. Across an iron bridge, they roll past the VFW and take a curving lane to an A-frame house that sits down along the Blue River. At the sound of rumbling engines, eyes look out from porches and parlor windows, gawking at the strange sight.

Off to the side of the house, a man pushes an old red lawn mower. His sweat-stained ball cap proclaims in big block letters, FREE MUSTACHE RIDES. He ignores Hunter and his buddies as they turn their bikes off and remove their helmets.

"Who's that?" Itch asks.

"Beats the shit out of me," Hunter says.

Nugget says jokingly, "Must be the Lawnmower Man."

The A-frame is painted a pale baby-shit brown. Off to the right sits a garage of the same hue with a candy-apple red 1970 Plymouth Barracuda parked in front.

Itch says, "That's a sweet fucking ride."

"Sid's gift when he came home from the service," Hunter tells him.

"How long you known this cat?"

"Since I was fourteen. Dad and I met him camping one year. They became friends. He piqued my interest in joining the service."

"No shit?"

"No shit. Served in Nam with the Army Corps of Engineers. Contact has been hit-and-miss. He lost his wife last year. I didn't make the funeral."

Standing on the concrete slab porch, they hear loud and angry words from inside the home. Hunter waits for a pause in the yelling, then knocks.

"Tired. I'm sick and tired of your bullshit. No. Now, wait a goddamned minute. I served my country. Come home. Worked my whole damn life. Then you and that surprise kid . . . What? Really? You gonna pull that card on me? Look, I don't gotta listen to this horseshit. Yeah, I think I'll have myself a beer. Hell, I might have two or three just to put out this big, smoldering piss-off you started inside of me. It's my God-given right."

Nugget has a confused expression. "Thought you said his wife passed away."

"She did."

"Then who's he getting stout with?"

Hunter lifts his hand to knock. "Guess we'll find out."

He bangs on the door. Shuffle and clomp from inside the house. The door swings open. Eyes light up.

"I'll be goddamned. *Hunter?* Holy shit. Who'd you bring with you, the Hell's fucking Angels? Get in here!" He envelops Hunter in a bear hug. Sid is a short but stout little man with a wild graying do like Einstein's—nothing on top, sheer rioting anarchy on the sides. He peers through thick square-framed glasses and asks, "So who are your buddies?"

"Itch and Nugget. Nugget and I served in Iraq together."

Sid's eyes ignite like two piss holes in the snow, "No shit. What regiment?"

"First Battalion, Hundred and Eighty-Sixth Infantry Regiment."

Shaking hands all around, Sid tells them, "Pleasure, guys. Make yourselves at home. Let's hit the back deck. Got some catching up to do." Taking them through the house, Sid asks, "So, just passing through?"

"Something like that," Hunter says.

The living room is simply furnished. Leather sofa. Flat-screen television. Card table in the corner. Pictures, in a time frame from snaggletoothed kid to squared-away soldier in dress uniform. Images of war, surrounded by bulldozers, airfields, and jungle giving way to those of his marriage to an attractive blonde line the walls. An off-balance ceiling fan wobbles overhead as they cross into the kitchen, recognizable as such by the sink and fridge and little else. No dishes or even a spoon—only a coffeemaker with a fat red plastic jar of Folgers beside it and a selection of bourbons ranging from Early Times all the way up to Maker's Mark and Knob

Creek. They walk out a sliding glass door to a wooden deck where a cast-iron picnic table sits.

Itch comments, "Badass table."

"Made it myself."

"Looks like some steady welds. You're a craftsman."

"Appreciate it. Not what I once was—the arthritis gets to me these days." Looking to Hunter, he says, "Well, either you're passing through or you're not. What's the big secret that brings you to Indiana? You relocated to North Carolina, right?"

"Yeah . . ."

"How about your dad? He still out on the West Coast?"

"He is, but . . ."

"*But*'s ass. You don't sound too sure about that."

"That's one reason I stopped by. He passed away."

Sid shakes his head, gestures for everyone to sit down at the table. "Oh, man, I'm sorry to hear that, Hunter. What happened? Was he sick? Seems like the 'big C' has gotten contagious over the years, or—"

"No. My uncle called. He lives out there too. Apparently, it was a mysterious house fire. That's all he'd tell me over the phone. That's where I'm headed—kinda taking my time, seeing some countryside on the way."

"Hunter, I'm damn sorry to hear that. Your dad—I know he wasn't around all the time when you was growing up, but when he was, he made the most of his time with you. Hell, he made it for anyone he encountered. I'm proof of that."

Thinking about it, Hunter knows that Sid is right. "He did. And we tried to keep in touch. But with us living on separate ends of the spectrum, it was tough. So now I'm riding cross-country with these two crazies, making a complete safari of the trip."

"How long you gonna be in Indiana?"

"Haven't really planned it out. Probably tonight. We'll see, maybe catch some breakfast tomorrow, then head out. Enough about me. What the hell have *you* been up to?"

Fidgety, looking around with a lost gaze, Sid runs his hand through his Einstein do and says, "Oh, you know, retired from earning my keep. Trying to keep this place in order since Annie passed of cancer last fall." After a quiet moment, he asks, "Say, any of you fellas want a beer?"

Hunter wants to ask who he was bickering with, but doesn't. Looks to Itch and Nugget, who shrug and nod yes, they suppose they could drink a beer. As reliable as the tides. Hunter pulls down the beginnings of a smile. "Sure," he says. "Thought about heading back into Corydon for some grub. You hungry?"

"Corydon? Fuck that noise. You just wheeled in; you sure as shit ain't backtracking. I got a better option. Let's hit the VFW. They got a fish fry tonight. Have some beers, catch up. What do you and your saddle gang say?"

Hunter turns. "Sound good, guys?"

Itch grins. "Let's do it."

Nugget says, "I'm game."

"Then get your bony asses up. We're driving the 'Cuda."

The black upholstery is clean and smells new—odd for a car that's fifty years old. Engine is loud and rumbling.

"Hear that?" Sid asks. "That, my friends, is the sound of a four-forty V-eight, triple deuce carburetors, and 727 TorqueFlite automatic transmission."

"Sweet fucking ride." Itch tells Sid as they pull into the graveled parking lot at the VFW.

"Appreciate it," says Sid. "Just replaced the seats few months back."

At the entrance, Nugget holds the door open for Sid, who

thanks him. Inside, the lighting is dim. In a far corner, the juke box plays "Swingin'" by John Anderson. Lining the ceiling are the names of veterans, Hunter supposes—men and women who have served in their country's armed forces. Walking over the scuffed floor of patterned red, white, and blue tiles to the bar. It is of a dark hardwood, chromed metal stools with cracked blue vinyl cushions. At tables with matching blue Formica tops, men and women sit in wooden chairs, shooting the breeze, sipping from sweaty cans of High Life and Miller Lite and glasses of whiskey, flipping ashes from cigarettes, the low hum of exhaust fans sucking up the smoke overhead, eyes piercing the three strangers who walk in with Sid.

"I'll grab us a table," Itch says.

"Go ahead," Hunter tells him. "I'll get us a round. Maker's good with you guys?"

"Long as it's on the rocks," Nugget says.

The bartender is a youngish gal, hair dark as potting soil but with tips dyed blue, pulled back into a ponytail. Her smoke-colored T-shirt has "UK" in bold white letters across the front. She comes with a sweet-feisty tone, chewing bubble gum.

"How you doing tonight, Sid? Looks like you got company from somewheres else."

Slapping his hand down on the bar, Sid looks at her and says, "Sure do, Felicia. And I'm doing pretty damn good, thanks for askin'. How about some drinks for my buddy Hunter and his friends, Nugget and Itch? They just rolled in from North Carolina."

"What's your poison, Nugget? Cuervo *Gold*, maybe?" She grins. "And what are you itching for, Itch?"

"How about Maker's?" Hunter tells her.

"I like your style." Felicia says. "On the rocks?"

Jokingly Hunter tells her, "Is there any other way?" He lays a twenty on the bar. Says, "Please."

Sid starts to protest. "I got this, Hunter."

"Your money's no good, Sid. I got it."

The bartender smiles, her pearly-whites glowing beneath the dim fluorescents while her green eyes flash the look at Hunter. She tells him and Sid, "Take a seat. I'll bring your drinks over." She winks with the chomp of her gum, then asks Hunter, "You related to Sid?"

"No. Why you ask that?"

"Oh, you just look real familiar."

Sid butts in. "You're such a sweetheart, Felicia, thank you." She starts to turn away, but then he asks, "When's that fish fry start?"

"Orville should be heating up the fryer in about an hour. Wanna put in an order?"

"Sure do, honey. We got four orders."

Pulling a pen from behind her ear, hot-pink nail polish glowing as she scribes on a small notepad. "You get three pieces of bluegill or catfish. You want slaw, fries, and hush puppies too?"

Sid asks, "The hush puppies breaded in cornmeal?"

"Yes, they are. Indiana's finest."

"I take them and bluegill."

And Hunter tells her, "We'll take bluegill, the puppies, and fries and coleslaw too."

Jotting everything down, Felicia tells them, "Ketchup and tartar?"

"Sounds good," Hunter says.

"Got it. Like I said, Orville should be firing it up in about an hour. I'll double-check before I get your drinks out."

"Appreciate it, dear," Sid tells her.

Turning away from the bar, Hunter feels every eye in the place following him and Sid to Nugget and Itch. An older guy in overalls, nursing a watered-down whiskey, raises it to Sid as he approaches.

Sid smiles. "Well, I'll be dipped in shit! How goes it, Archie? I thought you's dead."

"Lies," he says, grinning. "I'm still kicking. If Charlie couldn't kill me, civvy life sure as shit can't."

"Well, I'm glad you're sucking wind up here on the surface like the rest of us. Thought for sure I missed your damn funeral. Been feeling like an asshole all this time for no good reason."

Archie laughs. "Oh, don't lose that feelin', because you're still an asshole—just not for that."

The VFW hall is filling up with regulars, who all seem to know each other. The vibe is easy, familiar.

"What you been up to?"

"For starters, I had me some breathing issues. Went to get checked out. Doc found I had some blockage, so I had to get me a stent. Added another pill to my collection."

"No shit."

"Yeah, so I's laid up for a week or better. Had to go up through my damn groin. About the most I been touched in the past ten years or better—only it wasn't none too exciting."

"I suppose not. Remind me to try and avoid that little procedure."

"Before that, there was my boy, having to bail his ass out of jail. Getting him back into rehab. Starts off on the meth. Get that taken care of, and next thing you know, he's dating a Spanish gal. Shit, she's a human being, good girl. Everyone's so uptight about how you address them and their nationality, you know. I kept calling her a Mexican and she kept saying she's Spanish, but anyway she don't pay me no mind—I'm old. Regardless, he goes off and gets on the heroin. She comes crying and beating on my door late one night, says he got busted. So I bail his ass out. Again. Next thing I know, he's lost his job, can't pay his rent. She's waitressing, but it ain't quite enough, and now the two of them is shacking with me.

But she's a good girl. Cleans and cooks, works, and keeps his ass lined out. And she helped me quite a bit when I was laid up for a week. She got him a job working with her at the Beef O'Brady's in Corydon. And so far, so good."

"Damn, I hope he stays clean."

"Me too," Archie says. Sips his whiskey and asks, "Who's your compadres? You running with the Outlaws motorcycle club or some shit?"

"Naw, you remember ol' Hank used to be a traveling salesman?"

"Yeah, his daddy had a farm down in Walnut Valley, right?"

"That's him. This here's his son."

"Hunter? Damn, boy, you done growed the fuck up."

"One and only," Hunter says. Offers a hand. "How are you doing, Archie?"

Archie shakes his hand. "Well, you just heard my troubles."

"Archie here flew choppers in Nam," Sid tells him.

"No shit. Appreciate your service, Archie. I was a helicopter mechanic over in Iraq."

"I be damn. What was that like?"

"Lot of sand, lot of heat, and a *whole* lot of shit."

"I bet. How's your daddy doing? Ain't seen him in years."

The two seconds' silence seems to last forever before Hunter says, "Why I'm here. I thought me and my buddies would stop in and see Sid on our way out west. He recently passed away. Lived out in California for the past fifteen years."

"Get old, you move to the heat, keep the circulation flowing. I hate to hear that. Your daddy was a good guy. Hell, we drank together quite a few times."

"Appreciate that."

"Well, we best be getting over here. Good seeing you, Archie," Sid tells him.

"Nice meeting you," Hunter says.

"Take care of yourself, Hunter. Keep safe on your travels, and try to keep Sid here in line."

"I'll do my best."

Hunter and Sid cross the marred tiles to their table and slide into their chairs. Felicia brings everyone's drinks out. Her denim cutoffs brush up against Hunter as she tells Sid, "Orville's heating up the fryer now, so your orders should be out in less than an hour."

"Sounds good, hon. Thanks."

"You're welcome. Need anything, give me a shout." As she says this, Felicia is still giving Hunter interested eyes. She walks back to the bar.

"Think you got an admirer there, boss man," Itch tells Hunter.

"That ain't happening. I got a girl. 'Sides, that there's jailbait."

"She's around twenty-five," Sid replies. "Serving drinks in a bar."

"Not interested."

Nugget takes a sip of his Maker's and asks Sid, "Who's the guy was mowing the lawn over at your place?"

"Dodd. Some call him the Lawnmower Man; others call him the local Sling Blade."

"See?" Nugget says, chuckling now. "Told you guys. What's it he says in the movie? 'Some folks call it a Sling Blade; I call it a Kaiser Blade.'"

Itch gives a theatrical "*Um-hmm.*"

"He's a little slow in the head." Sid says. "Mows just about everyone's lawn in Milltown. Does a damn good job. Keeps to himself. But everyone keeps an eye on him."

Itch asks, "What's up with the ball cap he wears? Says 'free mustache rides.'"

"It ain't what you think. Damn horrible thing happened years ago. His sister went missing. He lived with her. She took care of him after their parents passed away. Neither of them was in too good of health. He's on the government's tit, drawing disability. But any rate, she was a whore. Slept with damn near the whole county. Useta be in here hanging around every night. She had her dives. She'd hit the bowling alley and Lisa's in Corydon. Then one day, she just up and disappeared. Eventually, she turned up down on Blue River, washed up on the bank next to a really good fishing hole. Coroner concludes she'd been strangled. Autopsy confirmed that, so I heard. Some said she was dumped in the river; others said she was dragged through the woods to the bank where she's found. When Dodd went through all her stuff, he found that hat. It was hers. It's all he has from when his sister was killed. Wasn't like she accumulated much over the years—hocked or sold most of her shit for dope money. But she had disappeared for better than a week. Rumor was she was raped—was bruising around her wrists and her neck, some said from a struggle. Regardless, it was just a horrible situation."

Hunter says, "That is pretty damn awful."

"It is. Never found out who done it, neither."

"That's some real BTK shit," Itch says.

Sid says, "BTK?" Fidgeting. He rubs his index fingers over his thumb.

"You know, 'Bind, Torture, Kill.' Serial killer from Kansas." Itch says.

Hunter says, "Dennis Rader."

Nugget says, "Guy did that shit for years. Traced one of his letters back to a computer where he attended church, busted his ass."

"Damn." Sid says, taking his hat off, running a hand through his wiry locks. "Imagine that. Been sitting with that same guy all those years every Sunday. Fucking creepy. I remember hearing about that in the news. Didn't keep up with any of it. But whoever killed

Dodd's sister had folks worked up for a while, thinking there's a killer amongst us. But most believe it was someone just passing through. Others believe it was Goat."

Itch coughs. "Wait a minute. She fucked a *goat*?"

"No, no. There's a guy in town who peddles pills, meth, and heroin. They call him Goat. Has a farm full of 'em. Some said she was into him for quite a bit on credit. He and her daddy was good friends. He grew impatient knowing she'd never pay him. She was tricking her hide to buy drugs, and then sometimes to get drugs from Goat. But that hat Dodd wears was hers. Her name was Shannon. He's worn that hat since she was found. Never takes it off."

"Fucking horrible," Hunter says, "Definitely gonna need another Maker's once this one's gone."

"Crazy damn world we live in," Sid says. Sips his whiskey. "Used to see all them mama-sans overseas doing that, selling themselves to us soldiers. Crazy times."

"Got that right," Nugget says.

"How about a toast?" Sid asks. Bouncing his heel up and down on the floor. There's a nervous energy about him.

Hunter says, "I'm game."

Everyone grabs their glass, and they rattle them together above the table. Hunter tells Sid, "To old times and camping."

"Amen to that," Sid says, and the glasses clink.

Each man takes a sip, and Sid asks, "What've you been up to out in the Carolinas?"

"Fixing and building bikes. Had my own shop for a while, working out of my garage. Then had a guy approach me about a new shop he's opening. Worked for him about five years. But it was wearing on me. He was no-account. Started taking me and the other gearheads working there for granted. Then I walked in on him abusing his hound dog. So I handed him some knuckles and boot leather. Took the dog, got home and got the news about Dad, and here I am."

Sid slaps the table, rattles everyone's glass. "Be damn, you don't take no shit, Hunter. Turned out to be a real cowboy!"

"Things had been headed toward me leaving for a while, maybe six months or better. Guy had turned into a real prick. I'd already done the same work from my home and made good money doing it."

"Then why'd you start working for this other guy?" Sid asks, wriggling in his chair as if he'd stepped on a hill of fire ants.

"Thought maybe he'd have a bigger reach. And he did. It got my name out there. Built a good number of new clients who kept spreading my name, so I should be good to start back up at my home again."

"That's good," Sid says. "What about a female? You ever tie the knot?"

"No, but I got a girl that lives with me. We been together three, almost four, years. She's a real piece of work."

Looking at Itch and Nugget. Puckering his lips after emptying his glass of Maker's, he asks, "How about you two citizens?"

Waving a hand through the air, Nugget tells Sid, "Hell no. Women are too much trouble. I just work, ride, lift, and run around with Hunter. Ol' Itch here, he's got a live wire."

"That right?"

"Not really. She just don't take no shit."

Sid nods. Gets up, tells Hunter and his buddies, "Gonna have to excuse me. Got a meeting with a man about a mule. I'll get us another round of drinks after the meeting."

Hunter watches Sid. Something seems off, but he can't put a finger on it.

"Everything cool?" Itch asks Hunter.

"Not sure. Something's not right with Sid. The shaking. Wandering eyes. Fidgeting in his seat. Reminds me of someone."

Reflecting back, it reminds Hunter of his grandfather—the early stages of dementia.

Walking back toward the table, Sid begins cursing, loud and obnoxious. He has a catatonic gaze about him. "Look, I done told you, I ain't putting up with your bullshit tonight. No. Get the hell outta my face. The boy can stay with my parents or yours, makes me no difference. You made the choice. Live with it."

Other patrons eye Sid, but that's as far as it goes. They just glance up, then go back to their conversations and their booze.

Hunter recognizes the look. The acting out. Remembering when he would be with his grandfather. Losing track of time. Staring at Hunter. Believing that Hunter was Hunter's father, Hank. Questioning him. Wondering when he was going to give him a grandson. Those times killed Hunter. Not being recognized. But not recognizing his grandfather, either. It was as if he had passed from one room to the next in a house—one room decorative and bright, the next room dark and shadowed. A shift of perspective and mood. During those times near the end, Hank was home, caring for his father. Sid's wife, Annie, who had been a nurse forever, helped Hank, giving advice and bringing food to help out.

Standing up, Hunter approaches Sid, who is yelling, "Now look at what you gone and done. Irritating and insulting my friends. They're all seated here looking at us." Looking at Hunter, he says, "I got it under control. It's all good. Just don't pay her no damn mind, Hunter."

Hunter looks at Sid, glances to Felicia at the bar. She presses her lips together and nods vigorously, as if to say this is the norm. "Pay *who* no mind, Sid?" Hunter asks.

Looking around, Sid all of a sudden snaps out of his trance, just as Hunter's grandfather used to do, and says, "The drinks. Aw, shit, I forgot about the drinks. I'll be right back."

Hunter touches Sid's arm and says, "I got it. Let's get you back to the table, get you seated."

At the bar, Hunter asks Felicia, "How long's this been going on with Sid?"

"Months. He has these spells. I've driven him home many nights. He starts talking and arguing with his wife."

"She's dead. I get it. My grandfather did something similar."

"Yeah, he apparently argues with her over something she did to him."

"Anyone ever reach out to his son?" Hunter asks.

"Blake?"

Confused, Hunter squints one eye small and asks, "Blake? Who the hell is Blake? I'm talking about Travis."

"Travis never comes around. I've called him before, but he's too busy. Blake's the younger son. He's come to pick Sid up several times. Pretty good guy."

Hunter didn't know anything about a Blake. Didn't know that Sid had a younger son. And he's never heard Sid mention him. He tells Felicia, "I've known Sid a long time. Never heard him mention a Blake."

"From what I know, his grandparents raised him. Annie's parents. Not sure what the story is." Felicia looks at Hunter. Bites her lip. She wants to say something but won't spit it out. She's holding back. Hunter can read it in her body language.

"What's going on? You act like you wanna say something. What's on your tongue that you can't spit out?"

"I don't know how to say this. You know how I questioned you when you first came in, about being related to Sid?"

"Yeah?"

"You and Blake . . . could pass for brothers. He looks like a younger version of you."

At a loss for words, Hunter feels suddenly trapped in an Alfred Hitchcock moment. "That's just a coincidence. Hell, I've known Sid since I was fourteen. He's never mentioned Blake. I only know of Travis. I'm forty-six. This is news to me."

Changing the subject, Felicia clears her throat and says, "You want another round?"

"Yeah. One more round for the road," Hunter says, digging money from his wallet. "Does this Blake live close by?"

"I think he lives over in Marengo."

"And you—what's your story?"

After setting four glasses on the bar, Felicia drops ice into each glass, then grabs the bottle of Maker's. Turns it upside down and starts filling each glass. "My story . . . Well, I'm from here, went to University of Kentucky for five years. My father got sick. I came home to help my mother look after him."

"Sorry to hear that. What's wrong with your dad?"

"Something similar to Sid. Alzheimer's disease. He got to be a handful for my mother."

"That's tough. I can only imagine. My grandfather suffered with dementia just before he passed and I left for the service."

"Yeah, tough, but then, that's why I've helped Sid. I don't mind it. He can't help whatever it is he's got going on. In my mind, he's recalling someone he loved and lost, who did something none of us know about. His mind won't let what she did pass."

"Hence why he's arguing with her."

"Love is tough," she says. "It can drive us crazy."

"You're right about that."

She cocked an eyebrow. "Any tough love driving you crazy?"

Laughing, Hunter tells her, "No. There's love, but it's not tough by any means."

"That's too bad," Felicia says, "you already having someone." She chuckles.

Grabbing the drinks, Hunter tells her, "Maybe in another life."

And Felicia tells him, "Definitely in another life."

Taking the drinks back to the table. Hunter approaches everyone, wondering why he's never heard about Blake.

JACK

Every footstep over the sunbaked hardpan road hurts Jack's feet. Like electric splinters traveling up his shins, knees, thighs, and into his hips and lower back. Sweat burns his eyes like strong soap as he approaches the dull yellow semi's red brake lights on the side of the road. He reaches for the pitted chrome door handle, pulling it open. The artic breeze of cabin air feels like heaven itself. Looking up into the interior, he sees a man with close-cropped black hair. Bent over the steering wheel, smiling, he asks in accented English, "Where you going?"

Jack tells him, "I am headed anywhere north of here."

"Sure. Get in." The man waves Jack aboard.

With one hand already gripping the door's handle, the other latches on to the vertical grab handle, and Jack steps up and swings himself inside. Pink-faced and groaning, limbs shaking, he realizes once he's in the seat that he should have taken off his pack first. To lessen his weight.

Thumbing the plastic latch across his upper chest, sliding his arms out of the straps, he shrugs off the pack and holds it on his lap. Twisting around in the seat, he pulls the door shut. Breathing hard. Cold air dries his sticky skin, forming a glaze of body and road grunge.

"You can lay your pack on the floor or throw it behind you—plenty of space back there." Jack lays his pack on the black rubber floor mat, pulls on his seat belt, and clicks it into place, and the driver puts out his hand. "Matías."

They shake. "My name is Jack. I appreciate your kindness. You're the first person I've seen all day."

Matías looks to his side mirror, the truck jerks into motion, and he starts working up through the gears as they gain speed. They are moving forward, and Jack is sitting in air-conditioned bliss.

"You're lucky," the driver says. "From the direction you're leaving, there are riots—people protesting back in Santiago."

"What are they protesting?"

"The high transit costs, and defending human rights."

"It's sad. In the United States, protests are usually about guns and school shootings and police violence against minorities. The world we live in has grown full of madness."

"It has, my friend." Matías looks over at him and says, "You look worn. How long have you been walking?"

"I am very tired. I have been walking in the heat for what seems like many, many hours. Again, I cannot thank you enough for stopping." Jack bends forward, pulls a bottle of water from his pack. Unclips it. Twists the cap and lifts it to his lips. Coating the dryness in his mouth, replenishing and hydrating his insides.

"It's no problem. I travel this stretch of road often. You say you're headed north. What draws you up there?"

Swallowing, Jack lowers the bottle, rests it on the seat between his legs. His brain feels sluggish, and he's slow to answer, letting the cool air blast over his flesh. Mini soccer balls hang like dice from the center mirror, and the dash is lined with bobble-head dolls of what Jack supposes are soccer players, all attired in numbered jerseys.

"Yes," he tells Matías, "I'd like to see Bolivia and then cross over to Peru and up into Colombia. I'm in no rush. I've nothing but time. I just want to see as much of South America as possible while I'm figuring some things out."

A red, white, and blue flag with a single white star covers the cab's headliner. It is the flag of Chile. And Matías tells Jack, "I can get you to the border. But first I have a delivery, to a local mine just outside Calama."

"Whatever you can do, I greatly appreciate. And I'll pay you if I can manage to find a Western Union. I was robbed in San Pedro, so unfortunately, I have no money to compensate you for helping me out."

"Robbed—that's horrible, my friend."

Waving a hand, Jack tells him, "I deserved it. I should have paid better attention to people. But then, I figure, they needed it more than I did."

Pursing his lips, Matías says, "You're American, no?"

"I am, yes."

"When I was a younger, I spent summers in America with my aunt and uncle."

"That's where your English comes from?"

"Yes, I learn from them when I was younger. So, what brings you to Chile? You don't really seem the hitchhiking type. What are you, sixty?"

"I am sixty-five," Jack says, smiling.

Laughing, Matías seems happy with himself. He tells Jack, "I usually pick up younger folks—hikers and *alpinistas*."

When he thinks about it, Jack has many reasons to be in Chile.

In South America. He is in search of something. Of himself. Of meaning. The meaning of what, exactly, he can't really say. All he knew when he came was that he wanted to see something other than the things he had already seen—something other than expensive suits and manicured buildings, boardrooms, yield reports, and balance sheets. Experience something entirely new to him, perhaps. And he tells Matías, "My wife recently passed away from cancer, and I have worked all these years and accumulated all this money. Working and saving, and of all the things I've bought—a big house, cars—none of it matters. I found myself alone and did a lot of thinking, and I recalled something my mother had told me. Just before she died, she told me to run away and never look back. At the time, I never understood what she was talking about. For the most part, I'd forgotten all about it. But there I sat in that house, with the flowers from the funeral all wilted, brown, and dropping all their petals on our sun porch. My wife was dead, and my mother's memory—her words hit me like a head-on collision. I realized I needed to heed my mother's words."

Matías looks intrigued. "What do you think she meant?"

Gazing out the windshield, Jack sees the wide expanse of bare ground and snow-dusted peaks with apricot slopes. The beauty steals his breath. After a moment, he says, "Since I've been here in Chile, I've had time to think, to really reflect on it. And I think what she meant was that I had more than enough money, and she saw what earning it was doing to me—what it had done to me, what it was causing me to do to my family. But I didn't see it. She knew I was being consumed by my obsession with wealth. I believe she was telling me to leave it all behind—leave everything I'd built and amassed—and disappear. And I'll be honest. In that room, after my wife's funeral, that's what I wanted to do, and that's what I eventually did. I went to a sporting goods store and bought hiking gear, went to the airport with my passport and a wallet full of money, and I booked a first-class flight to Argentina. Hitchhiked from the airport to Chile."

The only sounds are the engine, the tires rolling over the roadway, the wind blowing around mirrors and stacks, and the blessed blasting air conditioner.

Matías tells Jack, "That is deep, my friend."

The sky overhead is a breathtaking blue unlike anything Jack has witnessed. Clear of smog and wind-borne dust, it sits like a brilliant sapphire bowl overturned on the world below.

Jack tells Matías, "But when she was in that hospital bed, raving half out of her mind, I never understood what she meant. I just thought it was dementia talking in the throes of her last moments of life. But here I am, all these years later, trying to make sense of what she told me back then."

"You're trying to understand your own existence—the most admirable pursuit."

Jack says, "I'm searching for something, but I've little idea of what it is."

"Well, it's not the answer I normally receive," Matías replies. "I am sorry for the losses of your wife and your mother. You know, my mother—she is still alive, in good health with a strong ticker—stays active, chews a little coca every day. Like me and my wife, Catalina, she lives a simple, low-stress life." Matías's face lights up as he reaches to his sun visor, where pictures are clipped. He thumbs them loose and hands them to Jack. "This is my Catalina and our son, Gabriel. They're my world, my friend. My everything. Twenty years we been married. How long was you married, Jack?"

Jack's eyes go misty, looking at the photos. Thinking back to his twentieth anniversary. Sarah had planned an elaborate dinner for them, had a chef come in and grill Japanese Wagyu ribeye and candied brussels sprouts, and special-ordered an exquisite bottle of Château Latour. Jack not only forgot their anniversary but was late getting home. Her look of sadness hurt him more than any rage-filled diatribe she could ever have launched. Smiling, he says, "They're beautiful. I am sure you don't need me to tell you this, but you are a very lucky man, Matías." Jack pauses, then adds, "I was married for over forty years."

Holding the pictures, seeing the smiling faces, moments in time captured, memories shared, to be remembered, Jack thinks of his stolen wallet. He didn't even carry a picture of his wife. His kids. Only credit cards, cash, and ID. How fucking sad. Jack had taken so much for granted. Underappreciated every moment, action, or endeavor that related to his wife and kids.

Jack hands the pictures back. Matías takes them, clips them back up to his visor. The only thing Jack had on his visor back home was a garage door opener.

Matías tells him, "Thank you, Jack. I am very proud. You know, you're lucky I come along. The heat out here gets unbearable in the day. And at night, whew, it gets cold. Where did you hike from? San Pedro?"

Flashes of dancing in the street. People gathering to watch. Music playing in his brain. Jack tells Matías, "Yes. I had this horrible meltdown after I got robbed. I just started walking, and I spent my last pesos on some food. And this song my wife and I had danced to on the anniversaries that I didn't forget, 'Unchained Melody'—it's the only time I ever really made for my wife, Sarah. But I started dancing, and everything was flashing before me, and this very generous woman offered to take me in. She gave me a bed to get some sleep. She was very kind to me."

"Welcome to Chile, my friend. The people here are the kindest, most generous you shall ever meet. And this area—wow, it is so breathtaking: the mountains, the skies. But the heat can zap you if you're not accustomed to it."

Matías is right. Jack was ill prepared for this. Forget the climate-controlled conference room. Out here, it's man and the elements. Yet again it makes Jack realize how soft he is. And he tells Matías, "The heat here will fry you up like bacon on a tin roof. It's like nothing I ever saw."

"It is. You know, the Atacama Desert is over six hundred miles long, but it's only sixty miles wide. It's the driest nonpolar place on earth. People here are lucky if they get an inch of rain in a lifetime. Scientists compare the dryness here with Mars."

"Walking out here, that's exactly what I thought," Jack says. "It felt like being on Mars."

"Do you have kids?" Matías asks.

"Two. A son, Duncan—he's an electrician. My first daughter died during birth. Our second daughter, Megan, we adopted at age eight. But she killed herself when she was eighteen."

"Oh, my friend, you have the string of bad luck. America. All chaos. No?"

It does indeed seem that chaos has always been just beneath the surface most of Jack's life. But Jack wasn't around much, and when he was, he wasn't paying attention to the warning signs.

"Not everything in my life was chaos. I worked my way into a venture and built it into a Fortune Five Hundred company."

"Fortune Five Hundred? What is this?"

"It's a list of the biggest US companies based on revenue."

"Revenue? You mean earnings?"

"Sort of. The five hundred largest money-making companies in the US."

"Ah, you're one of those soft-bodied suits? No, wait." Matías chuckles. "The suit is your armor to keep you from getting crunched.

That makes you more like a crustacean—hard on the outside, soft on the inside."

Jack laughs. That's certainly one way of perceiving it. He tells Matías, "Never heard it put that way, but I did wear my share of expensive suits."

"So you sit in an office, behind a desk all day? You're like a Donald Trump or Elon Musk—a zillionaire?"

"Most days, I did sit at my desk. I had meetings to attend, dinners with clients and potential clients and investors. And I traveled a lot, spoke to other companies and corporations. I'm no Elon Musk. I do have a substantial amount of money, but none of it means anything now. None of it can bring back the things that I've lost over time."

"I couldn't sit behind a desk all day," Matías says. "I'd never make it. Here, behind this wheel, seeing the beauty that is Chile, it's like freedom. A real breath of fresh air."

"It wasn't that bad, but I was never home. I missed my kids going to school, their games and concerts and their interests—never really watched them grow up."

"You missed their influences."

"I did, and I realized it way too late. Now my wife's dead and my son is grown, and he wants nothing to do with me. I'm all alone. I have nothing and no one."

"My son—he's an outstanding soccer player. He will be the next Elías Figueroa."

"I'm sorry I know so little about soccer or sports in general. I have no idea who Elías Figueroa is. In my world, it was all about facts and figures and what the markets were doing."

"Figueroa—he's retired now, but back in the day, he was the most elegant soccer player. *Mucho* professional, kept his cool every second of the game. Represented Chile forty-seven times, was in three FIFA World Cups—the international association of *futbolistas*. Won the Bola de Ouro twice—the Brazilian player of the year—and the South American footballer of the year three times. I could go on and on."

"Do you play soccer, also?" Jack asked.

"Only with my son, yes. When I'm not out here on the road. It's tough, but I make the most of my time when I'm home. Lucky for me, my employer pays me well and holds family in high regard."

"My son, Duncan . . . I had high hopes for him. In school, he played basketball. He was a star athlete, really good. He was a point guard. He had college scouts from the Big Ten schools looking at him."

"Ah, I know *básquetbol*. We also call it *baloncesto*. Michael Jordan, no?"

"Yes. He's a very smart and interesting man. I have actually met him."

"You met Michael Jordan? The greatest basketball player who ever lived?"

"Yes, I have. He's very smart. Invested his money in a shoe line, clothing, a sports drink, and he owns a basketball team. While he was busy being one of the greatest athletes of all time, he was also planning ahead for his future."

"Did you and the great Jordan shoot the hoops?"

"No, we did not play any basketball. We talked at length about how to prepare and invest in his future, because he knew that one day he wouldn't be playing basketball, and he needed to have a plan."

Matías is wearing an ear-to-ear shit-eating grin. He says, "You know Michael Jordan, and here you are in my truck, hitchhiking through Chile! I feel like I am escorting a celebrity."

Still coming to terms with just what a for-shit husband and father he was, Jack tells Matías, "I'm far from a celebrity. I'm a lost individual who neglected his wife, his daughter, and his son." And thinking of his son, Jack adds, "You know, my son Duncan decided to go into a trade school of all places. I wanted him to attend an Ivy League school and get a degree in business to take over for me. Now he's an electrician—a fucking *tradesman*, of all things. I wanted him to do something more."

"Electrician—that's an honest trade," Matías says. "Working with your hands and your mind." Points to his brain. "No?"

"Yes, a very honest line of work. But I think he did it to rebel against me. For never being around, for being absent when his mother first became sick."

Downshifting, slowing down, Matías hangs into a curve that becomes a rutted road. The truck's suspension bumps and lurches, and he tells Jack, "Sit back, my friend, and enjoy the ride. The view. My delivery is just down this road. Then I can get you to the border of Bolivia. One thing we have is plenty of scenery. Maybe we can hit a truck stop, grab some food and drinks."

Not having any money, Jack lays his head back against the seat and yawns. Tired. Not even thinking about food. The sun has zapped and sapped his energy. Cold air from the truck's vents relaxes him, and he realizes he hasn't thought about his job since he landed in South America. Hasn't thought about what he used to do. The constant go, from the moment he woke until he laid his head to rest late every night. All he has contemplated since arriving in Argentina is loss. His daughter. His mother. His wife, whom he misses the most.

What would Sarah make of him? Of his hitchhiking from Argentina to Chile? He never did anything adventurous with her. Never traveled outside the country. Only all over the United States. Taking her to the best hotels and resorts, eating the best food, buying the best clothing and jewelry. Everything nice and safe and sterile.

Jack's breathing slows, and the rise and fall of his chest becomes free of tension. He feels nothing but smoothness until the semi slows down and Matías pumps the air brakes.

Jack has dozed off. He's in and out of sleep, aware only of the semi's idling engine. He wonders what Sarah would make of any of this. Of what he is doing. His quest of self-discovery. He has arrived at a time of life when things no longer make sense. Crazy how he had thought he had everything figured out, only to realize that he didn't know *anything*. All those years working twelve- to sixteen-hour days, six days a week—they went by so fast.

Matías mumbles, "What the hell's going on here?"

Jack is in a state of numbness when he cracks open his eyes—a weary gaze out the windshield, where trucks are blocking the road. Shapes of men exit from the trucks.

"Oh, I don't like this." Shaking Jack's arm, Matías says, "Wake up, my friend. Wake up!"

As his senses fire up, Jack feels the truck shift on Matías's side—the weight of a man reaching up and yanking the driver's side door open. A second later, Jack feels the same thing on his side.

Hands reach in and fumble with Jack's seat belt release. Both men are thrown to the orange dust. Bright sunlight stings Jack's eyes. Still trying to catch up to the situation, he hears Matías saying, "What are you doing? You can't do this."

"*¡Cállate, puto!*" a man growls, and Matías wisely shuts his mouth.

Hurt flows through Jack's limbs. Hands are maneuvering his body, rolling him facedown in the dust. Twist and pull, wrist over wrist, and the next thing he feels is plastic zip ties lacing and cinching his wrists together. Looking up, all he can make out against the glaring sun is a blur of dark skin and dark hair. A hood goes over his head, and his heartbeat ramps up as it occurs to him that this could be how it all ends.

Hands guide Jack from lying facedown, up to his knees, then to his feet. Shoving him from behind. "*Anda, gringo*," a voice commands him. *Walk.* One foot in front of the next, he shuffles forward nervously. A hand grabs his shoulder, jerks him to a stop. There's the sound of a latch. The unbarring. Something being released. Next thing Jack knows, hands are gripping him from the front, pulling him up into a vehicle. He feels whatever he's standing on—a tailgate or truck bed—give and sway with another person's weight. "Matías?" Jack says.

"Yeah, it's me, Jack," Matías pants. "This ain't good, my friend."

Then a door closes, and Jack feels the cold grip of panic.

ANNE

The figure lays facedown, haloed by a crimson pool as dark and glossy as used engine oil. Kneeling, Anne reaches out and gingerly touches the back of Mitch's head.

Jerking upward, he plants his palms on the bloody floor and pushes up to his knees, searching for balance. He gazes into Anne's eyes. One side of his face is swollen and purplish, reminding her of a turnip. Blood drips down from his temple as he says through gritted teeth, "Little bitch, why'd you fuckin' hit me?"

"You grabbed at me, got rough. I was defending myself."

"Bullshit!" he rages, thick white spittle in the corners of his mouth. "You're stealing from Dad!"

Mitch lunges toward her, head jabbing like a venomous snake. Anne scoots backward. Staggers, off balance. The back of her head bumps the cabinet door.

Following her, Mitch gets to his feet, awkward, zombie-like, limbs rigor mortis stiff, and comes at her. "You little bitch. Stealing from your own kin, leaving me for dead."

His words echo in Anne's head. Clamping her eyes shut, she twists her head from side to side. "No! No! No!" she screams. She doesn't want to do this, to get trapped in this game of victimhood. Turning to run, she slips on the slick of Mitch's blood. Her forehead clips the countertop. Lips and teeth scrape down the cabinet door. Her chin smacks the floor. Vibrations rattle through her face. Neck. Shoulders. From behind, she feels her brother's hands climbing her legs, digging into her calf muscles.

And as she had done to the attacking dog when escaping over the fence, and to the rail-yard worker when escaping under the fence, she kicks. She jerks. She fights. No longer wanting this life, this violent trajectory of actions from a family that kept her down. She kicks and kicks as the hands keep digging, squeezing, then shaking her entire being awake.

Crunching upward and sitting on her ass. Chest heaving, lungs burning. Eyes watering. She stares at the blurred outline until it coalesces into Cinnamon. Feeling a warm weight pressing against her thigh, she looks down at Cinnamon's hand.

Words of concern fall softly from Cinnamon's lips in the twilight of what Anne guesses is morning. "You all right?"

Clambering out of the snagged and dirty sleeping bag, Anne looks around. Seeing the fleecy-white guts and the interior of red and black plaid, she realizes she isn't home. "Yeah. Just a bad dream."

"Been trying to wake you for a few minutes. Anything you wanna talk about?"

Anne considers her words before she speaks. Can she trust the girl? She feels that she can. Feels comfortable with her, as if Anne, too, belongs in this world of hers. There was this mutual feeling of belonging. Acceptance in this new domain of life. It is something foreign to her, something she isn't accustomed to. Anne keeps reinforcing this acceptance, this fresh start. Telling herself this is a place devoid of judgment. Of rules. Of hurt. Inhaling deep, she holds her breath, then exhales slowly. Cinnamon's touch is gentle, comforting. Moving closer now.

Anne said, "When I decided to run away, my brother walked in on me in the kitchen. I was preparing to leave. There was an exchange of words. An argument. It got heated and—"

"Physical," Cinnamon interjects. "I know. You mentioned something about siblings. Plus, there's your eyes looking like bruised fruit. Kinda hard to miss those symbols."

Anne had forgotten about the black eyes. "Right." She laughs. "I was defending myself and hit him in the head with a cast-iron skillet. Dropped him to the kitchen floor. There was blood. I panicked. Ran. And I don't know if—"

"If he's alive or dead. Girl, don't sweat it. *You're* not the abuser. You're the victim. Don't you dare feel sorry for your brother. And you can't undo what has already been done. You got a new life now. A new family. A new beginning. You were protecting yourself, and that's not a crime."

Running her tongue over dry lips. Closing her eyes, all she can see is Mitch's face. The puddle of blood. Opening her eyes, she says, "You're right, but it don't make it no easier."

"Look, the life you ran from don't sound much different from what I escaped from. What I've come to learn is this: if life was easy, you wouldn't be here now. Everything that happened before has prepared you for this moment."

Pausing on Cinnamon's words, Anne still feels something for her brother even though he was abusive toward her. She says, "My biggest fear is I killed my brother and now they're looking for me. What I want is . . ." She hesitates. Can't put it into words, form it into a sentence.

Cinnamon tells her, "Just say it."

"I no longer wanna be me."

"Then don't be. Change who you are." Cinnamon squeezes her knee. "Now, come on. Let's get some coffee. Take your mind off all this sappy-ass talk. We've got all kinds of time to think and talk about heavy shit later. We need to see about getting into town before Dredd and everyone is woke up. Earn some money. We ain't staying here any longer than we need to, 'cause longer we stay, crazier shit gets."

Working her way up from the hard ground. Standing amid the clutter of books, water bottles, and buckets. Trot is curled up, snoring away beneath tree branches spread out like rafters supporting the worn blue tarp of a roof. Cinnamon looks at Anne, who spreads her arms and embraces her. Patting her back, Anne says, "Thanks for listening."

"I'll always listen," Cinnamon replies. Releasing her, she says, "I mean, what are friends for? You're in a place that's new, and I know it seems strange. You'll come around. Find your comfort zone. You're not used to love and compassion from others. I see it. You're like an abused dog. It all takes time."

Walking from one tarped and tented area to another, a younger guy with black hair flying off in all directions stands over the fire pit, where a kettle sits bubbling on a wire stove shelf spanning two concrete blocks. "Morning, Vargas," Cinnamon says.

Vargas gave a peace sign. "Morning. Water's heated. You want some morning brew?"

"If you can spare it."

"Anything for you, Cinnamon. Your buddy want a cup?"

"Please," Anne says, now with a bit more pep in her tone.

Vargas slowly pours the steaming water over a paper filter full of dry grounds, into a large chrome container. Taking his time. . .

"I used to work at Starbucks. You like the pour-over method?"

"Not sure I ever had it before," Anne said. "All we had at home was a stained Mr. Coffee pot."

"Well, this here is no Mr. Coffee. This, in my humble opinion, is the best."

Cinnamon digs through some mugs off to the side in a red milk crate and hands Anne a chipped black mug with an image of Scooby Doo. She says, "Vargas is badass when it comes to kettle coffee."

Steam billows up from their cups, and Anne takes a luxurious sip that warms her insides.

Cinnamon tells her, "Today, you learn to earn. Part of Dredd's DIY way of living."

"The *do-it-yourself* living."

"So you got the Dredd lecture. He's the hobo saint who was rebirthed to rescue us all. Always preaching about freedom, noncommitment—a nonconformist for the lost souls, the dropouts, and the drifters."

"What's his story? I mean, what did he run away from?"

"Look, the Kerouac and the Beats that he drones on about are just bait. It's a hook. He was a professor."

"A college professor?"!

"Yes. He was fighting the good fight. Didn't believe in what the establishment offered. He protested for equality. Wanted things to be free—everything from school to health care. In the end, he wanted a civil war against this great oppression we supposedly live under. He felt he could live how he wanted and influence others and get them to do as he wanted, all without working. You stay here too long, you'll see that the utopia he preaches about and the one that actually exists aren't one and the same. We ain't living in an era of oppression. What I ran from was an abusive home life, just like you and most everyone else. Most of those who come here these days are a mix of hippies with a side of millennials. We just don't want attachment to pop culture and consumerism. What Dredd says is we're the revolution. But in reality, we just wanna live a simple life free of interference."

"That's pretty deep."

"No deeper than a freshly dug shithouse hole. I just want you to know what's real and what's bullshit. In the end, we still have to earn our way. Preaching won't get us food, shelter, or clothing. The American Dream isn't a bad thing until you add the politics of left and right, skin color, poverty, and all the elements from the recipe of complicated living. In the end, how about just being a good human being."

"So, if we're not following Dredd's ruling class, what are we doing?"

"How I look at all this is simple: train hopping equals mobility; flying a sign equals cash; dumpster diving or running the trash cans equals clothing, food, water cups, nourishment. This removes us from the norm, from working long hours for shit pay. We got zero debt, no rules, no authority, and as females, we embrace our dirty bodies. It defines who we are, and it protects us."

Knowing she has a gun and money in her pack, Anne worries about getting ripped off. She trusts Cinnamon, but she is keeping her gains to herself. When the opportunity presents itself, she'll share it with her new friend. And then it hits her: Where is her pack?

"You look concerned," says Cinnamon. "What's wrong?"

"My pack—don't remember where I put it."

Smiling, she says, "It's on the sleeping bag. It was your pillow."

Anne sighs, relieved. "Shouldn't we wake Trot?"

"Yes, we should. The more hands we got, the more trash cans we can cover. Does he drink coffee?"

"I think so."

"Let's score him a cup. Get with Canary and the twins—her

little brother and sister. The younger the mouths, the more pity you get from the drivers. We can catch a bus, hit town for the morning rush hour of the working folks."

The smell of exhaust fumes is thick at the light. Engines rev, idle, and rev again over the rough pavement of badly patched potholes. Gears shift, and brakes squeak. The smell of tire tread blends with the aromas of bacon, eggs, hash browns, sausage, and fresh-brewed coffee from the nearby cafés and greasy spoons. Anne does her best to ignore it all while she stands with a plaintive look, trying to appear needy and poor. Her dirty pink backpack between her ankles, a wad of cash and a pistol buried in its belly, standing with Canary's little sister Sweet Tart, Anne holds a worn and stained cardboard sign that reads, "Homeless and hungry. Anything you can offer would help me and my baby sister."

Vendors of sandwiches take up space on other corners, prepping for lunch-hour traffic still hours away. The city's workforce shuffles by on foot as well as on wheels. Crossing streets. Walking down sidewalks. Sipping coffee. Facing the new day.

Ten years old, with a crazy rat's nest of porter-beer-colored locks hanging down around a pale face of sticky streaks, dimpled cheeks, and chapped lips. Dirty yellow and white Care Bears T-shirt. One hand waves; the other holds a small coffee can, ready when a car stops at the red light. Watching for a meeting of eyes from the driver. Some look straight ahead, hoping the light will change to green before they lose their steely resolve and glance in the girl's direction. But when eyes meet, even for an instant, windows roll down and strains of pop, rap, country, R&B, or talk radio waft out along with cigarette smoke, cologne, or coffee breath. And following that, a hand waving a green bill or a fistful of change. She runs up to the vehicle, holding out the can. Watches the crimped paper money drop, hearing the coins rattle down. She thanks them for their generosity, hops back up on the curb, watches them pass, and waits for the next eye contact.

A couple of hours in, several homeless people come pushing their shared buggy of copper wiring and scrap. Piled and hanging from the cart are odds and ends of clothing, tools, boots, bedding, and folded cardboard. An older man of color with ashen Brillo-pad hair and jaundiced eyes and a woman with mousy hair and spider-veined, needle-tracked arms. Their teeth are thick with accreted gunk from years of street living. Stepping closer, their glowering eyes burn through Anne and Sweet Tart.

"Shit y'all think you're doin' on our corner?"

"Guess we didn't know you owned the corner," Anne says.

"Got squatter rights. It's ours."

Anne reached over to Sweet Tart, held the girl tight to her side. "We ain't going nowhere. We can share. We're just about done."

"Share, my ass. You definitely done. Whatever you got in that there can belongs to us."

"I wouldn't share the sweat off my ass with you. And whatever's in this can belongs to *us*. We're the ones who earned it."

"We'll be seeing about that," the greasy male snarls.

Anne kneels down, digging a hand into her backpack. Fingers press and search for the cold weight. She says to the man, "You might want to think about backing the fuck up!"

Swaying closer, he looks and sounds half drunk. "Or what, little girl? I've beat my daughter's ass more than a time or two, and I'd be happy to beat yours right along with this half-pint you got for backup."

Vehicles keep driving past, eyes watching the little sideshow on the corner. The traffic slows, with a blinking of red brake lights, and stops. Anne's heart picks up the pace, her heart thumping against her breastbone. As her hand caresses the pistol's grip, her eyes turn to slits of rage. The man's tone reminds her too much of her father and mother. She won't be belittled or threatened by this man. She will stand her ground. The man sways, each step bringing him inches closer. Reaching for the can that Sweet Tart hugs to her little chest.

Anne pulls the pistol free. Stands up. Withdraws her other hand from Sweet Tart. Two-handing the .38's weight. Just as she used to on her father's friend's property, target-practicing while the two men got shit-faced. Training the gun on the intruder, she says, "Or I could give you another hole to breathe from."

The greasy man's eyes register surprise. "You wouldn't shoot a poor unarmed man."

"And you wouldn't steal from two girls trying to earn their way in life, would you, you pathetic walking pile of shit?"

Standing statue-still, he seems to contemplate his next action. Cars roll by. Eyes gawk. But Anne ignores their glances, keeping her focus on the man in her sights. She tunes out the sounds of the surrounding city, letting them blur into an indistinct white noise. All she can hear is the frenzied beating of her heart, driving a bass rhythm in her eardrums. All she can see is this piss-poor excuse for a man as everything around him fades to black. Her finger moves from trigger guard to trigger, and she braces her arms and body for the kick of the pistol. Imagining the hole the bullet will bore through his chest, and how much blood will drain from it, when a voice yells, "You heard what she told you."

The black dissipates from around the man as the outside world comes back into view, and she feels as if she just resurfaced after being trapped underwater. The greasy man turns around to find Cinnamon, Trot, Canary, and little brother Apple giving menacing looks.

"Look, sistah," he says to Cinnamon, "we got no beefs with you. It's this hippie and her half-pint."

"I ain't your sister, old-timer, and they're with me. Part of my family. You know what's best, you'll take your buggy and your Aunt Hazel heroin bitch and move the fuck on."

Outnumbered, the greasy man raises his palms and starts to backpedal, bumping into his frail female partner. And they turn away, pushing their cart.

Anne kneels down and slides the pistol back into her backpack. Her whole frame quakes and jitters with nerves. She feels hollowed out. Her stomach swims in a state of queasiness. Cinnamon grabs her forearm and guides her back to an upright posture. "Where the shit did you get a gun?"

"My father. I wanted to tell you—just couldn't find the right time."

"I think you just did. You're just full of surprises. Keep it on the down low, girl. We need to get moving. Too many eyes. Last thing we want is attention from the local PD."

Feet shuffle and bodies move to another street. Deeper into the city, where Cinnamon, Canary, Apple, and Trot lift dumpster doors open and climb into the big square steel containers, ripping apart bags, searching and sorting through the trash of local eateries before the morning pickup. Sometimes finding clothing, fruits, and vegetables from the day before, filling their packs.

Walking down other streets, they rummage through trash cans, dumping out cups of unfinished soda unless they are over half full. Removing lids, they take a sniff followed by a swallow. Keep the cups to reuse. Finding paper sacks of half-eaten breakfast sandwiches, breakfast burritos, biscotti, scrambled eggs, and pancakes. They take them, share them, eat them, offering to the kids first, then splitting the rest with one another.

In this manner, they work their way down sidewalks, from one street to the next, scouring the area. By twelve o'clock, they have collected all they can carry, looking like a band of gypsies. With the bills and coins they had made, they hit a local grocery on their way back to catch a bus out of the city. They grab coffee, Spam, potted meat, tuna, bags of rice, ramen noodles. Anne checks the local and national newspapers for mention of the brother she had left for dead, and is relieved to find nothing.

Once they had paid and left the store, Cinnamon tells Anne, "This should stock the camp up for a while. We've done our part, but we'll need to go again. Stock up for our departure. So before we get back, skim anything you feel is of value, and hide it. 'Cause Dredd always gets first dibs. And he ain't the sharing type unless you got something to offer in return."

Anne realizes that even here, with these people, there is a pecking order. It isn't all free love. Everything is open to interpretation. There is politics.

Figuring out the route, waiting on the bus, Cinnamon tells Anne, "These are our skill sets. Our means for self-reliant survival. You got what it takes. Damn sure are braver than most I've ran with. Hauling that damn pistol out on that homeless dopehead. He looked about ready to shit hisself."

"I wasn't giving him any ground. Not about to let him bring harm to Sweet Tart or me. Told him we could share the corner."

"Out here, not too many homeless types wanna share with someone that ain't from their camp. One thing you learn: a woman has to be firm and direct with her words and her actions. You did right, not giving an inch. Last thing a female can do, or you'll end up raped, dead, or both. Can't turn a blind eye to another's ways. They's types out here that don't have a care in the world for how they treat you to get what they want. Out here, there's no consequences for their actions."

On the bus, eyes judge. Heads shake and turn away. Bodies

maneuver to avoid being touched by Anne and her new people. She experiences being looked at as though she were something not quite human, some unknown species.

Getting off the bus, they walk back to the encampment. Breaking off the road, heading through the woods, following their trails back to the jungle, they arrive carrying new supplies.

Dredd sits on a threadbare, sunken couch, surrounded by several young girls. "You bear gifts," he says grandly.

"We do," Cinnamon tells him.

"What a haul. Must've been one of those days when the traffic is thick and hearts are bleeding, feeling guilt for their privileged ways of living."

"People were generous," Anne says.

"I see that." Dredd's grin undresses her, and he says, "Come on, then. Let me see the fruits you have gleaned and gathered."

Everyone starts laying down their plastic sacks filled with loot before Dredd. Emptying their backpacks of what they gathered in town. Dredd starts sorting and digging through the clothing, holding things up as if mentally trying them on. He pulls a bright green Granny Smith apple from a sack and bites into it, chewing and sucking the juice from it.

"This is amazing. Really fresh."

All eyes in the encampment watch and wait to see what supplies Anne and the others have gathered on their foray into the city.

Anne feels a revulsion simmering inside her. After she and the others stood and earned and picked through everything that Dredd now consumes and appropriates, it is far from fair or equal. As if sensing Anne's disgust, Cinnamon tugs at her elbow, pulls her attention away. Shifting her head, she nods for Anne to follow her away from the lunacy of Dredd's dictatorship.

They wander into the sleeping area. No one is around. It's dead quiet. Cinnamon digs into her backpack. "Found a little something in a barber shop's trash."

"What is it?" Anne asks.

"New identity." Cinnamon holds up a pair of battery-powered hair trimmers. "You wanna change your look?"

"I don't want to be a skinhead."

"You really think I would waste that beautiful face by turning you into a Nazi?"

"No," she says. "But what's your idea?"

"Come sit and I'll show you, long as the battery holds a charge." Cinnamon pats the blue milk crate beside her. Pulling a lock of hair up, she clips the ends, layering the sides, letting it hang over the ears. "Let's make you look like a badass in a Mad Max movie."

Nervous, Anne tells her, "Surprise me."

Standing before her, Cinnamon leans forward, holds a swatch of hair between two fingers. Starts on the left side, pulling it long, thumbs the clippers. They start buzzing, and the vibration feels pleasant against her head. Locks fall to her shoulders and the ground. Going up about midway, fading it right on down to the pale skin beneath, leaving the longer lengths on top. Then she goes to the opposite side and repeats the same method.

Blowing and brushing away the clipped hair. Clicking off the trimmers, Cinnamon lays them on the ground, goes to get something from her backpack, comes back. She then takes the length on top of Anne's head, pulls it over to her right side, and begins braiding. She has taken from her pack colorful friendship bracelets of various lengths, which she braids into Anne's hair.

With this radical change of do comes a feeling of elation, electricity flowing and surging through Anne's body. The way she is being pampered. Re-created by Cinnamon. Appreciation. An act of caring for her. Something she doesn't remember feeling with her mother, father, or brothers and sisters. She is becoming a new person. Shedding her old skin. Cinnamon is changing Anne's public proclamation of who she is.

Looking around, Cinnamon finds a cracked hand mirror, offers it to Anne.

"Take a look."

Anne holds the reflection of herself in the mirror. Feels the welling tears of happiness. Thinking that two or three days ago she was in Tennessee, miserable, unaware of what she was doing or where she was headed. Constantly at odds with what she was born into. The years of fighting, mistreatment, and abuse. And here she is, immersed and accepted into a new family. A real family.

"Well?" Cinnamon asks.

"I don't know what to say," Anne says, eyes brimming with tears. "It looks badass."

"So you like it?"

"I love it!" Anne says. "What's next?"

"We need another day of panhandling. Gather some more money. Supplies. Then we can catch out down to Louisiana. Hook up down there and head out west. Warmer climate. More desolation. There's other encampments I think you should see, more good people to meet. Canary and her little brother and sister wanna go."

"Sounds good to me," Anne says, ecstatic. "What about Trot?"

"What about him?"

"Can he go with?"

"Of course. But when I say we gotta go, we go."

"I understand."

Darkness has set in like a black fog, held at bay by the campfire's light. Figures sit around on milk crates or cross-legged on the ground. Some are eating fruit gathered on the day's foray into town. Others are napping. Kids read by lantern light or play with toys.

In the darkness, a twig snaps. Shapes of men and women come out of the shadows, and spotlights flick on as chaos erupts within the encampment.

A male voice says through a bullhorn, "This is the police. You are surrounded. Stay where you are."

Before anyone can catch up to what is going on, bodies come forward from all directions. People try to disperse and scatter. Rolling around on the ground. Hands reach; arms jerk. Punch and fight. Batons come out and thump into bodies. Screams fill the air as the night explodes in fear and anger and violence.

Anne and Cinnamon spring to their feet under the tarp where they have lain resting. Grabbing their packs.

"We gotta find Canary and the twins. But we gotta stay together."

"I'm right behind you," Anne tells Cinnamon.

"Keep hold of my pack," Cinnamon replies.

Running out of the tented area, they find a battle royal combined with a WWE WrestleMania and a Lollapalooza concert. Anne's eyes scan the madness. One hand holding on to Cinnamon's pack, she sees Trot. He takes a fist to the face just as someone slams a lawn chair across the cop's back. Dodging bodies. Grabbing hands. Voices screaming and shouting. They get to Trot, help him to his feet. "Where's Canary?"

"Last she told me, she's putting the twins down for the night."

Snaking through the mayhem, following a path to another tented area, Canary comes, a twin attached to each hand. Sweet Tart cries on her left; Apple sniffles on her right. "What is going on?"

"It's a fucking raid from the pigs."

"What's the plan?"

"We gotta get out of here," Cinnamon says.

"Lead the way," Canary says.

"Grab a buddy and come on." Coming from the tent, three cops are stepping toward them with mace and batons. Anne picks up a rock. Hurls it. One of the cops lifts his forearm and deflects it. And before the cops can pursue them, everyone is reaching down, grabbing whatever they can find that is loose on the ground. Sticks, rocks, bottles, and toys start raining down on the cops, who kneel and turn away. Cinnamon yells, "Follow me." Turns and jumps and maneuvers through blackberry brambles. "Come on, be careful. You gonna get scratched by thorns, but it's to our advantage."

Working through the briars and into the darkness, following the pound and shuffle of feet. Cinnamon leads everyone through the trees and undergrowth. Breaking through the night. Full moon overhead. Panting and rushed breathing, everyone feeling the adrenaline and fear of the unknown. The twins are crying. Canary tries to shush them, tells them it'll be okay, that they're just playing a game of tag or hide-and-seek.

Behind them comes the clomp and shouting of the police. Their voices yelling at Anne and Cinnamon and the others to stop. The madness in the jungle encampment fills the night with shrieks and screams. Glancing back, there is the flash of lights. Red and blue strobes of the cop cars, and the bright amber of the spotlights. Overhead, muffled noise of an engine, growing in volume. The roar resolves itself into the rhythmic beat of rotors as a bright light beams down. It fades as they cover more ground.

"They got a fucking helicopter!" Trot yells.

Panic grows, and Cinnamon tells everyone, "Keep moving. We'll be fine."

Maneuvering through the woods, Anne has lost all sense of direction, but Cinnamon keeps leading them deeper and deeper into the trees and brush. When the woods open up into what looks like a field, Cinnamon stops. "Everybody, stay down and keep quiet."

Everyone drops to the ground. They listen in silence. The sounds from the encampment have grown distant behind them. Heavy breathing begins to slow as Anne looks forward to where there are no woods. Just darkness. Her eyes adjust, and she can make out what she believes to be railroad tracks.

"We gotta be smart, make sure there's no one out here looking for us. Watching for movement. We need to get to the other side of the tracks, find a place to hide, jump a train when it leaves the yard."

Anne sits beside Cinnamon in the pine needles and leaf litter, Trot behind her, Canary and the twins beside Trot. Somewhere behind them, footsteps are approaching. Rushing feet snapping sticks and crunching dry leaves. Starting, then stopping. Everyone's nerves are rattled.

Anne unzips her pack. She feels Cinnamon's eyes on her; her hand feels in the pack for the gun. Cinnamon lays a hand on her forearm. The sounds of feet shuffling over the forest floor behind them grows closer and closer, like a hound dog on their trail. Sniffing them out. When the footfalls are practically on top of them, Anne grips the pistol. Cinnamon squeezes her arm to wait. Everyone's eyes are on the dark, wheezing outline that approaches.

HUNTER

His words came, loud and vehement. Raging and mad as a marine drill instructor preparing his soldiers for combat. Sid, pink-faced and nearly slobbering, had excused himself once again to go to the restroom, only to return arguing with someone who wasn't there. His dead wife, Annie. Accusing her for what she had done to him. The child. *That fucking child.* What kind of idiot did she take him for?

Hunter had tried to cut off the booze, take Sid home, but he kept pleading—"One more, haven't seen you in ages."

Itch and Nugget traded expressions of concern. Asked Hunter, "What's up with your buddy?"

All around them, other eyes stared, but no one spoke. Others sipped their alcohol, ignoring the ruckus as they carried on with their conversations.

Hunter said to Itch, "Not real sure. Bartender says this is par for him. My best guess, dementia."

The other patrons seemed content to wait out the belligerent tirade, letting Sid's lunacy flame and burn, waiting for the madness to peak, dwindle, and burn out.

Hunter excuses himself and gets up from the table. He walks over to Sid, whose mind is somewhere other than the VFW, lost in some tormented netherworld. Another time, another place. He takes Sid gently by one bony forearm. It is as if an electric pulse of rage travels through his limbs, through his body. Hunter steers him back to his chair and tries to calm him with words. "Sid, let's get you back to the table, finish your drink. Head back to your place."

Sid isn't registering any of it. "I always thought the world of your father," he says. "Then came that kid. You was gone. In the service, maybe. Can't remember. God, it's been so long ago."

"Kid?"

"Blake. He's a damn good son. Turned out better'n the other one."

"By 'the other one,' you mean Travis?"

"Yeah, always too busy for his old man, playing golf with his buddies. But the other one, Blake, turned out to be a good kid. It's just the way he was conceived that angered me."

"Conceived?"

"It's . . ." Hesitating, Sid says, "Complicated. Too heavy to talk about right now."

Calmed by Hunter's soothing tones, Sid is no longer stuck in the past. Hunter is done for now. He had paid Felicia for their final round of drinks, so he helps Sid out to the car. Drives back to Sid's house. He had planned on crashing there. But now, with the crazed night and Sid's back-and-forth arguments with himself, Hunter is leaning toward hitting the road, finding a cheap hotel. But then he thinks about how he and his dad couldn't leave his grandfather unattended. He would need to call someone to stay with Sid. He wasn't about to leave him to his own self-dismantling devices.

Searching through the house for a phone number. On the

gunmetal fridge, he finds the name "Blake," with a phone number beside it. Thinks he'll make contact with the mysterious son. Last thing Hunter wants is to leave Sid alone with his demons tonight. Making the call, he explains who he is. That he had gone out with Blake's father. That Sid had had episode after episode at the local VFW and that Hunter feels he is maybe getting worse. That he thinks someone should come stay with him, seeing as he'd been drinking.

It eats away at Hunter. His father had always told him to trust your gut. Don't leave things unattended or you might live to regret it later. And they never left his grandfather unattended. Hunter would never forgive himself if he were to leave and Sid created a situation that caused him to bring harm to himself or others.

Waiting for Blake to arrive, Itch and Nugget keep an eye on Sid, who brakes out a deck of cards, and they start playing euchre at a table in the living room. Beams cut through the dark, flashing across the windows, throwing shadows on the walls of Sid's house. Hunter opens the front door, and everyone stares in surprise. Hunter shakes his hand. He feels as though he has reached into a mirror, and his reflection has met him halfway.

"Thanks for calling," Blake said.

"Not a problem. Really didn't think it was safe to leave your dad here alone."

"Agreed. I do worry about him. But he refuses to move in with me." Blake comes inside, looks at Sid seated across from Itch. "How we doing, Pop?"

"Oh, I was hoping to get about three sheets to the wind, but this peckerwood and his buddies thought I was acting a fool. Brought me home, and you know the rest. Now I'm trying to learn them on euchre."

"I see." Blake tells Sid.

Itch and Nugget nod, smile, and say, "What's up?" Then Blake says to Hunter, "Heard a lot about you."

Hunter tries not to stare, but the kid is a younger version of him. And he tells Blake, "Funny, I never knew about you."

"My grandparents raised me at first. Little bit of bad blood between Pop and Mom around the time I was born. They eventually worked things out. Travis and I talk, but we're so far from having any common interest, it's just words filling the time."

"I hear that. So you live and work around the area?"

"Live down in Marengo. Got a custom bike shop up in Paoli. Saw your-all's bikes out front. Some sweet fuckin' Harleys."

The coincidence is unsettling. His appearance, and a bike shop to boot. Hunter says, "Thanks. We're all gearheads. I do custom work too."

"Small world. But you no longer live around here?"

"You ain't shittin' it's a small world. No, I live in North Carolina."

Feeling that he should sober up and get some of the fog out of his head, he remembers the coffeepot he had seen in the kitchen. "You want some java?"

"Probably not tonight. Little late for me."

Hunter can't take any more of this situation. It was like a real-life episode of *The Outer Limits*. He needs to extricate himself from it, regroup. Excusing himself, he goes into the kitchen, grabs the red Folger's can. Unscrews the lid. He finds the filters, places one in the coffeepot, and scoops out the coarse grounds. Loads up the filter. Adds water. Closes up the pot and presses Start. Listening to everyone talk in the opposite room, for Hunter it is like looking into an alternative universe, a reengineered version of himself. His mind goes frantic with repetition. How could he never have known that Blake existed? Keeping in touch with Sid over the years. How could Sid never have mentioned Blake? The other question is about his father. He had to know, which brings more repetition. More questions of why he never mentioned it. He wonders whether his father had ever met Blake. Had he known about Blake and never told Hunter? With his death, Hunter would never know. But the real question is, When did it happen?

Leaning his forearms on the counter, Hunter watches the coffeepot sputter and steam. He takes a cup from the cabinet and fills it up. Hollers, "Anybody want a cup of joe?"

Nugget and Itch yell, "Sure!"

"Then get your dead asses in here. This ain't no Hunter's Diner, and I ain't spoon-feeding you mugs."

Coming back into the living room, Itch and Nugget are shaking hands with Blake. Acquainting themselves. Passing small talk. Then Blake goes down a hallway to Sid's bedroom, comes back with a change of clothing, and starts to pack Sid up. Itch and Nugget go to the kitchen to grab a cup of mud.

Blake tells Sid to get up, that they are going back to Blake's house. He tells Hunter and his buddies to make themselves at home, to stay the night. There is no sense in driving this late with booze flowing through their bloodstreams.

Hunter said, "Really, you and your dad should stay here. I think we're good after a cup of coffee."

"Look, like I said, no sense in driving if you been drinking. Just trouble waiting to happen. Cop in this area pulls you over, out-of-state plates, he's gonna take one look at the tats and the bikes and haul your asses in. Sleep it off, and get on the road when you get up. Seriously. Way Dad talks about you, you're practically family."

Hunter thinks about it and doesn't want to argue. He shakes Blake's hand and thanks him. Tells Sid they will talk soon.

The moment the door shuts behind them, Itch turns to Hunter.

"What the fuck, dude! Looking at him was like looking at you. Like a fucking episode of *The Twilight Zone!*"

"How you think *I* felt?"

"Guess your dad has some explaining to do, only he'll never get the chance," Nugget says.

"No shit," Hunter says. "No shit."

Early morning, it didn't matter how much cold water Hunter splashed on his face, it wouldn't wake him up. And it wouldn't wash away the hangover that pounded and fogged his brain, or the unknown—the mystery of Blake. The sun of a breaking day warms the blacktop on Highway 64. Even with sunglasses, it dazzles the eyes.

The three bikes roar down the old highway. Taking the exit in Sulphur, they hit the interstate, making good time. Breezing through road construction on Interstate 64, crossing from Indiana into Illinois, taking exit 110 for US 45 to Norris City, East Delaware to County Highway 1, Enterprise Road onto a highway, passing through small towns. Hunter has questions about his father. Trying to recall their visits with Sid when Hunter was younger. It eats at him, knowing that Hank had had an affair with Sid's wife. Fathering a son, an unknown brother to Hunter. But had Sid believed the son was his own until he realized how much the boy looked like Hunter? It doesn't seem possible. But Sid knew about it, knew whose son it was. He is still arguing with his dead wife about it. The craziest part is Sid's never mentioning Blake to Hunter during all their years of keeping in contact.

Both Nugget and Itch had done a double take when they saw Blake. They joked around after he left, raising those same questions that Hunter was chewing on—questions that might never be answered. And then it came to Hunter: his grandfather. When they were staying with him and dealing with his dementia, Annie had come around quite often. And there were plenty of times when she was alone with Hank.

Throttling their bikes down, they approach a boxy black four-wheeled carriage, wooden-spoked wheels turning behind the hooves of a big trotting warmblood. Holding the reins is a man wearing a white shirt, black suspenders, and a broad-brimmed straw hat. He has a beard but no mustache. The woman beside him wears a black dress and white bonnet. The motorcycles slow to pass, giving the horse a wide berth. Itch says, "Holy shit, man, it's Quakers."

Shaking his head, Hunter says, "Amish, actually. They migrated to this area around the mid-eighteen hundreds, I think."

"Well, look at you, Mr. Historian!"

"You know me. It's all about the intel, the history."

"Knowledge is power, brother. Knowledge is power."

They ride for another two hours, following the highway into Effingham. Everyone is a little hungover and sleep deprived and could do with a little pick-me-up. Some caffeine. They park the bikes in front of Joe Sipper's Café and walk up to the long glass-windowed counter with blue anodized aluminum along the bottom. A display case of cakes and baked sweets. Hunter asks the cute ponytailed brunette sporting a fake-and-bake tan for the strongest brew they have: a red eye with two shots of espresso. He turns to Itch and Nugget. "Guys want the same?"

"Sounds good, brother," they reply.

The girl tells them to take a seat, saying it will be about five minutes.

Seated along the wall, they watch the midday patrons—reading their papers, eating sandwiches, sipping caffeine, and tapping on laptops. All three travelers are tired from too much booze and drama. They could use a nap at a rest area, but Hunter wants to make the border of Missouri. Find a hotel and clean up for the push through Kansas, Colorado, and into Utah.

A guy comes in—clean-cut, dark umber skin tone, wearing khakis and a Yankees baseball T-shirt. The girl behind the counter says, "How we doing today, Coach Wiethop?"

"Oh, surviving. How about you, Jenna?"

"Steady. You want the usual?"

"Yeah, please. Two shots of espresso and six ounces of hot water and room for milk, but no milk."

Turning around, the coach makes eye contact with Hunter, glances over at Itch and Nugget. Takes in the tattoos. The look of road-worn heathens with a hangover. Then back to Hunter. He leans an elbow on the counter. "Passing through?"

"Yeah," Hunter said.

"Those must be your bikes out front."

"What gave it away?" Hunter deadpans.

"You guys part of a club?"

"Naw, just gearheads. My father passed away. Taking a long road trip to California."

He said, "Sorry for your loss. Where you coming from?"

"North Carolina, but we stopped in Indiana last night—tried to visit an old friend."

Stepping over from the counter, he puts out his hand. "I'm Rod. Everyone calls me 'Coach.' Teach English and coach baseball and basketball down at the high school."

Shaking his hand. "Hunter. And these are my buddies, Nugget and Itch."

"Nice to meet you," Rod says, shaking their hands.

"From here?" Nugget asked.

"Naw. Went to college in Evansville. Took a job here after grad-
uating and never left."

"Coffee's ready, Coach," Jenna says. "And so are your new
buddies'."

Rod grabs two coffees. "Not sure which is whose."

Hunter stands up. "They're all the same," he says, passing them
to Nugget and Itch.

"Wanna grab a table?" Rod asks.

"Sure," Hunter says, walking over to a table. The four men
pull their chairs out and sit down. "Got the day off?" Hunter asks.

"I wish. Took a half day. Some legal issues. School's trying to
railroad my ass."

"Sounds like it sucks pretty bad."

"Oh, it does. Been teaching and coaching for twenty years,
won too many championships to count. And all of a sudden, they
don't wanna renew my contract. Trying get a favor in for a family
member, I think. Fucking politics."

Sipping his coffee, trying to clear the fog from his brain, Hunter
asks, "Can they even do that?"

"Not legally. But they're damn sure trying. Got a board meeting about it tonight. Taking a vote."

"Thought you had to go to the city to get bad politics." Hunter
chuckles.

"Right. I don't get it. Nobody seems to understand any of
this shit. I mean, this is a small town. A rural area. Democrat,
Republican—makes me no difference. I'm a middle-of-the-road
guy. Married, go to church on Sundays, no kids. I'm a person of
color. My wife is white. Never been an issue. I'm not playing the
race card, either. I knew when I moved here that this was once a
sundown town."

Itch says, "Come again? A 'sundown town'?"

Nugget says, "A town where people of color best be gone by sundown."

"That's bullshit," Nugget said. "In this day and age, that mindset should be obsolete."

Rod made a sad grin and shook his head slowly. "Preachin' to the choir, my man. And I've never had any racial issues or tensions since I got here. In my opinion, ninety-nine point nine percent of the folks around here aren't racist. I haven't met that point one percent yet, though I'm sure they're out there. But all the folks I know are good hardworking folks. And I don't wear my skin color as a chip on my shoulder. Only thing that counts is values and moral fiber. Bringing up race is petty. You bring it up, then I guess *you* got the problem. I know my history. Where I came from, what my folks and their folks suffered through, and what they overcame and what they accomplished."

Hunter sips his coffee, then says what his father had always told him. "This country wasn't built on good—only fought for with good intentions. Took a lot of blood and sacrifice for what was right and just. I'm with you. Big problem for most people these days is no one knows their history or where they come from or what their ancestors struggled and fought for."

"I agree," says Rod. "It's taught less and less. But enough of all that. I'm just keeping my fingers crossed and praying the good Lord is looking out for me."

Hunter says, "My father always believed that regardless of how bad things got for a good person, eventually the good would come back around to them. That the rough patches were just a test. What goes around comes around."

Rod laughs. "I hope your daddy is right. I lean toward Geronimo's philosophy: what doesn't kill us makes us stronger."

"Yeah. Regardless of how a person handles a situation, there's always gonna be racism. It's in every state. But is everyone racist? No. I believe the real test is this. You're a teacher. You've made strong impressions on students. Good impressions, I'm thinking, if you've been teaching for twenty years at the same school. So that'll come back in your favor."

"Well, I hope you're right. You know, with teaching, the problem is everything starts at home. Takes two parents to raise a child. But nowadays, both gotta work. So you gotta put in the time. Know where your kids are at. Communicate with them. They gotta have a father and a mother. Regardless of marriage, they both gotta be there for the kid. And like you mentioned, teach them about where they came from, what their family has endured. And then, as teachers, our job is we kind of pick up the slack and hopefully build on that solid upbringing. That foundation. But if the foundation is lacking, man, it becomes an uphill battle."

"The real problem is those who run our cities and towns," Nugget cuts in. "Career politicians. Keep taking and taking from us. Dumb down our education. Always trying to divide us. Someone looking for the right words to get your vote."

"Taking our money. Couldn't pay me to work with that mob day after day."

Itch says, "You could always get a job teaching the Amish."

Rod cocks an eyebrow. "You know, about four thousand Amish live around Arthur, Illinois."

"We passed a buggy on our way here," Hunter says.

"Way their history goes, they started in Switzerland. Got frustrated with their church. Wanted a stricter and simpler life. Came to America in the sixteen-hundreds. Some groups settled in Pennsylvania, and another group rooted here in Illinois. They're all really good people. Hardworking. Keep to themselves. They do a lot of carpentry work for people. Roofing and add-on decks. Really quality work. But anyway, so you-all staying here in town or just grabbing a cup of coffee and heading back out?"

"Coffee and the road. Like to make it through to Missouri. Get a hotel, a shower, some z's, and hit Kansas sometime tomorrow."

"Wow. That's one long never-ending drive to cruelty."

Finishing his coffee, Hunter says, "That's why we need to be making some tracks."

Standing up, Rod sticks out his hand. "Well, it was nice crossing paths with you guys. You do kinda stand out in a crowd."

Hunter laughs. "It was a pleasure meeting you. Good luck tonight. And stay positive. I'm sure some of the good you've done over the years will come into the discussion tonight in some shape or form."

"Thanks. I'm gonna try to keep positive, and I can only pray for the right outcome."

They gas up at the IGA. The road is long and speechless. They fall into the Zen-like groove of wind and road, and time relaxes its hold until, as the sun begins to set, they hit the edge of Missouri. Find a hotel just before dark, get unpacked, shower. Turn on the TV, flip through the channels, and land on the local news. There smiles a familiar image. Rod, the teacher from Illinois. The newswoman interviews some students Rod had coached. They speak in glowing terms about how he had helped them, how great a coach and friend he is. A mentor. And Hunter smiles. His words had proved true—what his father had told him long ago, that good comes to good people. It is only a test of character. Thinking about it, he wonders about Blake. Perhaps learning about him, taking this journey, is a test of Hunter's character, but he also wonders what other secrets his father took to the grave.

JACK

The smells of oil, solvents, and greased engine parts are strong enough that he can taste them in his mouth. On his tongue. His body lies flat, head twisted sideways, his neck stiff and achy. He feels the rattle and creak of the suspension with every bump. Jarring and pounding his aging body. Dry heat opens his pores. Sweat dampens and sours his clothing with fear. The fear of not knowing what has happened or what will happen. Of who these men are, what they want, and where they are taking him and Matías.

Fear presses Jack to search for answers. He whispers, "Matías, who are these people?"

"I swear to you Mr. Jack, that I have no idea," he whispers back. "This isn't normal."

There's the sawing hum of insects ramming and landing on the cloth sack over Jack's head. Somewhere in front of him, in the cab of the truck, he listens to muffled voices arguing back and forth. It's been going on for minutes that may have turned into hours.

Worry claws and digs in his gut, and he wants to puke. The

noises and the smells sicken him. This is something he is not acquainted with. Being kidnapped. Being in pain. He has lain in the same position with his arms bound behind him for so long that a feeling of numbness is starting in his limbs, spreading like an infection to his entire body. Unable to bend or move, he feels the deadness creeping up one thigh, while a charley horse starts in the other.

In business, when there was a breakdown in communication, when problems arose, to find a solution Jack did one thing: he asked questions. He whispers to Matías, "What were you hauling in your truck?"

"It's on the bill of lading. Chemical for the mines."

"Do you believe that someone would want this chemical that you were hauling?"

"It's possible," Matías whispers back. "Someone always wants what I haul."

"But who would want it?"

"Narcos or *traficantes*, maybe. I do not know; I've never been abducted."

"So there's the possibility that what you're hauling can be used to make drugs, you think?"

"It's a possibility, I suppose."

As the bumps rattling Jack's bones bring him more pain, Matías's words bring more worry. The words *narcos* and *traficantes* and *drugs* bring worry, awakening a revulsion deep in his consciousness. Images from the world news, of mass graves being discovered, beheadings, bodies hanging from overpasses, men brandishing automatic weapons with their identities covered by death's-head masks, soldiers of drug wars along the border. This is not what Jack was in search of. How did he manage to get himself *abducted*? And where are they taking him? What is going on? The more Jack questions everything in his mind, the faster his heart beats and the more his worry escalates.

Every so often, he twists his neck, readjusting the position of his face to keep the cloth from blocking his airflow. The condensation from his breath has dampened the sack to the point that the cloth grows heavy and makes breathing difficult.

Being overweight and out of shape doesn't help. Lying facedown, gut pressed up against his diaphragm, the fat around his upper body adding stress to his lungs and heart. Add to that his limited mobility, the heat, and the condensation gathering in the hood's fabric, and he feels as if he were suffocating.

Trying to imagine something positive to take his mind off the situation, Jack focuses on his breathing. His inhalation and exhalation. Trying to slow his pulse, control his nerves. An exercise he learned and practiced many times in one of his many leadership seminars over the years. Inhaling deep and holding his breath for five seconds before exhaling, imagining he is somewhere else, somewhere with a cool breeze, maybe a swimming pool or a lake, comfortable seating like a lounge chair or a recliner, all peaceful and low-stress, blue sky overhead. Someplace soft. His mind begins to calm, to slow down and drift. The tension in his body eases. His eyes close, and his body lies limp. He is walking on a beach of gray sand. In the distance, bright surf rolls and pounds. The sky overhead and out over the sea is deep-space blue, cracking with heat lightning. A balmy breeze soothes his skin. At the edge of the sand sits a figure. Hesitant, Jack moves toward the shape. Getting closer, he sees the smoke-colored hair shot through with blond. It is Sarah. Dressed in a thin, gauzy white cotton shirt, swimsuit beneath, tanned arms are hugging her knees to her chest. Jack kneels to touch her, and she says, "Don't."

Waves crash. Smell of the sea. Licking his lips, he asks, "Why can't I touch you?"

"Because I don't want to be touched by you."

The sea breeze brushes his face. "But why? What have I done besides love you?"

"What have you done?" She laughs. "Love? What *haven't* you done, is a better question. You did not love."

"I'm confused by your response," Jack tells her.

"You weren't confused when you chose your sacrifice."

"My sacrifice?"

"Your work. You chose to work, to earn more and more money over being with your family. That was your sacrifice. You sacrificed *us*."

"I provided so my family could live in comfort, allowing you and the kids to live without struggle."

"A life devoid of struggle—that's what you call it? You abandoned your daughter until she took her own life. Turned your back on your son until he rebelled and chose his own path. Left me to deal with the pain of cancer that consumed and dissolved my entire being while you worked. You call that love?"

Tears begin to form in Jack's eyes. His body begins to tremble. "I worked for you and the kids. I was there with you in the hospital as much as I could be. I got you the best doctors, the best care possible."

"The best that money could buy. Of course you did. Like I said, you chose your sacrifice. Now I'm gone. Live with it."

Bending down, Jack's lower back hurts; his breath quickens. Reaching, he grips Sarah's shoulder. She jerks away from the touch of his fingers, and he grabs at her once more, pulls her toward him. Her shoulder detaches from her body. "Way to go, Jack, tearing my life apart once again. Causing more pain that money can't put back together."

"No!" Jack screams. "I'm sorry. No!" Holding the arm, he

watches it turn to sand that sifts through his fingers, slides through his grip. He reaches for Sarah once more. Her face turns to him, devoid of flesh. Of eyes or lips. Only sinus bones and a skull with tufts of hair blowing in the warm wind.

Sarah tells him, "You never did listen to me, Jack. Just sowed more pain. Uprooting and tearing everything apart."

Frightened, he falls backward. His hands spread over the beach to catch his descent. He is weak. And Sarah slithers and crawls toward him. Climbs on top of him. His hands touch her body, feel the bony structure of her dead soul as it slowly dissipates. Running through his fingers, she turns to sand just as her arm did. The wind catches it and blows it away.

"Jack? Jack?" His name being repeated. A distressed whisper, over and over. He blinks and opens his eyes. Everything is shown to him sideways, through black cloth. The smells of the truck have returned. He hears the squeak and creak of the suspension, punctuated by his own panting breath. The scent of rotted lumber hangs in the air. The weight of his gut on his bladder makes him feel the need to urinate. But Jack holds it. And he says to Matías, "I am awake. I passed out and took my thoughts somewhere else."

"I thought you'd gone mad over there. You were dreaming. Kept talking in your sleep. Repeating 'Sarah, Sarah.' I thought you had truly lost it, my friend."

"Don't rule that out just yet. I'm old and wounded, and I am haunted by the loss of my daughter, my mother, and especially my wife, and this situation is scaring the shit out of me."

"My friend, you carry too heavy a burden."

The truck has stopped. Sounds of vehicles. Of people. Muffled.

Door hinges creak. Footfalls on the ground. Hands grope the rear of the truck, unlatching the door and sliding it upward. Hands grab Jack's ankles and calves. Pulling and tugging him across the splintered wood where he lies. His teeth grit. When his feet hit the ground, hands hold him while he finds his equilibrium. His knees are numb, and they give. He cannot feel his legs. His entire body is Jell-O from lying in an odd position for so long.

"Get the fuck up, fat man," a foreign-accented voice demands.

Whimpering, Jack tells the voice, "I am trying, but I cannot feel my legs."

"You're gonna feel something if you do not get your ass up, fat man."

Beside him, Matías is pulled from the rear of the vehicle. "What is it that you want?" he asks their captors.

"Shut up."

Hands pull Jack to his feet. Blood has begun to flow back into his legs and arms. He can feel circulation returning to hips and ankles. Hands guide and push him. He can see nothing. Cars are driving around. There are streets or roads around them, Jack believes. There is the sound of kids and the snorts of pigs and the bleating of goats, or maybe llamas. The smell of dirt and leaf mold. Trees and timber. Congealed with exhaust fumes and something being cooked. Shaking, Jack fears the worst. Imagines a pistol's barrel pressed to the back of his skull. The click of its hammer. Somewhere in front of him, a door opens with a grinding drag. Hands press him forward. The smells change from exhaust to the indoor smells of foods, musty water, and unwashed bodies. He hears the clatter of shoes, clicking sounds. Water dripping. Lights coming on. Another door opens. The sounds reverberate less now as they enter a smaller space. They are in a hallway. Another door opens, and they are pressed into what feels like a small room. Claustrophobic. The door closes, and the voices become muffled once more. Talking. The conversation grows distant, angry.

Sitting on a floor that is wooden and smells of urine and

excrement. The muffled voices return, growing closer and closer. The door opens.

"*¿Quiénes son?*" an intense but direct voice demands.

"Who are they?" Matías murmurs, translating for Jack.

Another man's voice, sounding rather less confident, replies. "One is the driver," Matías translates. "He says the other is a passenger."

The intense voice, angry, speaks again, and Matías reports in a whisper, "Why the fuck did you take them? Bring them here?"

"Uh, we thought maybe a ransom?"

"*We? Ransom?* Are you asking me or telling me, you fucking idiot? All I said was take the chemical. Take the fucking truck. Offload everything and leave the truck. Nothing more. No fucking driver. No fucking passenger. I don't traffic people—at least, not old, fat fucking men and local drivers."

"What do we do with them?"

"Ahh, maybe you should have asked that question before you decided to bring them here."

After a pause comes the sound of hands fussing with a wrapper, then the rasp of a lighter being flicked. The smell of tobacco smoke follows. After a sighing exhalation, the intense voice speaks again, and Matías translates. "I'll tell where you *can't* take them: back to fucking Chile." Another slight pause, and the voice says, "To the farmhouse, with Carlos. They can help him until I decide what to do about your fuck-up."

Routed and taken back out the way they came, passing the same familiar smells and sounds. Rough hands load them back into the truck. Jack feels like passing out from fear, exhaustion, and the infernal heat. And Matías tells him, "If this is a dream, we're in hell, my friend."

And Jack tells him, "Earlier, when I nodded off, I dreamed of my wife, Sarah. She was on a beach."

"Did she have flames all around her?"

"No, she did not. But everything was gray and black, and she spoke harshly to me about the way I provided for her and my children."

"That's good. She offered truth."

"Why is that good?"

"Because flames could be an omen for an ending. Black and white could be an omen for the situation, meaning this is how it is between two sides. No middle. Like a lesson."

Wherever they are headed, the road has become rougher than before. An upward climb followed by rocky descents. The undercarriage rattles as if it might fall off. From the cab, Jack can hear the men arguing.

For some reason, Jack wonders about his backpack. Did they grab it, or leave it in the truck cab? Everything happened so quickly he never paid attention, thinking that wherever their captors were taking them, he would at least have some of the provisions packed by Maria. A change of clothing. Food. Water. Something familiar.

Time passes. It feels like hours. Jack tries to control his breathing, his worry. Tries to think of somewhere calm. Until the truck stops. The rear door slides up again, and once more, Jack and Matías are dragged across the truck's floor. The black hoods come off. Jack can breathe. The air is thick. Heated and sticky. Daylight crimps and burns his sight at first. His eyes blink and water. A hand stabilizes him until he can stand without support. There is the ominous click of a blade. The plastic zip ties that bind his wrists fall away. There's a nudge. Handing him something. Jack's hands take the weight. It's his backpack. He hugs it to his chest. His vision is full of blurred shapes. Still adjusting. Hands push and poke at him.

"Walk," a voice commands. Then a hand leads him by the arm. Walks him forward. Until the voice tells Jack and Matías, "Stop."

Jack's eyes squint and burn. Little by little, his eyes adjust to the brightness. He's in a town or a village. Surrounding them are six buildings that look like two-story barns with decks on the upper level. They are constructed from odds and ends of lumber and tin. Sections of plywood and two-by-fours and two-by-sixes. Worn chairs sit out before the structures, and clotheslines run from one end to the next. An array of different-colored shirts, pants, and undergarments hangs from them. Out in the space between the buildings, the common area is like a courtyard. Old tires and hunks of stone lie where they were discarded.

A short, stubby man with an impressive gut peeking out beneath a stained and holey T-shirt stands expressionless, studying Jack and Matías. A mop of black curls is sweat-pasted across his forehead. He wears dirty blue workpants, and black rubber boots up to just below his knees. "This is Carlos," says the man who just hauled Jack and Matías out of the truck.

Jack nods. Unsure what is happening or what he should say, he takes a good look at his kidnapper: dark acne-scarred skin with dead eyes, a knife scar from one corner of his mouth down to his neck, pinstriped short-sleeved button-up shirt and loose-fitting, lived-in Levi's jeans.

"This is your new home," he tells them. Then looks to the potbellied man and tells him, *"Alfonso dice que los traigamos aquí . . ."* Then followed a brief torrent of incomprehensible Spanish, ending with *"pasta."*

Pasta? Jack glances at Matías, who smirks.

The kidnapper leaves. Carlos waves at his new charges to follow him and leads them to a small, run-down outbuilding constructed of boards, concrete block, and a rusty tin roof. Inside are two beds. A bucket. He points. And Matías tells Jack, "Our new home. Our bedding and bathroom."

Jack drops his pack on a bed. Then the man leads them back outside. Jack looks around them. They are surrounded by green, steaming jungle, in a place that doesn't even exist on a map. Carlos grabs two large cloth sacks, hands one to each of them, and leads them down a narrow forest path. Across the dirt road, they cut through an expanse of trees and bushes, to a clearing where small children stand picking green leaves from rows and rows of bushes. "Coca plantation," Matías whispers to Jack.

Carlos turns and nods at Matías. *Yes.* Confirming his whisper.

Carlos talks to Matías in Spanish. Matías then tells Jack, "We are to help the *niños* harvest these leaves. Fill the sacks Carlos gave us. When they're full, we go back and empty them in the courtyard, walk back up the trail at the farm, and do it again. We do this until dark."

Coca. Jack is on a plantation for cocaine—not a place he ever planned to be.

Carlos walks them to a plant, shows them how to strip the yellow-tinted leaves without damaging the leaf buds that will grow in to replace them. Drop the green blades into the sacks. *Looks easy enough*, Jack thinks, and he nods his head in acknowledgment. He starts on one row; Matías starts on another. Jack hasn't done any form of physical labor since he was in high school, and even then it was just washing dishes—not all that physical. His sausage-fingered hands grip the limbs at the base, work down over the length of the limb with a pulling motion. Working and stripping an entire plant. He watches the children and tries to mimic their movements, their form. The repetitive actions are rough on Jack's delicate uncalloused hands. They become sore and red, then begin to swell. Blistering. Then bleeding. But he stays with it, going down the row, the sack growing ever heavier. Then walking to the courtyard to exchange the full sack for an empty one. Then back to the plants. His back and knees are pulsing with hurt. He is drenched in sweat. The arches of his feet throb. He feels his hamstrings start to cramp and knows. He needs salt. Electrolytes.

He tears strips from his shirt to wrap around his cracked and bleeding palms. Sweat burns and stings his eyes.

Matías asks Jack, "Have you ever done gardening?"

"Not since I was a kid. My mother had the green thumb in the family. Planted a massive garden of tomatoes, peppers, beets, corn, green beans, and eggplants every year."

The sun beats down on Jack and Matías, draining them of fluid. Jack feels light-headed. He feels a swirling sensation in his brain, as if he might pass out. Just keel over from heat exhaustion. All around him, children are doing the same thing he is doing, only better. Faster. More productively. Laughing and running back up the path to the courtyard after filling every sack. Emptying it and returning for more work.

Carlos waves to them, and Matías and Jack sit down beside him. He has a bucket of well water and a large wooden ladle. Dipping the ladle, Jack sucks the liquid into his mouth, slaking a throat that feels coated in grit.

Matías asks questions. Translates their conversation back to Jack. He asks how long Carlos has been doing this type of farming.

All his years, he says.

Jack tells him to ask, Why not try coffee or cacao?

Carlos tells Matías, not enough money for his family. This type of farming, this crop, is all they have. It pays for food and shelter. Clothing. Education.

Looking at Carlos, his wife, his kids, Jack isn't judging. For once in his life, he sees and understands what poverty is. What real labor means. What it's like to be on the other side, to know you may not be around to see tomorrow. It isn't an easy feeling to accept. And all the money he has in his bank account is useless here, now.

Jack tells Matías to ask Carlos how long he has lived here, in this way.

Carlos tells them, since his birth forty years ago. His father left the land, the farm, to him.

Jack asks, "Where are they?"

Carlos chuckles, says they're in the Vrae Valley, working on his coca farm.

Overhead, a helicopter thumps by. Jack points. "Who's that?"

Carlos tells Matías that it's the government and their military. They try to police the area. But it's too vast. They've got protection from the Shining Path guerrillas.

Jack read about this area in the world news reports. It is a lawless and unforgiving land.

When it becomes too dark to see, Carlos tells them that tomorrow they will load the leaves to start making paste.

There was no comfort that night as Jack lay in bed, bathed in his own sweat and stench. Staring at the ceiling, he waited for the mosquitoes whining around his head to light, so he could swat them. Stomach growling. Carlos had left them a bucket of water and another bucket covered with a cloth. Bread and mangoes were inside. Lying on a hard bed with a thin mattress, Jack was too sore to move. Reaching for a mango, biting into flesh so sweet it overloaded his taste buds, he chewed, savoring it. Swallowing the exquisite-tasting fruit, he was sickened by the situation. How this farmer and his family lived. Their struggle. Mouths to feed, and no help from the government.

Closing his eyes, he felt a warmth course through him. He hoped Sarah would visit him. Trying to find a smile, something positive, he would tell her his ambitions, his desire to help Carlos and his family. He just didn't know how.

ANNE

Hunkered down, everyone is on edge, insides clenched tight. Behind them, feet clomp and crunch, snapping twigs and rustling branches. Nerves taut, Anne starts to ease the pistol from her backpack.

The shadow limps into view, gasping for breath. It's Dredd. Everyone's heartbeat begins to subside, and they relax out of their crouched positions. Coming out of hiding, Cinnamon grabs Dredd by the arm, pulls him down to their level. Hissing, "You gone crazy? Get your ass down and shut up."

Wheezing, he tells Cinnamon, "Fucking insane. Damn pigs were beating and arresting everyone they could. Tore the entire encampment to pieces. Everything we built. Lost!"

"Well, we're safe now, long as no one followed you."

"We're never safe. The man is always trying to keep us down. Tread on our freedoms. Fucking pigs."

"Well," Cinnamon says, "until a train comes, we got no other options but to lay low, keep our eyes and ears open."

"You're probably right," Dredd replies. "We hide and we wait. It's not like we can fight back without more bodies."

"Fighting never solves anything," says Cinnamon. "Movement is the best course of action."

He draws on the silence, doesn't offer a rebuttal.

Everyone stays hunkered down, one eye closed, the other open. Ears listening for footfalls. But they never come. All that comes is the morning dew, and nervous yawns anticipating the law to come barreling through the woods at any moment. The thin predawn light creeps in, turning the woods gray and the sky pink. A robin starts up; other birds take up the hue and cry, waking the world around them. Then, below the growing hubbub of chirps and caws, the distant crawl of a train. Something positive. Their escape.

Cinnamon starts shaking everyone awake. Stiff limbs unfold, working out the kinks, inciting the blood to circulate. Bodies get upright, emerging from their camouflage. Then everyone runs out of the wilderness, toward the berm of pale rocks supporting the rails.

Kneeling, Anne lays her hand on the cold iron. She feels the faint, almost subliminal vibration, which grows until she knows she is not imagining it. The train draws nearer, louder, closing the distance.

Cinnamon looks back to the woods. Seeing everyone standing out in the open, she waves at them to fall back, to kneel and hide and avoid drawing the train crew's attention. She squeezes Anne's hand, and Anne feels her warmth. Their eyes meet; they smile. Canary holds her brother and sister, one on each side, their little hands fidgeting with the sprouting weeds and fallen leaves. Trot sits beside Anne, and Dredd is alone, sulking in his own negativity. Everyone's nerves are taut. There's a certain energy that builds, anticipating a train's passage. It never wanes, never gets old or commonplace. It is a rush of stormy weather traveling through your body.

Rounding the bend, the train slows. Everyone waits, lets cars pass. At last, they stand back up when they start to see cars worth hitching on to. Adrenaline firing their veins, they follow Anne and Cinnamon's lead. They bolt for it. Digging hard into the ground, racing over the earth, taking each rise and dip in stride. Their packs bouncing, jostling, as they come on like a band of gypsy commandos. Sprinting to match the locomotive's speed, they come alongside the clattering cars. Anne reaches for the grainer's steel ladder. Her lungs burn, and the dog-bitten ankle aches and throbs, but not enough to slow her down. She is getting on this train. Grabbing the rung, she pulls herself up onto the metal porch. Turning, she reaches down for Cinnamon. Their eyes lock. Lips smile, Anne tugs hard, lets her weight fall backward, and the girl swings up. Behind Cinnamon comes Canary and the twins, who are running hard, their little legs pumping. She helps them, along with Trot, who brings up the rear. He gives one twin a boost up onto the porch's platform, then the other. Then Canary swings up, and finally, Trot clambers aboard. Just as they fall onto the train, it starts to gather speed.

Last aboard is Dredd. He looks spent. Grabbing for the ladder, one hand slips off, and Anne considers stomping the other one. She sees him for what he is, just as Cinnamon told her, not for what he pretends to be. He's a chameleon. But she grabs his wrist. It is not her decision to make. She helps him get his hand back on the rung. He recovers, brings his other hand onto the ladder. Anne falls backward, her weight pulling Dredd onto the train. He falls beside her, breathing hard, smiling, greasy dark curls framing his face. He talks over the rumble of the train. "Thank you. That was very noble of you. You could've let me eat gravel, left me behind."

And she could have, but she didn't. She only hoped she wouldn't later regret helping him.

Everyone coughs and heaves, looking to the cutout circles within the metal car. The double barrel. Everyone crawls through the hole to get out of sight. Inside the compartment, it's like the last train Anne hopped, when she met Cinnamon. Dirty and dusted by railroad travel. It smells of bodily fluids. A few dirty blankets and a plastic bottle of urine. The inner walls are tagged by others who have hopped the train. Initials and dates. Everyone is road worn and weary. They're tired, pushed to the brink. They have just lost something they had built and grown used to. Now they are uprooted, in search of something, but with no real consensus on what that something might be.

Their sleep-deprived minds are erratic and stressed, unable to hold a clear thought. Anne leans the back of her head into the metal wall, clutches her backpack to her chest. Closes her eyes, feels the vibration in the back of her skull. Reverberating through her body. She wonders where they are headed, where the train is going. She twists her neck, looks to Cinnamon, who sits beside her. "Any idea where the train's headed?"

"Once we get a ways down the tracks, I'll peek out. See what looks familiar. See if I can guess a direction, a destination."

"Let's hope it's Louisiana," Dredd interrupts. Seated directly across from everyone and looking like a stain. His shirt is torn, his face scuffed by dirt, lip scabbed. "One of those pigs busted me up good. But he got his. No worries, my people," he tells them. Always about him. "We will rebuild. Start anew." Holds a fist up.

No one knows where the train is headed. But Cinnamon tells Dredd, "Settle down, Che. My best guess is, we're headed to Louisiana. It's the only thing that makes sense." Talking over the clatter of wheels on rail joints, she turns to Anne. "My hope is we can hop another train line in Louisiana, head out west." She eyes Dredd across gap between them.

Shaking his head, crinkling his busted lip, chewing on disgust, he tells her, "I think we should stay in Louisiana. It only makes sense."

The smells of dirt and unbathed bodies pervade everything.

Cinnamon's eyes narrow to slits, and she tells Dredd, "If you wanna stay in Louisiana, stay. We're not interested. We got other plans."

"We? These are *my* people. We just lost our entire encampment to a bunch of fascist pigs. Got beat down and roughed up. Barely escaped, and now you're all of a sudden the newly elected leader? You been out on the rails. Away from the group. Now you return and you're running the show?"

"You don't own nobody," Cinnamon retorts. "Someone wants to stay with you, they more'n welcome to. Unfortunately, there's nobody on this train that wants to. You always preaching about freedom, then we get a say in this."

"Look, you're too new to have an opinion. I know what's best for everyone on this train. I've given my life's blood for everyone."

"Life's blood," she snorts. "Last I remember, it was a group effort. Everybody chipped in, put their time in on the street corners, the garbage cans and dumpsters. Everybody but *you*. All of us went out and earned and sorted through trash. Brought it all back for you to rummage and take. Throw us whatever you don't want."

"It was my encampment."

"No, that's where you're wrong. It was *our* encampment. Meaning everyone. We're a family, not a dictatorship."

Dead silence. Dredd's eyes go evil, and he tells Cinnamon, "There's good folks in Louisiana. They'll take us in. You'll see."

"Then stay with them. We don't need to be taken in. We've already seen what you're about, what you offer, and it ain't about family or freedom."

Anger burns in Dredd's eyes. Reaching across, he grabs Cinnamon's ankle. "It's not your decision."

Kicking free of his grip, she tells him, "You're right. It's Canary's and Anne's and Trot's. It's free will."

"I'm with Cinnamon," Anne says.

"Me, too," says Trot.

"So are we," Canary tells Dredd.

Again silence. Anne watches the dynamic play out. Cinnamon doesn't trust him. Apparently, never has.

He speaks. "So that's how it is. Cinnamon returns. Brainwashes everyone into a mutiny against me. Even the new girl, who hasn't even given me a chance, who doesn't even know my kindness. What I've created, sacrificed, and endured. Wow. Fucking wow!" Turning his face sideways, away from Cinnamon and the others, looking out another hole cut into the compartment, he watches trees flit past. Anger animates the grime, vessels, and tattoos on Dredd's face. Closing his eyes, he pouts like a spoiled adolescent. Resting his head on the dirty, graffitied compartment wall, he sulks in silent rage.

Cinnamon leans into Anne's shoulder. Anne grabs her hands, laces her dirty fingers within Cinnamon's, feeling her warmth, a need and a want. Cinnamon whispers into her ear, "We're gonna need more money. But I'm not telling Dredd jack shit. There's a chance we may need to stay in Louisiana a day or two. Hit the city, then catch out. We don't gotta stay where he stays, though. Plenty of street encampments."

Turning to Cinnamon, Anne looks into her eyes and smiles. "No go," she whispers. "I got us covered."

Surprise lifts and brightens Cinnamon's smudged features. "How? You been holding out?"

"No. I . . . it's how I nearly killed my brother with the skillet.

He caught me stealing from our father's nest egg. Attacked me and, well . . . he got a skillet upside his fucking head, and I got the cash in my pack."

Giggling, Cinnamon tells her, "Damn, girl, I like your style. Just full of surprises."

In that instant, Ann sees the desire in her new friend's eyes and feels a sudden yearning to kiss her lips. But she doesn't. If Cinnamon can fight back her want, she can do the same.

And Anne whispers, "Anything to get us out west. See some different scenery. To be free from restraint."

Cinnamon tells Anne, "I know folks out in Kansas. We get there, we can squat a few days. Trust me. You'll love it."

Anne feels the warming glow and tingle, and she says, "Long as I'm with you, I'm happy."

HUNTER

Smell of cheap hotel soap, warm wind on his face, thoughts of the half brother he had never met. A father with a secret, and a past Hunter never knew about. He wondered what else he might never know.

They had been on the road all morning, rolling under glorious blue skies. Thoughts came and went, drifting comfortably, flowing from one to the next. Time and the road were similar. They passed by, no matter what. Houses were set in far from the road. Metal roofs. Pole barns. Livestock. Flat land in a pastoral panorama that stretched as far as the eye could see. He thought back to when he was a kid. Hank gone all week, Hunter staying with his grandfather. He'd been an infantryman in the marines. Held his own in World War II and the Korean War. Granddad had been a man of the land, of God and country. A real patriot. He checked the tags of his clothes to make sure they were made in America. If not, you'd best return them, or he'd take them out to the rusted old fire barrel, douse them with gas, and light a match. It was an old way of thinking that started the day after Pearl Harbor. In today's economy, the poor guy wouldn't have anything to wear. Such prejudice seemed quaint now. Today, prejudice was more about sides telling you what to believe, then ridiculing you for not following their choice. All this in a country where thought was supposed to be free. In Hunter's mind, the only thing that carried weight was truth.

The endless ribbon of road kept coming, and so did Hunter's train of thought. Remembering the years as his body and mind grew. And as his grandfather's began to fail. When the sickness came, Hank was forced to stay closer to home. Hank was good with money. Kept a nest egg and small investments. There were days when they took his grandfather for walks on the property he owned—well over a hundred acres. He was still sharp on the past, clearly recalling events and situations and people. Hunting and training hound dogs. Gardening. Grilling. A long and happy marriage. Kindness to others. Raising Hank. But seeing Hank and Hunter side by side in the same room, his grandfather got confused. Wondering why there were two Hanks, one aged and one young. Two versions of his son.

Hunter could only imagine what his grandfather would have done seeing all three of them—Hank, Hunter, and Blake—together in the same room.

When the dementia consumed his brain, he came apart quickly. His mind left and his body followed.

During that time, Hunter's father taught him that whatever the sickness, whatever the odds, one could still offer compassion, hold on to hope. Don't give up. Being positive offered good energy. *Your grandfather's tough. Served in two separate wars. Saw and did more than either of us could imagine or endure.*

Taking in the flat, open expanse of pavement, Hunter realized that even though his father hadn't spent every day with him, he made the most of the time they did have. It was quality, not quantity. Hank had instilled morals and values within him—the pillars that formed who he was today.

Still, Hunter wondered about the times his father had been away. Was he really working? Was he traveling? Where was he? What was he really up to? When Hank was around, he was good to Hunter. A big Eastwood fan. Loved his films. Taking Hunter to the Dirty Harry films. The spaghetti Westerns at the dollar cinema. Seeing all these Wild West landscapes now reminded Hunter of *High Plains Drifter. The Outlaw Josey Wales. A Fistful of Dollars.*

Signs for Abilene, Kansas, came breezing by. Throttling down, they passed through the town. Pieces of fact entered Hunter's mind. Traveling through part of the Louisiana Purchase, the thirty-fourth state. "City of the Plains," they called it. They cruised past the Alamo Saloon—gray wood framed in dingy white, with a front porch, red wagon wheels. They passed the Heritage Center, the Brookville Hotel, Rittles Western Wear with a huge spur outside the building. Amanda's Bakery and Bistro invited them with tantalizing smells, but everyone wanted a beer and some bar food—something off the roadside. Maybe shoot some pool, toss some darts. Unwind.

Taking Old US 40 outside Abilene, they come up on Midway Bar and Grill and pull off into the gravel parking lot that spreads out like a dusty reserve of unknown histories. The bar looks more like a late-1950s California ranch home crossed with a pole barn. Vinyl siding on concrete, with a wooden picket fence around back. Turning their engines off, they dismount in front of a sign that reads Welcome, Bikers.

Unbuckling their helmets. Boots crunching over gravel, they enter like cowboys in off the trail. Stepping onto the concrete floor, they breathe in the welcoming aromas of fried cheeseburgers, chicken, and fries. Behind the bar, beneath the red glass lighting fixtures, limps a guy in his midthirties—Ho Chi Minh beard stringing down to his sternum, faded tats, and flabby arms that still have the look of strength. He wears a Gojira T-shirt.

"Welcome to Midway Bar. Name's Al. What can I get you fellas this evening?"

Hunter swivels the black vinyl bar stool around, lays his helmet on the floor, sits down, props a booted foot up on the brass rail. It feels good not to have pavement racing beneath him. He says to Al, "Miller Lite, double cheeseburger, and an order of fries, glass of water on the side."

"You got it, brother. Bottled water okay?"

"Yeah, long as it's cold."

"Only way we serve it, brother. And you two?"

Nugget and Itch ask for some version of the same.

Off to the side is the game area, with crazy designs running over gray flooring, a circular table with green chairs surrounding it, an oak bar attached to one of the walls. Underneath a creaking ceiling fan, a green felt pool table commands the room's center, and an old-school Ms. Pacman and Galaga video game combo stands against the left wall.

Behind the bar, the usual clears and darks for well drinks line the shelves. From the back comes the sounds and tantalizing smells of burgers frying. The three travelers are road worn, their frames still humming from the long ride with no stops. Hunter is still tilting his mind, trying to shake loose answers about his father that aren't there. Al lays the beers in front of them, pops the cans. Their openings foam up. Placing a cold bottle of water beside each, Al asks, "Where you-all from?"

"North Carolina." Hunter replies.

"You're out a pretty fair ways. Just a road trip, taking in the sights?"

Hunter listens to himself say, as if by rote, "Father passed away. Headed out to California."

"Sorry to hear that. Know much about Kansas?"

Hunter's eyes home in on a sign clipped to the napkin holder: "Support your local bartender, helping ugly people get laid." He chuckles.

Itch says, "Lot of cowboy stories and the Wild West, is all."

Hunter sips his beer and laughs, tells Al, "Give us a quick history lesson."

"Will do—"

"Oh, sorry, I'm Hunter. This pickle dick beside me is Itch, and the other's Nugget."

"Cool. Nice to make everyone's acquaintance. Appreciate you-all stopping in. So, Abilene became the first real cow town of the West. Joseph McCoy hogged up two hunnerd and fifty acres. Built a hotel, named it Drovers Cottage. Had stockyards that could handle two hunnerd head of cattle. Stables, too. Kansas Pacific brung in a spur line—let cattle cars be loaded. Sped to their destinations. Next thing you know, Abilene's the first cow town in the West. And that was that."

"No shit?" says Itch.

"None," Al assures him. "From 1867 to 1871, the Chisholm Trail ended here. Wild Bill Hickok was marshal in 1871."

"Wild Bill?" Nugget says.

"Yeah, but it was short-lived. Lost his job for shooting his buddy. Lot of history around this area. Shame. People don't much care about the history no more. They're more interested in their damn phones, thumbing away all day on social media sites."

"I hear that," Hunter says. He hasn't touched his phone since they started riding. A couple of times, he had thought about phoning Olivia. Checking in with his uncle. But he has yet to do it.

From the back, a bell dinged and a voice yelled, "Orders up!"

Al turns toward the back and soon is back with three plates—one in each hand, another balanced over his forearm. Laying a plate in front of Hunter, then the other two in front of Itch and Nugget, he says, "Ketchup?"

"Think I'm square."

Itch says, "I'll take some."

"Will do." Al walks over to a cooler, pulls out a bottle of ketchup, and slides it down to Itch. "Thanks."

"You're welcome. Need anything, just holler. I'll be in the back." Al pauses, then says, "Also, after you scarf down, you're more than welcome to shoot some pool or play some video games. Make yourselves at home."

Without another word, the famished road warriors dig in.

Nugget comes up for air first. "Damn, burger is outstanding!"

Hunter swallows, mumbles his agreement, and takes another bite. Itch, meanwhile, is too focused on the task at hand to speak.

Five minutes and no words later, they are finished. Picking up their beers, they walk into the game area. A skinny man and a big-boned woman are shooting pool. She wears her brunette hair pulled up with red ends. On her neck, a tattoo of a beating heart. The skinny dude stands leaning what little weight he has on his pool stick. Tapping his beat-up boot on the floor as if he has some-where to be.

"Hurry up, bacon bit. I don't got all day."

Bending forward, resting the cue between her fingers, aiming and sizing her shot on the cue ball, she says, "How 'bout you kiss my white ass, Danny."

"It's big enough the whole damn town could kiss it all at once. Hell, they could lap that sumbitch. Run a marathon."

Hunter feels a little twinge of annoyance. His father had always taught him to respect women, saying that regardless of size, looks, or wealth, the female form always has beauty. His father had always shared stories with him about his mother. As a girl, she had struggled with weight. Caught a lot of crap from her schoolmates. Until she lost all her weight her senior year, then bore a child, only to find she had a wild streak. She became a stripper and disappeared.

Laying his beer on the bar, Hunter crosses the room. Approaches the guy. "Pipe it down, show some respect."

The guy says, "Who you think you are, butting into my affairs? Know who my daddy is? The marshal. I don't gotta take shit from some inked-up hillbilly. So go on, mind your own, you Harley-headed fuck."

The wormy guy turns his back.

Hunter steps toward the dickhead, then feels Itch's hand on his shoulder. "It's all right," Itch whispers. "He's just an asshole, brother. No need to smash him here—plenty of time later, if need be."

"I got your 'asshole,'" Danny says without turning around. "Don't make me warn you again."

"I bet you do, ya little ferret," says the woman, who has turned around now. "You're the only asshole stinkin' up the atmosphere in here."

Danny steps in to the lady, raises his hand.

Hunter plays the situation out in his head. If he doesn't react, the female gets slapped. Disrespected. Hunter needs to deescalate the situation. Hunter comes forward. Grabs Danny's bony wrist, twisting him backward. Hearing a pop and crack, a little pain to get his attention. Change his mindset. The crack and pop float in the air like a drummer's rim shot. Danny sags at the knees, his mouth opening. He whines like a preschooler whose toy the bully has taken away. He drops his cue and it clatters on the hard floor.

Hunter holds a firm and controlled grip, keeps the pressure on

Danny's wrist, kneels down with Danny, speaks loud and direct. "Dude! Let them hands take a rest. Think about your actions. They'll have consequences. This is your lady, respect her." And Hunter releases Danny's wrist. Stands up. Danny pulls his hand to his chest, running a thumb over the skin like a wounded animal licking its wound. Angry-faced, heated. Danny sizes up Hunter and his buddies. Knowing he is outsized and outnumbered. Hunter holds Danny's eyes until the anger deflates. Something in Danny changes and he looks to the ground. Pouts.

The woman stands with her cue in one hand, a Coors Light in the other, looking at Danny. "Yeah, little respect would be nice. Do as this man tells you," she says. "And keep off me, 'cause you're about as welcome as a turd in a punch bowl." Taking a sip of her beer, she makes a face. "Warm as piss." She says. And turns the bottle upside down on Danny's head.

Still on his knees, Danny is drenched. Hunter shakes his head, smirks, "Karma." Hunter offers a hand to Danny. "Come on, get up. Word of advice, it'd be in your best interest to play nice with your gal pal before she slaps the bad language out of your jowls."

Danny inhales deep, swallows his pride, runs a hand over his face. Injured and embarrassed, he seems to realize the error of his ways. Takes the proffered hand. Standing up, he looks at Hunter and works his mouth for a minute, struggling to find the words he wants. "Sorry," he finally says.

"No need to apologize to me. It's your girl you should be making up to."

Looking pissed off and beaten, to his girl Danny says, "Sorry. Got a little carried away."

"Booze talk," she tells him. "You're hotheaded, always get carried away."

To ease tensions, Hunter says, "Let me buy you-all a beer."

It seems crazy, when Hunter reflects on it, that the woman his father most respected—his wife!—up and left him when Hunter wasn't much older than three or four. He doesn't remember much about her, just flashes of images he tries to piece together. He had never seen her again.

Seated back at the bar, Danny and his girl pass on the beer. Chastened, he holds the door for her on the way out.

Al sets everyone's beers before them. He says, "Don't get why folks gotta treat others with no respect. Takes a lot less energy just to be nice and treat others right."

Hunter thinks about his ex-boss. What a tool. He had treated everyone like shit, even his dog. Some folks just had to learn things the hard way. "I'll drink to that."

"You know, I treat every customer that comes in here the same, regardless of how shitty or nice they are."

Hunter says, "My father always taught me, good or bad, kill 'em with kindness. Someone wants to be rude, selfish, or flat-out ignore you, speak to them with a smile. Look them in the eye and say hi, ask them how they're doing. Feed them goodwill."

"Sounds like you had a good dad."

Lost in thought. More than once over the years, Hunter had questioned how good his father had been. This trip has opened his eyes. Forced him to reflect, to recall memories. Situations and lessons he had learned without realizing it. Where they came from. His moral values. Discipline. It came from his father. From Hank. And he says to Al, "I did." *When he was around.*

After paying for their food and beers and hitting the head, Hunter, Itch, and Nugget fire their bikes up, buckle their helmets on, and head back down the road. Alcohol hangs heavy on everyone's judgment, the air mixing with the beer buzz. Gripping the handlebars, feeling the power of the bike under him, Hunter can't get Blake out of his mind. Stopping at the bar, having a few beers, and eating had let him forget, step outside himself for a bit. Abandon those thoughts. But they are back in full force now. Hours pass.

They blow into Colorado on Interstate 70 as darkness closes in. Hunter's vision plays tricks on him when he notices something from out of nowhere. Thick, muscular neck, head with horns like the devil's, broad and bulky with wide-set eyes, thick mane of brownie-colored shag. *Christ, it's a bison!* And the next thing Hunter knows, he's Evel Knieveling sideways with sparks fountaining up from metal on pavement, sliding beneath the beast, sideways glance, feeling of moist hide and hair passing over his face. Hunter holds on for life, riding it out, and everything goes dark.

JACK

Morning feels like a newly arisen blister. Ache reverberates through his body like a metal file rasping at his bones. His hands are cracked and oozing. He is doing something he hasn't experienced since he was a child: using his hands to pick up, grip, or lift anything of weight. To perform physical labor. He can not recall the last time sweat stung his eyes.

The dank room had grown unbearable, thanks to Matías. He is squatting on a bucket, hunched forward, sweat beading on his face. The noises coming from him don't sound human. A cigarette perches on his lip. Smoke hangs in the air around him, and Jack is grateful for the way it helps mask the stench.

It takes all of Jack's concentrated will not to retch. Like everything else on this pilgrimage, it is unlike anything he has ever encountered.

Pressing his feet to the ground, he limps out into the morning air, where the heat punches him in the face. Looking out over the courtyard, the surrounding forest, the quiet. Watching the fog rise like smoke from the valley of green vegetation. A hand touches his shoulder from behind. Jack jumps. It is Matías, carrying the bucket. "*Con permiso*," he says. "I'll dump this load of *mierda*. Let you have your turn."

Letting him pass with his reeking burden, Jack turns his face away and wills himself not to inhale. He hears gurgling from his own belly and wonders whether it is growling or complaining. He had eaten fruit and potatoes before he slept. Not a great combination. He misses his Wagyu filets, medium rare. But here he is, awake. Troubled. The starch isn't sitting well in his gut. He hopes the feeling is just hunger—the last thing he wants is to come down with something dire from the water and the food. Searching his mind, he wonders how he will get out of this place—or *whether* he ever will. And if he can't get away, can he survive here in this way, living a simple life of enforced servitude? Or is he just living on borrowed time ever since he was abducted? After everything he had built and worked to achieve, for once in his life he is unsure of anything, especially his future.

Matías returns with the bucket. "Today, my friend, we make the paste."

Paste, Jack thinks. What did that even mean? He remembers, as a kid, helping his mother hang wallpaper. Using a brush to apply the soupy vanilla-colored liquid with tiny lumps in it, slathering it on the back of the paper and pressing it to the wall. Maybe this paste can be viewed as the base, the beginning that will meld everything they'd be doing together.

Carlos emerges from one of the structures across the yard. He wears a stretched-out yellow shirt and a faded Yankees ball cap. With him walks a young man in his late teens or early twenties. He came from the two-story barn that was constructed beside Carlos's place, carrying a green plastic bucket covered by a towel.

The young man nods at Jack and Matías, then offers the bucket to Jack. Taking it from him, Jack nods and says, *"Gracias, señor."* He pulls the towel back. Inside are potatoes and some kind of meat. It is warm.

Carlos speaks to Matías in Spanish. And Matías turns to Jack. "That's our food before we start our morning. Today, we learn to make this white colored *pasta*."

The word sounds so foreign, so odd.

"We eat; then we smash the leaves. That's all he tells me. Like you, I've never done this. I drive a truck for a living."

They sit in the courtyard on a makeshift bench constructed of old closet shelving and tree stumps, the bucket between them. The meat is dry and sparse. Jack picks it from the tiny bones and chews it with the little potatoes he pulls from the bucket, skins still intact. Eating with his fingers, he feels like a wild animal.

Matías, who is less squeamish, chews, spits bones, and licks his fingers, his cheeks full like a chipmunk's. He asks Jack, "You like?"

"When a person is hungry, no judgment about the food you are placing in your body. So long as it nourishes and replenishes, it is a good thing."

"It's guinea pig."

Jack controls his gag reflex. He is eating a fucking *hamster*. He wonders how many of these little furry critters it takes to produce this meal. But it is protein. It will sustain life. He swallows and takes another bite.

One by one, Jack, Matías, and several small children swing the sacks of leaves over their shoulders and carry them up into the jungle behind their barnlike living quarters, where they dump the sacks into knee-high wooden corrals constructed from scrap lumber. Then children in red and yellow rubber rain boots spread them out evenly. After an hour of walking back and forth, transporting all of yesterday's harvest, Jack's quads burn and his back aches. Carlos explains to Matías that the leaves had taken nearly four months to grow. This is the next phase. Matías translates this information to Jack.

The young man who had brought their food stands in high black rubber boots. The red bandanna up over his nose makes him look like a horse thief. Carlos explains to Matías, who relays to Jack, "After we walk on the leaves, smashing them, one of the other kids dumps the large blue gas can of bleach and water into the leaves, then mixes the liquid up within the squared corral. Walking on all the leaves softens them to soak up the bleach and water for ten hours." Carlos's son uses a long broomstick with a long rubber blade on the end to swish and mix the leaves and liquid. The resulting sludge reminds Jack of cooked greens.

Even after dilution with water, the fumes of chlorine bleach are thick and intense. Jack's and Matías's eyes burn and water; their noses drip. Jack's throat is painfully raw.

Once they finish mixing the leaves, they leave to let them soak. Following the path back to the courtyard, they sit outside. Insects buzz and whine around them. Jack watches the kids play with a flattened basketball, tossing and kicking it as if it were supposed to be flat. They laugh and run without a care in the world. They have no understanding of class or poverty or what the rest of the world has to offer. No TV. No internet or smartphones. Here, those luxuries are unheard of. Jack feels the size of an ant. The wealth he had amassed, the privilege he worked his entire life for—all of that is lost here. A myth. Feeling sorry for himself, seeing how weak he is, he asks Matías, "Do you think your family knows what happened to you? Being hijacked and kidnapped?"

Sweat beads on Matías's forehead as he lights a cigarette and takes a long drag. "Hard to say. Here, when something bad happens, it might take twelve or twenty-four hours before it reaches a person's loved ones, their family." Pulling hard on the cigarette again, he says, "Here, time stands still. News travels very slowly. For all she knows, I'm out on a bender with guys I know and work with."

"That's awful. Weren't your wife and son expecting you to arrive home from making deliveries?"

"Yes. But I've gotten other deliveries and not phoned until the next day. Working for extra money. You know, we just live simple. There's no set time for my arrival. One day don't mimic the next."

When evening comes, Jack is stinking and miserable. His stomach churns, and he has a cramp embedded deep in his left side. They walk back to the lab. Off to one side is a row of big blue plastic drums. Carlos gives Jack and Matías bright yellow rubber gloves several sizes too big for their hands. They look like dish-washing gloves. After pulling them on, they begin taking big bundles of the leaves and throwing them into a wooden tub, where they are sloshed back and forth with the squeegee while a kid dumps kerosene into the leaves. Jack and Matías gag and cough from the breath-stealing fumes. Matías explains the process to Jack as they stand covered in sweat, their nostrils singed by the harsh vapor.

The lab is open—no walls, just tarps or canopies over a floor of packed dirt, with wooden posts cut from trees to support the corners. Jack watches the kids with their grime-printed smiles, rubbing eyes and faces irritated by the fumes. He feels his entire being dissolving.

He asks Matías, "What kind of life is this?"

"The only one they know."

"But how can they live this way?"

"How can they not? This isn't America. Here is different. Here, people make bigger sacrifices for smaller gains. Those gains usually have to do with feeding your family, keeping a roof over your head. Waking to see another day. This is all they know."

Urging Jack and Matías to get up, Carlos points for them to come and watch. They have loaded the slurry of kerosene-soaked leaves into fifty-five-gallon drums perforated with holes, then rolled the drums, heavy with the liquid, to several rectangular wooden frames. Taking a long shaft welded to a steel disk only centimeters shy of the drum's diameter, Carlos shows Jack and Matías how to twist the contraption down into the drum, tighter and tighter, pressing the liquid from the leaves into large plastic buckets below the drums. It reminds Jack of a giant coffee press. The kids stand with Carlos's son, making sure the rivulets of liquid drain into the buckets. Carlos directs Jack and Matías to carry the buckets of liquid to men who dump cans of kerosene into each, while a kid uses a long stick to stir the mixture. It forms a bubbling soupy paste that is then dumped into large cloths that look like bedsheets, over large stainless-steel kettles. As the liquid drains off, the paste thickens up into a solid the color and consistency of spackle. But this white stuff will be filling nostrils, not nail holes.

As he bends over, helping Matías dump the liquid waste, Jack can't tell whether he is high from the raw cocaine or poisoned by the solvents in the air. They carry buckets and a sheet-metal trough to a ditch that leads to a nearby stream, poisoning the fish, polluting whatever it touches.

The paste will be packed, Carlos explains, then rolled in plastic by morning for transport to a connection within a Colombian cartel. There, it will be further broken down and mixed with other chemicals to create cocaine for distribution.

That night, lying in the heat, sore from the day's labor, Jack thinks of the children pulling leaves from the coca limbs, nimbly stripping one plant, moving to the next. Never missing a leaf, filling one bag after the next, lugging them back to the courtyard. Lifting containers of fuel, bleach, kerosene, never complaining. Lifting. Filling. Pouring. Grunting. Never spilling a drop. Never resting until Carlos gives the word. The kids work to help their older brother. Their father. The family is an integrated unit, an engine of human enterprise.

Carlos gave the command to take a break, and they flopped down on the dirt floor. This world was foreign and unfamiliar to Jack. Things he had never seen or even imagined. The war on drugs was something he has been only vaguely aware of, seen on the news or glanced at in the paper as he turned to the business section. But he has never really thought much about the *business* of narcotrafficking. Or maybe he has always found it easy enough to pretend it isn't real.

He thinks about his mother and how strong she had been, leaving his father for an unknown future. She was tough. And the working-class environment he had grown up in was sheer luxury compared to the living conditions that now surround him. Yes, it appears that *everybody* is tougher than Jack.

The fear and uncertainty of that life had pushed Jack to rise above his past, to earn all that money. He realizes now that he never really suffered. Beyond making tax-deductible donations to various not-for-profit organizations, he has done little to nothing for humanity.

Lying on the thin mattress, he hurts. He feels as if a contagion has entered his body, inflaming and stiffening his tendons and joints. A discomforting pang from all that he has seen. He thinks of those children. Of Carlos and his wife and this life they live. How they work. Carving out a meager existence with just enough money to feed their family. Supplying a cartel that will earn a thousand times what they pay Carlos. Somehow, Jack had to help these people. They are killing themselves to make paste that in turn creates cocaine. And for pennies, while their bosses earn millions. Where is the balance in that?

When sleep comes, it envelopes him like a glove, and he fall into a dark recess of heat. Walking through some unknown cavern of life. Seeing Carlos's kids kicking a flat soccer ball. The air glows like purple mist. He yells for them, but they run. Bugs blink fluorescent in the night air, hovering and humming by his face. A woman's hand reaches for the children. "No!" Jack yells. "No!"

She smiles. Taking the kids' hands, leading them away with her. "No!" Jack yells again.

He has to save those kids. They walk faster. He huffs. His weight is getting to him. He is old and out of shape. The jungle opens up into an area of shacks thrown together from odds and ends of lumber and corrugated metal. Some are the color of rust, others various shades of despair. From a distance, the kids giggle and laugh. Jack hurries his steps. Every movement is laborious and taxing on his body. His lungs hurt. His hand reaches for the makeshift door that is hinged with belt leather nailed to the wood. There is no knob, only a round peephole cut through the slab of lumber. He two-fingers the hole and jabs a splinter into his finger. Pulls the door toward him, his fingers wet with the drop of blood. Inside sit kids, who turn to him. The girl standing in the center turns to look at him, and it is his daughter.

Then come the screams. Lifting his body from the bed, Jack is dreaming. Hands are shaking him, Matías standing over him. "Men are raiding the village."

Placing his feet on the ground, Jack peeks out through the cracks of the wall, then turns to the panicked faces of Carlos and his family.

Matías says, "We have to run."

"What about Carlos? His family?" Jack asks.

"What about them? We stay, we risk death. Those are either soldiers or FARC guerrillas."

Outside the shack, a woman screams. Children cry. Male voices bark loudly. "Orders." Matías whispers. "They're giving orders." Arguing in Spanish. Jack feels his insides shiver and quake. Matías stands staring at him. If they run, they risk being shot. And even to be seen escaping can bring risk to Carlos and his family.

Jack has a decision to make, and no time to deliberate.

ANNE

Inside the Louisiana line, they catch out just as the train leaves the yard, evading a bull. Dredd gets on at the last minute, angry. Something boiling and brewing. Stowing away on an open boxcar. Jamming the door in its track with a rusted spike. Inside the car, wooden floor splintered and pocked by whatever it has borne over the decades. The walls are scrawled with graffiti—initials, symbols, and dates of passage.

Discomfort pervades the air. No one has slept. Pushing his greasy hair back, Dredd tells Cinnamon, "Shouldn't have brought her." Darting a look at Anne. The tension in the air is so heavy and thick, it has its own texture. "Everything was fine until she arrived. You-all go out, come back with a major haul, and next thing you know, it's pigs on the prowl in search of some blood."

"You're wacked, Jack," Cinnamon scoffs. "Nothing has been fine for a long while. Why I never stay around more than a day or two."

"Bullshit. Canary, she's my girl. Always been loyal. Like you once were, Cinnamon. I took you-all in. Gave you a home. Structure. Taught you about real freedom. Oppression."

Anne and Canary sit with their backs to the wall, packs between their knees. The twins rest their faces on Canary's lap. Trot stands over Anne, lights up a smoke. Out the open door, the world of wilderness flies by in a green blur.

"I started hopping trains long before we crossed," Cinnamon spits. "You were probably still trying to help freshmen girls achieve enlightenment in the back of your VW Microbus."

"Oh, fuck you, little lady. Funny how this Anne shows up and next you know, the cops do too. I got the memo, the bullet points, the headline. Know what I think?"

"That's the real issue, isn't it? No one cares what you think anymore, and they haven't for a long time."

Dredd's face hardens and he says, "She's a mole. That's what I think. Know what we do to moles?"

"Oh, back the fuck off, Dredd. She's no mole. She had a scuffle with some street vagrants when we were in town earning. Cops probably picked up on it. We never paid it much mind. Could have followed us back to the encampment, staked us out without us knowing it."

"Really, a scuffle. And you're just now telling me? After we done lost everything. Placed everyone's lives in jeopardy. Uprooted everything we built."

"No one is in jeopardy. Anyone got arrested is out by morning."

"I take you in and this is how you repay me. After all I taught you two. Everything we worked and built—it's gone, girls. Gone. Disbanded. No fucking more."

"I was leaving anyway," Cinnamon tells him. "Just passing through. I wasn't staying."

Fiery faced and disgusted, Dredd yells, "Maybe you're the mole." His eyes bulge.

Balling her small fists, Cinnamon pushes herself to her feet. "There's no mole," she barks back. "You're fucking AWOL! Hear me? And you're fucking controlling. You act like a fucking dictator, like everything you preach against."

Coming to her feet, Anne reaches for Cinnamon, "Let's calm down. Take a breather. Everyone's spent. It's been a long journey, rough night." Taking her hand, Anne tugs her gently. "Come on. Let's sit."

The twins start to sniffle and hide their faces.

Dredd sits in the opening, his back turned, legs dangling out of the train. Rattling of steel over steel.

Anne and Cinnamon sit back down, wanting to find some calm. Middle ground. Looking to Canary, Anne pretends Dredd is no longer present, and she asks what Canary's story is. Where she came from, how she met up with Cinnamon and Dredd.

Canary's father died when he was late getting home one night. Stopped by the grocery for garlic bread. Her mother had made some Italian dish and forgot the bread. For whatever reason, he wasn't paying attention to the parking lot. Guy walked up on him. Wanted his wallet, so the police believed. Her dad wouldn't give it. So the guy whaled on him—a tire iron upside his skull. It was the equivalent of slamming his head into a brick wall, cracking his skull like a boiled egg. After he spent a week in ICU, her mother pulled the plug, and he passed. Insurance money raised her and the twins until Canary couldn't take it anymore. Her mother went from being a full-time Realtor to a full-time functioning alcoholic. Once, she had cared for her children. Cooked their meals and cleaned their home. But when Canary's father passed, her mother's spirit followed. It was broken. Damaged. She no longer cared for anything except her next drink. Red wine was her favorite, but she wasn't afraid of vodka, either. The bloody Mary was a favorite.

Drinking started when the alarm went off. Didn't stop until she blacked out for the night. Her addiction was consistent. Well maintained, day after day. She sold houses. Stocked the liquor cabinet. Dated men of questionable character who made Canary uncomfortable. Coming into her room at night. Fearing for her brother and sister. She kept reading and watching videos online about train hoppers and their culture, the family structure and freedom they championed. And she made a decision. Late one night, after her mother blacked out, Canary packed them up and off they ran, into the dark. Thumbing a ride to the tracks in Liberty, Kentucky. A small town. Mainly white working-class country folks. Hopping out the Norfolk Southern yard. From there, they learned more and more about hopping trains. Hooking up with different groups, she learned the ropes. She met Cinnamon when switching trains in West Virginia and introduced her to Dredd. Ran with them. Was accepted. Earned her keep with the dumpster dives and panhandling for change. And here she was.

Out the open boxcar door, the scenery was dark like the mood inside the car. With his back turned, Dredd yells, "Those early days, you meant something. You were mine. All mine. Both of you."

Pulling his legs up, pressing his palms to the wooden floor, he pushes himself up. Turns around and faces everyone.

Anne squeezes Cinnamon's hand. She can't believe this bullshit Dredd is stirring up again, not letting the dog lie. She can't keep quiet any longer. "You don't own people," Anne says. "This is America. Everyone has choices."

Dredd mutters, under the train's bounce and rattle, "Contriving . . . controlling . . . *cunt.*" He points at Anne, then bounces his finger on an imaginary line, pointing at Cinnamon and Canary. "Pathetic. All of you."

"What is wrong with you?" Anne asks.

"Wrong with *me*, you ask? Really. You come in and steal my people. Destroy everything I built." Making a fist, he punches the air. Stomps his feet hard on the boards, as if he were marching. Dust whirls up from the floor. Dredd is becoming manic. Reminds Anne of her brother and father, getting mad when they didn't get their way.

The twins tighten their arms around Canary. They're scared and trembling. They're not taking to the arguing, nor is Canary. Her eyes fill with tears.

Behind Dredd as he stomps and terrorizes everyone with his tirade, behind his craziness and his bloodshot eyes, the world isn't serene or green. There are no soft blue skies and poofy marshmallow clouds. There is no tableau of beauty. Only narcissistic anger.

Everything in Anne's head falls silent. Her hand reaches into her pack, and her thoughts drift. Going back to the kitchen. To her brother. His reaching for her. Her defending herself. Grabbing that skillet. Turning. Making contact with her brother's skull. The splash of concussion. Eyes roll double-gumball whites. Anne shakes, convulsing internally. She's lightning in a bottle. Enraged as Dredd comes forward. "I don't gotta play these fucking games with you bitches," he says. "I own you. Each and every one of you. Took you in. Gave you a home. Food. A fucking *life*." He kneels down, pushes, and breaks the twins' grip on Canary with his right hand, backhands Cinnamon with his left. Knocking her into Anne, who loses her balance and falls into Trot.

Forcing himself on Canary. She screams, cries. Claws at his face. The twins reach and punch at Dredd's arms. He swats them; one wails. Cursing, he smacks and slobbers all over Canary's face and neck. He's gone full lunatic, pushing his grossness onto her. Trot reaches for Anne, tries to get her upright, help her regain her balance. The train clatters along over the tracks. Canary pulls her knees into herself for extra leverage, to help her hands push and fight against Dredd's gripping and grabbing. Anne swats Trot's hands away from her. Feeling the heft, she pulls the pistol from her pack. The twins are bawling. Anne stands. Comes at Dredd, whose face is buried in Canary's chest. Sure-footed, Anne sees nothing but Dredd's shape. Everything around him is blacked out. Bending down, she presses the muzzle into the side of Dredd's skull, just behind his ear. His hands are dug into Canary's hair. The click of cold metal behind his ear gives him pause.

Anne's tone is equal parts anger and disgust. "Get your filthy hands off her. And stand the fuck up."

Dredd chuckles. Releases Canary. Pushes her away from him. Works his way to his knees, then stands.

"You ain't gonna shoot me."

"There's an easy way to find out—just don't do exactly what the fuck I tell you to do. Now, get your sick, sorry ass away from her."

She motions with the pistol.

Hands raised. Moving away. "Little girl like you even know how to shoot a weapon like that?" Quicker than a flinch, Anne points out the open door, fires the pistol. Flame gouts from the barrel. The twins scream. Canary clutches them.

Cinnamon yells, "Anne. Stop!"

Anne positions the pistol to blot out Dredd's face. "Back the fuck up."

Moving away from everyone, Dredd stands with his back to the opening, the world rushing by behind him.

Anne remembers her family. The belittlement, the mistreatment. Tells him, "You're no different from the family I ran away from." Her eyes well up with moisture. "Always making others less. Abusing them." Stepping toward Dredd.

He steps back. Tells Anne, "Let's put the piece away. Maybe talk. I got a little heated. Lost my shit."

"*Now* you got a change of heart, that it?"

Anne steps closer, catches a whiff of the discharged round.

Behind Anne, Cinnamon screams, "No!"

Dredd backs up one more step, only there is no step to take. He reaches, but there is nothing to grab but warm, flowing air. And out the opening he goes. There is the meaty smack of his body hitting a tree as he disappears.

Turning back to Cinnamon, Trot, Canary, and the twins. Lowering the pistol. Everyone huddles. Sniffling. Crying. Horrified. The act of violence is past. Gone. Done. Over.

Anne collapses to the floor. Cinnamon follows her down and embraces her, helps her to her feet. Anne's breath slows. Stepping toward the wall, reaching for her pack, she slides the pistol back into it. There are no words. Watching the trees flit past, everyone closes their eyes. Searching for sleep. Canary and the twins are settled. Trot sits smoking with his back to the wall. Anne opens her eyes. The discomfort is gone. Dredd is gone.

One thought runs through Anne's mind. Like a pustule, Dredd has been lanced and drained. These girls, these *people*, were never his personal property. He doesn't hold ownership or sway of any kind over them. Over anyone. Anne has made sure of that, made sure it is known. This is her family.

HUNTER

Denim rips. Flesh parts and tears. Heated pavement smeared with blood and the face of a woman. Of Hunter's half brother's mother. Of Annie. Memories come in distorted shards and fragments. Tiny chunks of time, buried and forgotten. There is the shudder of sound, snapshots of a place surrounded by black. The black eases, and the picture enlarges and become clearer.

There was a bedroom with framed photos over the dresser. A bed, where Hunter's granddad sat up, his liver-spotted hand running over his hairless pate. Lips part. "Just wanna die. Call me Misery," he barked. "My name is Misery. And just I'll lay right here and run my hand over my big bald head."

Laughter rang from beside his bed. Annie's face was a living repository of peace—soft and easy, delicate, kind as a human could be. Her blond locks were pulled back, her figure shapely and fit. She fluffed the pillow behind Hunter's grandfather's head, telling him, "Stop talking nonsense. You got family here. You're surrounded by love every day."

His grandfather called her "Nurse Annie." His daughter-in-law. Hank laughed. He stood on the opposite side of the bed. It was an old sleigh bed his grandfather had cut, measured, planed, and constructed by hand. Drilled the holes, cut the dovetail joints, stained the wood.

The sun shone through the two windows. The walls were a muted shade of burgundy, framed by white crown molding.

Searching his mind, Hunter had forgotten about this. Repressed it for some reason.

"Come on, Pop, quit talking crazy," Hank told his father. "Annie's got a husband."

"Horseshit. You take me for a dope? She is my daughter-in-law. See how she makes eyes at you and you return the gesture?"

The dementia had confused his grandfather. Every day was something new for him to reacquaint himself with. Something more to rediscover, to figure out. The pictures helped. Bringing back snippets of memories. But it was the present that was beginning to fall apart.

"No, Dad, she isn't. She got eyes for Sid, her husband. They got a son, Hunter's age."

Looking at Hank and then at Hunter. Blinking his eyes. Rubbing his bald head. Then twisting both fists into his eyes. "Need some damn meds for this double vision. Seeing two of you sons o' bitches. One young, one old."

"Really?" Hank said. "Well, maybe two halves make a whole."

Hunter was searching dusty corners he had not been in a long time. Things he had forgotten. Uncovering pain. Other aches he need not go looking for, because he couldn't miss them if he tried—the pain that burned in his right knee, for instance.

Voices dropped and echoed in his mind, and he felt as if he were in a cave or a hole in the ground. Hands gripped and pawed.

Looking around at his vault of memories, he couldn't recall a time when he had seen them, Annie and Hank, alone together.

Always in the company of his grandfather or himself or Sid. Squeezing his eyes shut, he dug deeper. Came to a door. It was cracked. His eyes wandered, meeting the break of light. Peeking into the room. Sounds of skin and bedclothes. Lips, wet. Hank whispering, "We can't. We can't. It's not right. Sid is a good friend."

Annie whispering back, "Things you don't know. I'm dying inside. I don't like it when you're gone on the road."

There is the sound of a big diesel truck engine. Loud, then throttling down. Shutting off. Cracks and pops of an engine cooling. Creak of a door. Footsteps. Voices. Reassurances. Hunter's eyes flutter open. Darkness. Headlights. Making out the shadows and shapes. Bending his neck. It's stiff. His face is taking a sideways glance, his bike the same, on its side.

"You're alive." Rolling his eyes. Looking up, it's Itch. "Hang tight, brother. You were out cold. 'Bout took out a damn buffalo!"

Things are coming back to him. The bison came from nowhere—a roadblock, an obstruction on the highway. Inhaling, he can still smell the great beast in his nostrils, taste it on his lips. Its fur sliding across his face. Hunter tries to push himself up, bend his knees.

"Take it easy. You slid under that damn thing."

"My bike?"

"I think it's okay. It's you we're concerned about."

Hunter starts twisting and stretching, testing, making sure everything gives or bends the way it's supposed to. There is some hurt. Burning sensations. But no cracking. Everything is movable. Nothing broken or hurt bad—nothing some soap and water and bandages can't handle. Pushing his palms to the highway, the pavement is rough and warm. Off to the side, in the distance behind him, sits a Chevy Silverado. Hands reach under Hunter's arms, lifting and grunting, helping him stand. Taking steps, he has balance. Equilibrium. Strong arms guide him, not letting go until he can feel blood flowing in his limbs. Moving toward his bike.

"I'm good," he says. "Seriously." His head is spinning a little, but everything is starting to mesh. His reality is beginning to solidify.

Looking to the pavement. Headlights show the trail to his bike. Paint and frame had left scuffs and scratches over the road. The road left some of the same on the motorcycle. *Fuck.* Hands keep trying to help. Hunter jerks from the grip, bends down. Light-headed, he tries to deadlift the bike from the road. A deep nasal voice tells him, "Take it easy, buddy. Let me and your compadres get it. Load it in my truck if you want. Take it to my place. I got a shop. Can give her a good looking over. Fix whatever needs fixing."

The dream, the memory of his grandfather, of his father and Annie—it is something Hunter had forgotten. Hidden, vague as it is. Small. Buried in his brain. Something he hadn't understood then. Maybe he couldn't process it as a kid. But now he holds a piece of *then*. And yet, it raises more questions. How often had it happened? How many times had Hunter seen it? Suppressed it all these years. How can Hunter open more of his mind to recall his childhood?

"Dude?" Itch says. "You okay, staring into the abyss or some shit?"

Hunter says, "Still letting pieces of myself fill back in."

Beside Itch stands the old-timer who had offered to help load up his wrecked bike, take it to his place. Attired in Levi's, white V-neck T-shirt, and faded Beechnut hat. Big wad of chew in his jaw. Thick salt-and-pepper mustache. Headlights shadow his frame. Hunter says, "We'll need a wide board—a two-by-twelve if you got it—to load the bike up into your truck."

"Happen to have one. Was busy with a project earlier today

on the farm. Name's Purnell. My place ain't but a dick stroke from here. You're more than welcome to rest for the night, look over your bike."

Hunter shakes his hand.

"I'm Hunter. These are my buddies, Itch and Nugget. Appreciate the gesture. That buff came out of no-fucking-where."

"You sure you're okay?" says Itch. "You took a mean skid over the pavement. Went straight under that son of bitch, then he just wandered off."

"I'm good. Let's get this bike loaded up. Go assess the damage."

Riding in the Silverado's front seat, Hunter can't see everything in the dark. But from what he can make out, Purnell owns a lot of land. Has horses. A big farmhouse. Huge barn. And a pole barn. He pulls into the big wooden barn, drives up the center, and kills the engine and gets out. The ground is packed down hard by hooves and boot heels. Bright overhead fluorescents hang from the six-by-six joists that support the roof. Off to the left, hay is stacked in a loft over horse stalls. To Hunter's right is a workshop. Concrete floor. Tools and tool chests, counters and vises, table saws and horseshoes, compressor, hoses, and air tools.

Behind him, Itch's and Nugget's bikes rumble to a stop. Hunter limps to the rear of the Silverado, where they meet him. Purnell lowers the tailgate. Places the two-by-twelve on the bed's rear. The bike is tied down by straps, one side keeping the other taut. Unbuckling the bike. Balancing it, the guys roll it down the board—not an easy task with a flat tire and a somewhat bent rim. Wheeling it off to the side, heeling the kickstand down, leaning it next to the area where the tools are located. Hunter eyes the big red tool cabinets. Wrenches. Hammers. Mauls and axes. Everything to operate a farm, from running fence line to overhauling a tractor.

Purnell tells them, "Bunkhouse is down on your right. There's bunk beds, sink, shower, bathroom, fridge with food and drinks. Make yourselves at home."

From behind him comes a female voice. "Everything all right, Daddy?"

Purnell turns around, "This is my daughter. She's the brains of this here outfit."

Walking in from the shadows outside, she has caramel-colored hair with Tweety Bird–yellow highlights. Her eyes wear no hint of liner. Sun-freckled face. Wearing a blue-gray T-shirt and jeans with worn-out Ariat boots. Smiling she says, "Let me guess: rider hit another bison." Glancing to Hunter's torn jeans, she says, "Looks like we might need to get you cleaned up if you got the time."

Hunter chuckles. "Got nothing but."

Purnell waves Itch and Nugget to follow him, "I'll show you guys to the bunkhouse back here, let you get cleaned up and settled in. See if I need to bring you anything or you can scrounge something up—got a little bit of everything back here. Up to you."

Following Purnell, Itch says, "Just appreciate your kindness, man."

Hunter sticks out his hand to the woman. "Hunter."

A soft but strong hand takes his. "I'm Tara. Come over here, and I'll take a look at you. Get you cleaned up."

He follows her to a room off to the left, where she flips a switch. Lights hum overhead, deleting all but the faintest shadows. The room is immaculate. It has oak floors, and white cabinets with silver handles running along the walls. A steel sink, and in the room's center, a table and a few circular stools.

"Take a seat," she says. "I won't bite." Opening a drawer, she takes out a pair of bandage scissors, pack of gauze dressings, white tape, and a small sponge. She pulls on a pair of purple rubber gloves and says, "Gonna need to cut up your jeans a bit. Hope that's cool?"

Hunter looks down at the bloody knee and grimaces. "Do what you gotta do to clean it up. Last thing I want is an infection."

Starting just above the wound, Tara cuts up to the pocket and spreads the denim apart. Clear liquid has oozed to form a sheen over the wound. She rolls her stool over to a counter and opens a drawer, taking out a plastic bottle of brown liquid. Rolls back to Hunter and he asks, "You a doc?"

"Nurse. I work part time at the county ER. I'm one of those educated farm girls. I know this business through and through. Helped my daddy make his fortune; now I want him to retire."

"Get out while the getting's good."

"Someone needs to make Daddy realize that. Don't need the money, I'm a registered nurse working part time, but it keeps me busy and licensed, just in case." She pauses. "This is gonna burn some."

"Sounds like a bad date."

Smiling, she says, "Comedian."

"Gotta find something to laugh about—I just dumped a thirty-some-thousand-dollar custom bike."

Pouring Betadine onto a swab of cotton, she dabs it on, staining the wound a reddish brown.

"That's gotta hurt," she says. "The bike, I mean."

"It's nothing I can't fix. But yeah, it sucks."

Looking at the wound, she says, "I'll put some antiseptic gel on it and bandage you up."

"Appreciate it. How long you lived here with your dad?"

"Over forty years—basically all my life. He inherited the place from my grandparents. Been in the family for over a century."

Out the doorway, at the other end of the hall, Hunter and Tara can hear Purnell telling Itch and Nugget to eat whatever they want and that there is beer in the fridge too—bottom drawer.

Blotting a trickle of antiseptic from his calf, Tara laughs. "He's always helping someone."

"Well, I appreciate it. My first wreck."

"Really? *Ever?* How long you been riding?"

"Ever," Hunter says. "Been riding for over twenty years. I work on bikes for a living. How many times you fall off a horse?"

"Okay, fair is fair. Maybe once. Grew up breaking them and studying their ways. Get to a point where you can read their movements and manners. Then you adjust."

"Exactly," he says. "That's how I am with a bike. You put all that time and money into something, last thing you want to do is destroy it."

"The last thing I want is my father destroying himself on this farm. Since my mother passed away, I've been on him to retire, sell this place. But he won't, because it's all he has left of her. Her memory. He's been offered millions, but he keeps turning it down."

"That's tough. Sometimes you gotta help them relocate. My father didn't know what else to do when I moved away. So I told him, go be with your brother, around family. He relocated to California."

Or was it something else? Having an affair. Another kid. His father had to know the score. Maybe he was running away.

Tara opens a tube of ointment, squeezes a small blob onto her gloved index finger, and smooths the antiseptic over the weeping flesh. Then she opens a sterile dressing pad and lays it over the wound.

While taping down the dressing, she looks at the tattoo on his hand. "Gotta be a story there," she said.

The crazy black outline of a skull with *X*s for eyes and "BBH" with a line through it for the teeth. He explains that it was what his grandfather kept telling him and his father when he was suffering from dementia, rubbing his "big bald head," as he called it. It was something that stuck. A way to remember his grandfather.

"You know, I've helped my dad my entire life," Tara says. "Built all this. Made a life of comfort out of hard work with horses and cattle. Had a couple make the Kentucky Derby. I just want him to enjoy some time without labor before something like that happens to him—cancer, dementia, Alzheimer's disease. But he won't leave."

"Why you think that is?"

"Mom. She passed. Like I said, this was her family's farm. He wants it to be mine. But I can't be reminded of it all anymore."

"Have you told him that?"

"More times than I got fingers on my hands. He doesn't want to forget."

"So he doesn't wanna let it go. Understandable."

"No, he doesn't. And it's not like she's coming back."

"Rebirth, you mean. Like a reincarnation."

"Yeah, like we're Tibetan or some shit."

"From what I can see, looks like a great place."

"It is, but it's too much. Too much space. Too much upkeep. People to pay. Lot of overhead." She looks at him sitting there with one very pale leg exposed, and smiles. "You work out?"

"Powerlift. Yeah."

"I can tell. Not just a biker with tats. You got some brawn, you and your friends."

"Oh, we train together, but yeah, I've earned my stripes."

"You serve?" she asks. Picking up the mess. Dropping the gauze and cotton and the bloody pant leg in the waste can. Putting medical supplies back into drawers and cabinets.

"Yeah. Iraq. What gave it away?"

"Your bearing. Manners. Respect for what you talk about. Not negative."

"I was a mechanic. Helicopters. Still saw my share of shit. Kids mainly. Killed daily. Born into war, they never had a chance other than us soldiers and liberation."

"And you'd let them down during the first Iraq invasion."

"I didn't have a say during the first invasion. Wasn't a soldier then."

"I didn't mean you personally."

"I know. I just hated leaving people, the kids especially. You never get used to that rumble and gunfire day after day. Gave me an appreciation for what we have in America. People here don't know how good they got it."

"Hard to believe that people could fight so hard to take away your freedom."

"Sometimes, I think we're *too* free."

Tara makes a wry smile. "Yeah, like building walls around what a person can or can't say. Just because we don't agree doesn't mean we're wrong."

"Where else can you work and eat and read and do as you wish? You speak out in some countries, and it's the last anyone will hear from you. People don't realize how sacred their freedom of speech is."

"I agree. Not to change the subject, but you got a change of clothes, I'm assuming?"

Standing up, Hunter says, "Yeah."

"The bunkhouse is at the end, on the right. Showers. Amenities. You should try to get some sleep."

"Appreciate it. I'll have a look at that bike before I hit the hay."

Walking out into the shop area, Hunter fishes out his cell phone. He hasn't turned it on since they started traveling. Hasn't checked in with Olivia. He squats down and looks over the bike. Blown tire and a bent rim. Scuffs and deep scratches—that will set him back even more than a new tire and a rim.

His phone vibrates as it comes to life. Looking at it, he sees ten missed calls. Three from Olivia and seven from his uncle. *Shit.*

Stepping out of the barn, getting some bars, he phones his uncle.

"Dave?"

"Hunter? When you gonna get out here?"

"Soon. Had a bike wreck, but I'm in Colorado."

"Sorry to hear that, but we really need you out here. Lawyer's wanting to get this wrapped up—too bad you can't do it over the phone."

"Let me straighten this bike situation up in the morning, and I'll get there as soon as I can."

"Hope to see you soon."

He hangs up.

Behind Hunter, Tara asks, "Everything okay?"

"Gonna have to figure something out in the morning," he says. "I gotta get to California."

"What's in California?"

"My father passed away."

"Sorry to hear that."

"Appreciate that. But anyway, I'm the executor of his estate. Uncle is wanting me out there."

"Well," Tara says, "I best let you get changed and rest up."

"Yeah. Listen, I appreciate all the hospitality."

"Maybe I'll see you in the a.m.?"

"Maybe so."

After changing his clothes, Hunter flops down on a bunk bed while Itch and Nugget sit up playing cards and drinking beer. He decides to phone Sid, see how he is doing. The phone rings several times before a younger voice picks up. "Blake?"

"Yeah?"

"It's Hunter. I was calling to check on Sid."

"He's doing better. Keep him off the booze, he's not as bad."

"That's good."

"Make it to California?"

"Not yet. In Colorado. I had an accident—just need to get my bike straightened out, and I'll get there soon." There is silence. Hunter can't bite his tongue any longer, so he gets to the point. "Did you ever meet your real father?"

"I did. And I've met my half brother, too, so don't be a stranger."

JACK

Blistered hands raised, Jack and Matías slip out the back of the scrap-wood shanty. Eyes turn with rifles trained on them. Men in deep-forest camouflage, with stern faces. Jack's heart is thumping fast as men move forward, hands reaching, grabbing, jerking and directing Matías and Jack, then Carlos and his family. Eyes look at them as if they are fools. As if maybe they should have run.

Booted feet collapse them to their knees. Jack goes down with ease, keeping his hands raised. The questions come.

"*¿Quiénes son estos hombres?*" "*¿De dónde son?*" "*¿Cómo llegaron aquí?*"

Carlos speaks, then pauses. He hesitates, eyeing Matías, who switches to English as he explains why he and Jack are here. The American is a journalist, Matías lies. Doing an investigative piece on the struggles of campesinos in Peru.

Doubt falls over the commanding soldier's face with a scar that runs from the corner of his mouth down to his neckline, jagged and pink. He's shaking his head. Turning to one of the other soldiers, he whispers something. The soldier walks to their military-green jeep, searches for something, comes back with a sheaf of paperwork. They eye the wad of papers, then eye Jack. Comparing something. The commanding soldier asks in barely understandable English, "Wha . . . is . . . joor . . . name?"

There's a knot of nervousness in his throat. Fearing for his life, he says, "Jack."

The man squints, says something to the other soldier, who points and nods excitedly, saying, "*¡Sí! ¡Yack!*"

Before they can decide on their captives' immediate future, an early-1980s Toyota Land Cruiser comes barreling down the road. All eyes turn to the interruption. In the passenger's seat, Matías and Jack recognize one of the men who kidnapped and delivered them to the farm.

Before anyone takes notice, Matías grabs Jack's arm. "Run, amigo! Run!"

Behind them, voices. Jack's feet pound the hard earth, heading toward the shack where they've been rooming. Dashing around the corner, up behind the shack, following the rugged trail of dirt and rock. Passing the makeshift lab of tarps, buckets, and fuel containers and veering into the jungle. Tree branches slap and scrape their faces and limbs. Everything is thick, overgrown. Jack swats the cloud of biting flies that envelops him. Already his chest is heaving and burning. His heart pounds on the back of his sternum as if it wants out.

Behind them, voices and shouts are faint. Matías points to the right, off the trail, and Jack follows.

Turning to him, Matías commands, "Jack, hurry. Come!"

Dodging plants and bushes, stepping deep down a hillside, until Matías missteps. His ankle rolls, and the land slants steep and straight down. Jack takes a similar tumble, and down they plunge, hitting rocks and limbs and brambles. Being gouged, scraped, and stuck. Until their momentum slows and they fetch up at the bottom.

Laid out, wheezing and breathless, Jack rolls over onto his stomach. The world around him spins into fragments. His head spins. Matías reaches for his arm. "Hold it together, my friend," he says. "We now have a fighting chance, but we must *move.*"

As they help each other to their feet, Matías cringes. "Oh, my ankle! *¡Carajo!* Fucking hell! I've rolled it."

Jack is realizing the seriousness of their plight. They have nothing. No water. No weapons. No money. No first-aid kit. No map and compass. *Nada.* Before them there is nothing but jungle. He wonders about bandits, outlaws. Goddamned cannibals. Survival.

Matías limps again. Tells Jack, "We gotta move."

They slog on, brushing through vegetation and making slow progress. No human sounds—only the droning of the cicadas and the movements of two injured and exhausted men.

Coming to a small, rocky stream of water that is ankle to midshin deep, Matías tells him, "We follow this down, and eventually, we find people. Some kind of settlement."

Out of breath, Jack tells Matías, "That's fine with me, but *then* what will we do?"

"We get lucky, find someone to get us to a town. Find a phone. Call for some help."

Jack is bathed in sweat and grunge. He never stank this bad in his life, can't even recall the last time he bathed. And they walk, navigating down the stream. Every bend of knee and lift of foot is becoming a struggle. Jack knows he's dehydrated. He can feel the dryness in his mouth, and the parching of his body. At least the stream water feels cool on his feet. Moreover, he's deficient in salts, minerals. Electrolytes. He looks down at the stream of water. It is moving along fast and seems quite clear and fresh.

He asks Matías, "How safe do you think this water is for human consumption?"

Limping along, Matías is smoking a cigarette. He says, "If the amoebas don't wreck your insides, someone else's insides will wreck them."

"Someone else's?" Jack says. "How's that?"

"Somewhere, this stream is connected to a village or farm or both. Regardless of distance, people are using this stream for bathing, washing. Remember the cocaine paste. They dumped the waste from what we made into the river that ran by the farm."

Jack just clenches his jaw and walks on. They keep moving, slower now. He feels a growing weakness in him, and panic builds in his mind. They have no idea where they are. How they will survive. Running his hands over his face, he wants to cry. Foot lifting, splashing in the water. Sound of ripples moving against them. The feel of sun beating down on their bodies, sapping their energy. Jack's hamstrings feel tight, and the blisters on his hands sting. Hips and knees hurt but at the same time feel disconnected, as if they belong to some other body.

He had heeded his mother's advice and run away, but way too late. Watched his wife die. Left everything behind. And here he is, searching for something. But what? The goddamned meaning of life? His ideas about life have been changing from the second he arrived in South America. Confirmed by his level of pain. Though he keeps telling himself he should give up, that he's had enough. And though he wants more than anything to quit, he doesn't.

Matías just limps and walks. Smokes. Glances up at the sun. He seems to have a hidden source of cigarettes, a never-ending pack. Never out of breath. Maybe that's what Jack has missed out on all these years: cigarettes. Maybe those old Camel ads were true after all—maybe they actually keep a person fit for surviving in a jungle.

Shit, he's going mad. Losing his grip. He didn't think it would be quite this easy. He has built companies up from nothing, saved others from bankruptcy. He can do this. But then, he never even took the stairs at work. Always an elevator. Pushing buttons. The easy route. Now look at him. Pathetic.

Stopping, Matías turns and asks Jack, "What are you fighting with yourself about back here, Jack?"

Son of a bitch has been leading the way, eavesdropping while Jack has been talking out loud. Thinking openly without realizing it. He really is losing the plot. Hardest part of living is knowing you are going to die and then getting placed in this lethal situation you may have caused sooner than expected. Maybe that's why people become thrill seekers. To overcome that. To push above and beyond what they believe to be a limit. Until you have no limits. At that point, you have conditioned yourself. Hardened yourself. Overcome what was humanly possible to overcome.

Jack asks Matías, "Am I talking aloud?"

"Only for the past two hours. On and on. Is this how you figure things out at your work?"

It is official, then: Jack has lost it. "I guess I do. I've been alone for some time. After my wife died, I just withdrew internally. I started to have conversations with myself. You know, just talking problems out. Dilemmas. Things that had happened at work. Interactions, occurrences, dynamics. I don't know, I guess it became a habit. It's very liberating to get the words out into the open."

"Out into the open, with no one to reply? And you withdrew to here, Peru? To the Vrae Valley, cocaine central? Ha! Jack, you're one crazy guy. You Americans—I don't get it. You have everything at your fingertips. Now look at us, out in the jungle, fleeing drug runners and soldiers, like Tango and Cash."

"Who?" Jack questions.

"Stallone and Kurt Russell—it's a movie from the US."

"Never seen it."

"What? How about *Big Trouble in Little China*?"

"Nope."

"Jack, you're shitting me. This is un-American. Are you communist?"

"No, I'm not communist. I just never had time for leisure activities."

"Ah, work, work, work. You never made time. Now look at you. Lost in a jungle in Peru, with a crazy soccer-loving truck-driver father. Abducted and forced to make cocaine. We're making our own movie, huh, Jack?"

"Yeah," Jack says. "Something like that. You know, when my mother said to run away and leave it all behind, I didn't heed her words quick enough. I ran too late. I'm retirement age now. I'm just an old man. This is too much for a man my age to endure."

"Ah, Jack, quit feeling sorry for yourself. There are people older than you in this jungle who survive on pure grit. Just keep moving. You're seeing the world for what it really is. That's good. We're like Indiana Jones."

From a distance down the stream come voices. Children. Men and women. Their words and laughter, splashing and bouncing through the trees, cause Jack and Matías to smile, move a bit quicker, even feel a little spark of hope. Pain subsides and is forgotten. Birds singing in the trees become audible. And as they make their way around the zigzag of the curving stream bank, passing large smoke-colored river boulders that block their view, they behold the figures of men and women and scampering kids. All eyes are on Jack and Matías.

The people are spread out along both sides of the stream. Washing. Bathing. Seated, their feet in the water, cooling off. There are piles of clothing. Wheelbarrows. Buckets and tubs. Jack is still amazed at how people live in such low-tech simplicity. But rising up through all his doubts and misgivings comes something he has not felt in some time: Joy. Hope. A surge of relief.

Matías leads the way up the stream, limping and waving at a man. Off to Jack's right, he sees a snake basking on a rock, its beige-and-black pattern unmoving, eyes watching their movement. Feeling revulsion and fear, Jack moves quickly—he despises snakes. But for the first time, he actually wonders about the snake's experience of the encounter. Did it fear him as much as he feared it? Or did it even deign to consider his existence at all?

Matías is approaching a man in a tattered Maradona T-shirt and stained dungarees. They shake hands. Exchange words. The man rests his hands on his hips. He has a potbelly and bony limbs. Pursing his lips. Nodding his head. The man then waves Matías and Jack to follow him. Leads them from the stream, where kids stand watching. Taking them into the jungle, where they follow a trail that opens up to a village. A woman hands them a bucket of water. It is the sweetest, most delicious thing he has ever tasted.

All that struggle to get here. Jack will never again take painless walking for granted. All his hurt starts to ease when he bites into a mango. Feels the juice that runs down his chin. Savoring the sweetness. The sugar. His mother's words play through his mind. *Run. Run away from all of it.* And he didn't, instead contenting himself to earn more and more. But more wasn't helping him, and he got weak. And now the only thing that will help Jack is *pure will.*

The locals wangle a lift from a visitor to the village, telling Matías it would be in everyone's best interest if he and his gringo friend left as fast as they were able. Loading into the bed of a Toyota truck, they share space with a crate of live chickens bound for a small town alongside a muddy river. The ride is rough with potholes, roots, and rocks the size of an engine block, and the truck creaks and groans at the abuse. Jack expects it to split in half, but it never does.

Pulling into the town. Getting out of the truck, they thank the driver and walk along the dirt main street, drawing looks from every eye. Jack gets the sense of being spied on, surveilled. It makes him feel jittery, uneasy.

Women in woven vests, with brimmed hats over their dark locks, sell fruit and meat pies as kids run and play. Eyeing it all, Jack has no money for the food that looks and smells so good. He realizes he is of lower social standing than these peasants. They have much to offer; he has nothing.

Matías believes they can find a way to contact his boss. Maybe his wife. Get someone to pick them up. They just need to find a phone.

Jack wonders about his work. Someone has to be wondering where he is. He has not kept in contact with anyone, hasn't even checked in since he went MIA.

As he walks along, more eyes look at him, then turn away amid whispers. He studies the buildings in the distance. Old mud-block structures with roofs of corrugated metal. They're unlike anything Jack has ever seen. Their boots scuff and scrabble over loose rock. Matías tells him of the flood season, how it washes out roads and entire hillsides, causing mudslides, burying roadways.

The sun is beating directly down on them now, and sweat burns their eyes. Matías forearms moisture from his face as he speaks with locals. Jack understands a word or two in every sentence—not enough to get a clue what's being said. A barrier. Fingers point, directing them away from the market, up toward the buildings above the town.

Jack is tired of walking. Every step hurts every part of him.

Walking past a shop window, he notices handbills taped to the glass and stapled to door frames. Pages with his face on them. Matías rips one down. "You're famous, my friend. Look."

"What does it say?" Jack asks.

"Businessman missing. Reward for his whereabouts."

"Reward?" Jack asks.

He goes to rip one of the pages down, and the next thing he knows, hands are pulling on him. Other hands push Matías out of the way. It seems he is of no concern to them. Uneasiness flows in Jack's veins. Pulling and pushing the grips and restraints away, he tries to run away. But suddenly, there's a hood over his head, and he gets a punch to the gut. Wrists are crossed and zip-tied, and he is being pushed into a vehicle.

ANNE

Actions play and replay like a movie reel in Anne's mind, moving forward, then rewinding. The look on Dredd's face. Stepping forward. Stepping backward. Forward, back. Knowing he had lost. She should have warned him. She felt guilt as some part of her emotionally reflected on right and wrong. Call it moral judgment. In the end, he was fucked. Beaten. Watching his quarter second of free fall. It came quick, the impact of his body meeting the trees. The thud. Smacking the wind right out of him. It was only sounds. Afterward, it was as if he had never existed.

Cinnamon's arms wrap around Anne, warming her ribs. They lie on their sides, Cinnamon's chest expanding behind her, pressing into her back. Feeling the constant rattle of steel wheels over joints in the rails, she looks out at the landscape of flat pastureland with a train of clouds floating above. Three strands of rusted barbed wire.

Cinnamon whispers into Anne's ear. "It's a relief. He's really gone."

"We've been freed," Canary says. She's sitting cross-legged with the kids lying off to the side. "All the things we had imagined, daydreamed about but never spoke aloud, like maybe he'd OD, get hit by a car, beat by someone who's fed up with him, someone stronger than any of us. And it's a girl with some grit who comes to lift off the burden."

Anne lies silent, appreciating the moment. Lost in her thoughts as she reviews her actions. She dealt with her anger. Cheeks burning, she felt it rise and immediately released it. Let go of it. Searched and found her inner quiet. But her violence rattled her. Violence she had inflicted on a member of her own family. She has her own demons, but what she isn't, is a pushover. A person can take only so much abuse before they either go under or rise above the abuse. Or they stand their ground and create change. She realizes that now.

And Cinnamon squeezes her, tells her, "You stood up to oppression. You realize that, right?"

"Violence begets violence," Anne replies. "There will no longer be a division of people. We're a family." Reaching for Cinnamon's hand, squeezing it, she says, "I need this." Lifting her head, looking at Canary, she says, "*We* need this. We need one another."

From the opposite side, Trot says, "We're so different but the same."

They fall silent, and there is only the sound of air rustling in the open door. Anne and Cinnamon get up. Anne presses her hands against the rusted metal of the car. Running her fingertips over the scrawls, trying to imagine the years and decades of hauling every sort of cargo imaginable and the procession of train hoppers, anonymous but for the initials etched or scribbled on these walls. How many of those who traveled here before her were also breaking away from an abusive or oppressive home life? Uprooting themselves from everything familiar just to take back control and walk away from a life they no longer accepted.

Closing her eyes, she can't unsee it. Dredd's face keeps

appearing in her mind's eye. Anne knows that she's on a hormonal roller-coaster ride. And it seems that Cinnamon can sense her unease. The girl grabs her shoulder, tells her, "It's okay."

"No, it's not. I might've killed him—killed someone else."

"Like your brother? Look, I don't think you killed either of them. If you did, it was self-defense. You're a strong person. They were weak people, trying to make themselves feel strong by bullying others. You were protecting us—all of us."

"I'm a *confused* person. My life has been tense and confrontational, filled with nothing but friction."

"Not anymore. Everything that has happened to you was preparation for this moment."

There is something about Cinnamon's touch—something that Anne has never experienced, never felt. Is it love? It is an emotion—Anne knows that. And it feels good. It is also a form of caring. Desire. Something her family never knew. They kept her down for so long, in a shell within walls built around all kinds of bad. A mother who never cooked or cleaned, never expressed concern or affection for her children. A father who worked, only to come home and drink and order everyone around, making demands, putting others down with all sorts of derogatory comments, stealing from them any vestige of self-esteem or confidence.

Turning around to embrace Cinnamon, Anne tells her, "I feel like a soldier who's been in battle since birth. For seventeen years. But being with you and Canary and Trot, I feel alive."

Cinnamon hugs her tight. Feels the warmth of her embrace. Her arms. Her body.

Anne wonders where she would be if Trot's family hadn't relocated to Tennessee. Where would she have ended up? In school she had people she called friends, but were they really? People she could trust? She had always questioned that. Like her followers on

Facebook or Twitter. Fake friends. Just names that really didn't know her, making snarky puns, one-liners, and comments for likes and follows. Fakes, all of them. Just a bunch of nobodies sitting behind a keyboard casting judgment, saying things they would never say to your face. It was toxic. None of them had any real concern for her. And the feeling was mutual.

They release each other. Even with all the dirt and stink, there is something beautiful about Cinnamon besides her smooth skin, her petite build, her toughness.

And she asks, "What's the plan? Where we headed?"

They will ride the train until they see the sign for Sanger, Texas, where they'll hop off. Divert eyes and attention. Gather some supplies. Find a place to camp. Then catch back out. Travel through Texas and head for Arizona. By Cinnamon's best guess, they're in Oklahoma now.

What Anne really wants is a bath. Just for a night. To clean up. Lie on a bed with fresh sheets, lie with Cinnamon.

"What about a hotel?" Her heart skips at her own suggestion. "A hotel?"

"I got money. We could find a cheap one for the night. Shower and relax. Catch out after that."

"Girl, you done lost your mind? That's *food*. That money is for your survival. We're called 'dirty kids' for a reason."

That glimmer of hope hidden beneath despair dwindles and drifts. Anne says, "I get it. Was just a thought."

Smiling, Cinnamon tells Anne, "I know we been riding for who knows how long. Feels like days mixed into months. But that's the rail. It's a grind. Like I said, once we get into Texas, we'll hop off in Sanger, get out and get some supplies. You'll forget all about Dredd. Move forward."

"I get it," Anne says. "I just . . ." She hesitates.

Concerned, Cinnamon touches her face. "You what?"

"I never been outside of Tennessee."

With a look of surprise, Cinnamon says, "Now you're shitting me for sure."

"No. Everything I've seen so far—it's all new. Breathtaking. It's magical, and it's frightening. It's all these feelings and emotions rolled up into a ball, tugging and pulling me in all directions. My family never took us much farther than the grocery store, or one of my dad's friends' places in the country to shoot guns while they drank beer and played cards."

"Holy shit. You never visited relatives?"

"No. Nothing interesting about my upbringing. No culture, unless you mean the culture of pissing and moaning and the occasional ass-whipping."

"I'm without words, in total shock."

Trot sits with his legs hanging out of the boxcar, smoking a cigarette. Turns back to Anne and Cinnamon and says, "It's true. She told me that, and I said, 'You gotta get out of this town. There's an entire world out there you ain't ever seen.'"

The day passes. Everyone sits with their backs pressed into the car's wall. Digging into their packs, sharing what snacks they have. Snickers bars. Apples.

Passing through landscapes and towns, they watch for signs. The train slows, stops to reconnect to other tracks. They wait and watch, see a sign for Durant. Then there's the crunch of gravel. Feet digging in. Lungs huffing. Trot glances out of the boxcar as a backpack tumbles in through the door opening. One hand braces on the door; the other slaps down on the floor. With a grunt, a young man swings up, hooks a heel on the floor, and lizard-crawls into the car.

Eyes meet as he flops onto his back on the stained and splintered floor. Cinnamon stands over him and yells, "Doc?"

Rolling over onto his elbows, he grins. Gets to his feet and says, "Well, I'll be dipped in dog shit. Cinnamon?"

Behind him comes more heavy breathing, and another pack thuds into the boxcar, followed by another body. Another and another. One by one, more train hoppers share space with Anne, Cinnamon, Canary, and Trot. Bringing more life, more energy, to the band of travelers.

Doc's black derby hat makes him look like a bartender in a Wild West saloon but for the orange feather stuck in it. He has tattoos under his eyes, but they are too smudged by dirt for Anne to make out the images. A thick, curly beard and mustache, dirty bandanna around the neck, T-shirt and vest, and raggedy Carhartts with a hammer loop. Combat boots complete the ensemble. His arms spread wide, wrapping around Cinnamon. "Oh my Lord, where have you been? It's been six months or better. Thought that crazy you bunked with from time to time had maybe eaten you."

"Good news is there's no more Dredd!" Cinnamon bubbles. "These are my friends, my new family."

Doc eyes Anne, Trot, and Canary with her brother and sister, hand in hand. Tips his hat. "Nice to make everyone's acquaintance." Then he introduces his crew of misfits. There's Spider, with his head shaved on each side up to the temples, where his locks go wild and wavy. Inferno is a youngish man with burnt-sienna skin and a spiked Mohawk that looks like black flames. He wears a sleeveless leather jacket, camo track suit, and combat boots. Sours is the lone female—dark hair with blond tips down to her shoulders, a stud through her nasal septum, a tie-dyed T-shirt cut just above a navel with a silver belly ring through it. She wears a baby face caught in a continuous pout. The Conductor has a face of stone, tattooed with ink lines that look like scratches under the patchy beard. He wears a cotton ball cap with fishhooks on one side of the bill and a small tire weight on the other side. He looks lean and sinewy in his sleeveless jean jacket, no shirt. Tattooed arms. He has an acoustic guitar strapped over his shoulder. *Where did that come from?* Anne wonders. Each of them nods. Everyone sits. Some put their packs behind their heads, stretch their legs out.

Words pass back and forth about where they've been. Where not to go. Catching out. Getting stuck on trains. Getting chased by yard bulls. Camping beneath bridges and overpasses. They share their candy bars and jerky and nuts and chips. Bottles of water. Converse about how they've lived. Survived without constraints. Anne listens, rapt. This is real freedom. Belonging to a real family. She vows never to be kept down again.

Doc looks Cinnamon in the eye and asks, "Tell me why Dredd is no more. I mean, we all know the guy was a maniac."

Doc's friends all chuckle at that.

And Cinnamon tells him, "He was. Why I never stayed more than a day or two at his encampment. But the conversations we had during each visit kept painting a worsening scene. And no one would step up."

Doc laughs. "He always bragged about being a radical in college. Bitched about handouts, then wanted a handout. You know, always wanted to preach but not do."

"Wanted to be a ruler, boss everyone around," Cinnamon tells them. "Once I saw the writing on the wall, I split. Those that stayed just got blinded and beat down."

Doc says, "When you realize what you bought into, you're trapped."

"And everyone was afraid to speak out. Why I kept my distance. Kept passing through. It was a like a rest area for traveling."

"You knew better. Saw through his lies."

"Yeah, but I didn't want others to keep getting hurt by his actions."

"You were smart," says Doc, the bright feather in his derby hatband bouncing with every nod and shake of his head. "Kept your distance."

"I did. Just made friends with those in his little flock. They didn't have anything else. Then I met Anne, brought her in with me. I warned her. But she already saw through his ways and didn't buy into his words. And she was strong enough to fight back."

"Sounds like a new leader."

"I'm no leader," Anne puts in. "Just want a family."

Doc grins at her. "Well, looks like you got one, for life."

Looking around at everyone, Anne realizes that they all have a story. A place they arrived from. Leaving behind their abusers. Fathers who beat them. Mothers who left them. Brothers and sisters who bullied them. Some had good home lives; they just didn't want what that home suggested. Didn't want the American dream, whatever that was. Everyone made their own interpretation.

HUNTER

Secrets. Everyone had them, especially his father.

"Don't be a stranger," Blake had told him. It seemed that everyone but Hunter knew about their connection. His words had echoed in Hunter's mind all night as he lay sprawled out on the bunk bed. Nugget and Itch stayed up, drinking Coors Light and munching homemade bison jerky, passing words with Purnell.

Come morning, he was out of the shower, wound cleaned and a new bandage on the knee. A blown tire wasn't an issue, but the replacement for the bent rim was going to take a while to get delivered, even if they managed to overnight it. Nugget had offered his bike to Hunter, saying he would stay behind, get the rim, and replace the tire. Fix everything and meet up with Itch and Hunter down the road. Tara said that would be fine with her and her father, that Nugget could stay for as long as it took. Hunter could even meet with him back here on his way home.

Now, hauling ass through Utah, the heat rises from the road as the sun climbs over the mountains. The road curves. Miles roll by.

Time counts down. Hunter wonders what else his father had kept hidden from him after all the years he was believed to be on the road, traveling and working. Bringing home stories. Life lessons from afar. From encounters with people he met and helped. Hunter supposes he will never know.

The landscape has a desolate beauty. Great sandstone towers rise from the desert floor. A bright green line of cottonwoods marks a seasonal streambed. An atmosphere of changeless calm. Little vegetation, just the vastness of blue overhead. It is something the eyes never tire of, and it delivers a breath of positivity to his senses, cleansing the mind.

Throttling down, Itch and Hunter pull off at a middle-of-nowhere gas station off I-70 for fuel, some water, and a piss.

Footing out the kickstand, taking off his helmet, Hunter misses the iron. He hasn't lifted weights all week. Thinking that maybe after sewing up the details of his father in California, he'll find a gym. Get the blood flowing. Get a good pump. Stepping from his bike, he takes a long look at the big red Pegasus from the building's glory days as a Mobil gas station, sometime back in his childhood. A Route 66 sign in the window reminds Hunter of something out of a movie like *From Dusk till Dawn* or *The Getaway*. He's waiting for the sheriff to roll up wearing a Smokey hat and mirrored shades.

They park beside the retro-looking gas pumps—old-school, with the latch on the side, metal housing, real counters, nothing digital. They walk into the store, the door jangling the little bell over their heads.

A sweet rush of cold air hits Hunter and Itch in the face. Counter to the left. Cigarettes lined overhead. Behind the counter, an attendant in his midtwenties sits on a stool holding his phone up in front of him, thoroughly engrossed in thumbing a message to someone somewhere. It seems everyone is connected by a smartphone.

"Busy day?" Hunter asks.

"Huh?" asks the attendant. Wearing a ball cap on backward, hair stringing out from beneath it. He wears a blue T-shirt with "Billabong" across the chest.

Off to the right are rows of chips. Jerky. Potted meat. Nuts and candy bars. Everything is packed in tight. Coolers straight back in the rear, beside the teensy bathroom. Itch hits the head first.

"Customers. You had many today?" Hunter asks, trying to make small talk.

While the attendant works out a response, he walks to the coolers, opens the door, and grabs two bottles of water.

"They come and go. Out here it's a slow death. Some days, there's plenty; others, it's a big minus. Don't make me no difference—get paid the same regardless of who trespasses."

"I hear that," Hunter says, eyeing the lunch meat and cheeses in the cooler.

Behind Hunter, the bell over the door rings. A kid walks in. He seems cautious, even leery, of the scene he's just entered. Sizing the area up. He has on a faded Soulfly T-shirt. Hole-worn jeans. Black Converse high-tops. He walks the isles in search of something to lift. Hunter recognizes it right away. He glances at Hunter, looking nervous. Approaches him. Nods. Sizing him up, taking in the ink on his arms.

"Cool tats."

"Thanks."

At the counter, Hunter is waiting on Itch when the attendant lowers his phone.

"Hey, that shit on the shelves ain't free. Take it out of your pocket."

Hunter turns to the kid, who pulls a package of Reese's Cups and a Twix from his pocket. Hunter feels sorry for him. "Grab what you want, kid," he says. "I'm buying."

"What do you want in return?"

"Nothing."

At a closer glance, the kid looks a wreck. Sweaty locks. Dirt beneath his fingernails, as if perhaps he lives out in the desert beneath a rock somewhere.

Coming from the bathroom, Itch says, "Already made a buddy, huh?"

"Something like that."

The kid grabs some chips to go with his Reese's Cups and Twix. A couple of Monster Energy drinks from the cooler. Placing everything on the counter, Hunter tells the attendant, "I got all of it. And I'll need two fill-ups out on the pumps. Here's fifty. I'll get my change when they're topped off."

After paying up and leaving the store, Hunter and Itch open their tanks, release the gas pumps, and start filling their motorcycles. They load bottles of water and some nuts into their saddle bags, and each chug a bottle to quench their thirst. The kid leans against the building as he downs a Monster drink and shoves two Reese's Cups into his mouth at once. Drops the wrapper on the ground.

After they top off the tanks as high as they can without sloshing on the paint job, Itch goes in and gets the change.

Outside, the kid is chomping away, his cheeks packed like a chipmunk's. He tells Hunter, "Them's some badass bikes." A crumb of Reese's falls from his mouth.

"Thanks. You from around the area?"

Washing his sugar rush down with the Monster, he says, "Yeah. Hitched up here. Live down the road a ways. You guys part of a gang or some shit?"

"No, just passing through. Headed to California."

"Ever been to Sturgis?"

"Few times."

"Bet that fucking rocked."

"It's had its moments. You need a lift back home?"

"Yeah. Think you could give me one? I'm just down the road a few miles."

Hunter looks at Itch. "You mind?"

Itch shakes his head. "I'm good with whatever you're good with, dude."

Hunter says, "I'm Hunter. This is Itch. Hop on."

Kid finishes off his Monster. Crushes the can, drops it on the ground. "Oh, I'm Cory."

"Nice to meet you, Cory. Think you could pick up your trash? There's a can right beside the door."

Hesitant, Cory says, "Yeah, I guess I could." Bending down, he picks up the can and candy wrapper and tosses them into a black drum with a plastic liner.

Getting on the rear of Hunter's bike, Cory hangs on to the back of the seat, just in front of the chrome sissy bar. Heeling the stand up, Hunter cranks the bike to life.

Warm wind pushes against Hunter's face. Giving the kid a lift reminds Hunter of his father helping a runaway girl. She was fed up with her home life. Her mother had died of cancer. Her father worked the barges, was never home. He was trying to provide. The girl stayed with her older sister, her boyfriend, and their crying newborn. But she hated the small, cramped living conditions. So she'd decided to run away, fend for herself. Hitchhiking across the USA. When Hunter's father gave her a lift, she told her story. She was hungry. Hank had bought her supper. Paid for a separate hotel room. And over the days, he had talked her into returning home. Gave her a lift on his way back to Indiana. He convinced her that the road was no place for a sixteen-year-old. The hunger she had already experienced was nothing compared to what awaited if she stayed in the wind. The world would chew her up and spit her out.

Hunter had to wonder if maybe it was a half sister he never knew about.

Tapping Hunter's shoulder, Cory yells in his ear, "Turn down the next dirt road."

Slowing down, hanging a left down a wide dirt track liberally strewn with loose rock. Everything is flat, with nary a tree or bush. Not even grass—just scraggly purple nightshades growing on bare dirt. They roll up to a frame house with a corrugated metal roof. Some boards are graying, others chipped and showing white. Windows are boarded up or covered with cardboard. An air conditioner hangs from a window, dripping moisture, creating a dark spot on the dead earth. Electricity runs from a pole off away from the house. Rusted steel tanks lay about the yard, held in reserve for some unknown or forgotten purpose. A camper stands on legs off to the side of the house. In the distance, a school bus with blown-out tires sits on its axles, surrounded by four or five cars that look beyond any hope of repair.

Downshifting and throttling down, they make less noise—just a low, soft rumble. Everything in sight is glossed and smudged with the aura of defeat. And Hunter wonders what he could possibly do to help this kid living in such squalor and despair. They come to a stop, and Cory gets off the bike. "Appreciate the lift."

Hunter doesn't want to leave him here. "You're welcome. Parents home?"

Cory looks nervous as a cat in a dog pound. "Yeah. Dad's inside."

Shutting his bike off, Hunter glances at Itch, asks Cory, "Mind if we come in?"

"I don't know," Cory hedges. "He might be sleeping or something. Not fond of strangers."

"He don't mind if you're hitchhiking?"

Dead sagebrush lines a dusty concrete pad. A not-quite-bald tire leans beside the cracked and peeling red front door. Cory twists the knob. The door creaks open. Stepping inside, Cory leaves the door ajar. Hunter and Itch follow several feet behind him, feeling a creeping sense of unease. Hunter tries not to imagine what's inside. And Itch starts whispering, "Don't like this. Don't like this. What if there's dead bodies? Maniacs. Cannibals sitting in there waiting on supper?"

"Pipe it down, Itch."

The dead air reeks like a thawed freezer. The thin floorboards give under their weight. The only sound is that of the little overmatched window unit. The house is in a state of neglect, looking as if no one inhabited the interior. Trash is thrown around as if the place were a squat for junkies or meth heads. Balled-up newspapers. Dirty dishes, stacked without organization. More dishes fill a sink the shade of beef broth. Clothing tossed and piled wherever. Kitchen counter and table are lined with pill bottles and Ziploc bags of pills.

What the fuck? Hunter asks himself. His Spidey senses are flaring. "Where's your dad?"

"Not sure. He was here when I left. Like I said outside, probably taking a nap."

Itch walks to the counter. "What's the deal with all these pills?"

"It's what he does."

"Really?"

"Yeah, really." The kid won't meet his eyes.

"Hold up," Hunter says. "No one's judging your situation. But what's going on here, what it looks like . . . I can't leave you here."

"You'll take me with you?" Cory says, the eagerness in his voice hard to miss.

"I'll get you outta here. This situation. These conditions. I'll get you away from this. It's not right, and it sure as shit ain't safe."

From the dark interior of the house comes the heavy clomp of feet, the click of a hammer.

"Ain't taking my boy nowheres. Cory, what kind of scooter trash you bringing in here?"

The guy has hair as messy as a hawk's nest, unshaven, neck beard, no shirt. Religiously pale.

"Bikers," Cory says. "Gave me a lift. Bought me some snacks down at Elmer's."

"You some kinda narcs, working with the local pork? ATF? The judge?"

The man's eyes are bottomless pits without a glimmer of mercy. Hunter says, "No. Just giving your son a lift." He studies the pistol. Taurus revolver. Six shots.

"Well, looks like you gave it. What you in my home for, snooping where you got no concern?"

"Wanted to make sure Cory wasn't alone."

"Really, that how it is?"

The guy looks three-steps-from-the-sanitarium insane. As if things are breaking apart in his brain.

"Yeah, that's how it is. Kid shouldn't be home without some supervision."

The guy looks ready to either cry or explode. "Trying to tell me how to raise my boy? My own kin? What, you the supervision police?"

"No. but—"

"But what? You got kids?"

"No, I don't. I—"

"Oh, there you go with this 'I' bullshit. If you don't got no kids, then how the fuck you gonna tell me how to raise mine?"

"Not trying to tell you anything. I just don't believe—"

"Don't believe in what? God? Satan? Freedom? Well, guess what. I don't fucking care *what* you believe, motherfucker!"

Anyone can see that Itch is getting tense. Balling his hands into fists. Hunter feels it. Recognizes it. It's pulsing through him as well.

"What's your boyfriend's problem? Why's he making fists? You want some of this, you bristly-headed son of a bitch?"

Everyone has a breaking point, and in Hunter's estimation, Itch is right about there. Hunter feels it too. Violence is coursing through them. Through their veins, organs, bones, connective tissue. Hunter feels as if he had just stepped into a real-life version of some cheesy horror flick. He's just waiting for a chainsaw or a meat clever to come from somewhere.

"Look, I wasn't trying to offend you. Just concerned for Cory's safety."

"What do you think? You waltz into someone's home, look at how they live. Critique them. Then run the fuck away? I don't fucking think so!"

Feet stomp across the floor. The man comes raging toward Hunter, gun raised. Pushes the muzzle against his temple, turning his head to the side. "Real tough guy, huh, until someone puts a gun in your face. What? What you gonna do now, Mr. Tough Guy? Huh?"

Seeing the gun, homing in on the situation, Hunter is reminded of his father, teaching him about fear and weakness. Hank had been selling a home security system to what seemed a hardworking middle-income couple, when something was said that offended the husband, who in turn got mouthy with his wife. Derogatory. Hank stepped in to defend the woman. Calm the husband, who then felt inferior. Went to the bedroom and came back waving a pistol at Hank, who didn't waver. Didn't back down. As he told Hunter, "You stand up to weakness." It was why the guy pulled the pistol on him: he knew he was in the wrong, thought he could intimidate Hank. But he didn't.

Recalling that now, Hunter tells the father, "Never said I was a tough guy. I told you, was just making sure Cory wasn't alone. Didn't know his situation."

Anger continues to seep into every fiber of Hunter's being. People have choices. Sometimes, they don't mesh with morals, with what we view as right or wrong. Having a pistol pointed and poked into your face—there is nothing right about that.

Hunter is fed up. Time is standing stock-still. This guy breathing on him smells like bad feet that had stepped in vomit. Spitting when he spoke. Strung out. Then something breaks internally. Itch hollers, "Get that fucking gun outta his face!"

Turning his attention to Itch, the guy says, "Or what?" He turns his head sideways. "What are you gonna do? Oh, I see, your boyfriend over here is the real tough guy."

Pulling the pistol from Hunter's face, he turns to point it at Itch.

Hunter doesn't wait. He drives a left cross into the guy's temple. His right hand grabs the guy's wrist, twists, controls the gun. Then his left shoots out, open hand to the throat. The guy makes a gagging cough, releases the revolver. Hunter grabs the pistol as the guy buckles at his waist. Can't catch his breath. Heaving for air, he sounds like someone with the whooping cough. His hands go to his throat, as if to pry open a shocked airway. His eyes weep, and a rope of spittle hangs from one corner of his mouth. He drops to his knees. Cheeks red but fading. He can't breathe. And Itch is on the guy. Treating him like a speed bag. Driving his knuckles into the guy's face.

Cory screams, "No! No! Dad!"

Hunter slides the pistol into his waistband, then pulls Itch off Dad, who lies motionless on the floor slats, surrounded by trash. Cory kneels down to his father.

Red-faced and glazed by tears, this is all he knows. This way of living. Survival. Hunter just hopes Itch hasn't killed the son of a bitch.

JACK

The battered old Toyota Land Cruiser coasts down the grade and labors up the other side, gears grinding, the engine easing and revving with each drop and rise of the terrain. Moments of his life flash and fade. Memories of his wife. His daughter. His son. All the things he'd missed: school events, birthdays, court hearings, doctors' appointments. Graduations. Anniversaries. With this realization, guilt floods him. Panic seizes in his gut. The arches of his feet ache as if they had been beaten with a truncheon. The pain travels up his calves, around his shins, running up the hamstrings to his lower back. He is a weak man.

The seat is leather, worn slick. He feels his body sliding around with every lurch and sway of the Land Cruiser. Feels the presence of two bodies, one on each side. They give off heat, though they do not reek as he does. Rather, they exude the thick, overpowering smell of cheap cologne. They seem to have bathed in it.

Will they kill him? Torture him? Do they want the reward? Is this even *about* the reward?

Rap music blares from the speakers, and someone speaks broken English with a Spanish accent. "You like Mos Def?"

"*Pues, sí,*" says the man sitting to his left. "And the Eminem."

The heat rolling in through the open windows feels like a thick, steaming blanket. At the same time, the AC is running, sporadically easing his discomfort with a welcome splash of cold. Someone in the vehicle is smoking. Every time he starts to doze off, his head drifts to his right, and an elbow bumps him in the head. "*¡Despiér- tate, cabrón!*" a voice commands, only for him to doze off again and slump to the left. Getting another elbow bump and another annoyed command to wake up.

Every hour or so, a hand slaps his face and lifts the hood up to his nose, and the mouth of a plastic bottle meets his lips. He greedily sucks down the cold water, wishing he could pour it all over himself.

More questions run through Jack's mind. Is this happening because of how horrible a husband and father he'd been? Is this payback? Some sort of karmic retribution?

The old Land Cruiser has been alternately revving and coast- ing for what seems like hours. And when the terrain finally levels out, the vehicle coasts to a stop. Sounds of movement. The doors all around unlatch. Open. Hands grip his arms, not roughly but not gently. Pull and lead him from the vehicle.

His feet walk over hard, dusty earth. Every step makes him flinch in pain. His feet hurt. His arms are pulled behind him. Add to these tortures the sweltering heat. The only noise other than the squabbling of sparrows is the snarling and barking of several scary-sounding dogs. Constant. Loud. There is the sound of a latch. Unseen hands guide him past a metal gate that groans shut behind him. A voice tells him, "Watch your feet. Step up."

And he does. Walks one step after the next, climbing a dirt trail. His knees creak, and his thighs burn. At last, the ground levels off, and he feels the heat slacken. Wherever he is being taken, it's cooler. The dogs' barking has grown distant somewhere behind him. He has entered an enclosed area. The air feels cool. And a voice says, "Take him to his quarters."

Led down what he believes to be a hallway, the sound of footsteps bounce off the walls. He stops. A door is unlatched. He is placed inside, told not to turn around. The sack is lifted from his head. The click of a knife blade and the plastic ties binding his wrists fall away. "Make yourself comfortable," a voice tells him. The door behind him closes, locks from the outside. Footsteps grow distant.

Jack stands stiffly, taking everything in. Outside light comes through a window with its wooden shutters pulled back. Below the window stands a black walnut table with a book on top. Beside the book is a pair of tan cotton pants. White T-shirt. Boxers. Gray Sanuk slip-on shoes. All nicely folded and stacked. The cherrywood twin bed in the corner is made with what Jack recognizes as Egyptian cotton sheets, with a small blue blanket folded at the foot.

Beside the table, on a stand of the same wood and design, sits a white porcelain basin. Below the basin are towels and washrags. The room has rock walls and cobblestone floors. The air is deliciously cool. His fingers tremble, touching the shoes. Lifting them, he sees they are tens—his size. Laying them beside the garments, he picks up the pants. They have a forty-inch waist, thirty-inch inseam. His size.

He feels stiff getting out of his smelly, ragged clothing. His bones pop and creak. Muscles are tender, aching as though they had taken a beating. After splashing water onto his face, he washes his arms. Chest. His balls. Ass. Thighs. Knees. Shins. On the windowsill, he finds a bar of soap. Lathers up. How the water feels is beyond his powers of expression. Possibly orgasmic. As he washes off the days of filth, his eyes begin to tear. And before he knows it, he is washing and bawling like a baby. Something he never thought he would take for granted again: a bath. The aching seems to ease with the pleasure he derives from such a simple action.

Soon, even the rinse water appears black with filth. At last, toweling off, putting on the new garments, he feels as if he might break down at any moment from the emotions that swarm him. He feels elated, as if streams of liquid light are flowing through his veins.

Outside the window stand men wearing black wraparound sunglasses, with automatic weapons slung over their torsos. There is a courtyard planted with flowers and shrubs, all sprouting and healthy. A thick stone wall surrounds the area. It looks to be six feet high, maybe a bit more. Jack wonders where he is. What is in store for him? Why is he here?

His palms sink into the mattress, feeling its cool softness. Lying facedown on it, his nose pressing into the sheets, inhaling deeply. They are clean, their fresh scent something he can not explain. He lets his body sink into the bed. It is like diving into a vat of cool, minty pudding. Soft and soothing, caressing and hugging his sore body. And again he finds himself in tears. Lying on the bed, enveloped in its comfort, he wants never to move, never to leave. His body quakes. His senses are firing on all synapses at once. He has lost all the things he took for granted. Stripped of everything—his daughter, his mother, and his wife—and here he is, rediscovering joy. Rediscovering the simplest of pleasures. Drifting off, there is only silence. Feeling himself falling down a pit, faster and faster, he cannot stop until, quite abruptly, he stands before a room with its door open wide. Inside, his daughter begs for help because the floor has fallen away to become a cliff. One hand holds on for dear life. The other hand dangles, reaches for Jack.

Oh, how he hurt! But he reaches for her hand. Takes it. It slips from his grasp. He can't hold on to it. It is slick to the touch.

"Why are you letting go, Daddy? Why?"

"I'm not. I can't hold on."

"Neither can I." She falls, and her screams echo up to him.

"No!"

Jack falls forward. Rushing into darkness, only to be standing before his home when it ignites. A window shatters, and in the open space, his daughter appears, screaming, "Help me Daddy! Help me!" Running to the front door, he grabs the knob. It is so hot, his palm sizzles. But he cannot turn it.

"Help me, Daddy!"

As he goes to try the door again, the home flashes over, engulfed completely, taking his daughter's shape with it.

Again the floor opens up and Jack is falling. Faster and faster and faster until eyes open. Quick gasp of air. He rolls off the bed, spills onto the cool cobblestone floor. His eyes open on a pair of snakeskin boots. He follows them up a pair of pressed denim jeans. Looks up at a man of Latino descent. Midthirties. Coal-black hair with a peppering of gray, trimmed and wavy. His hands glitter with gold rings. He smiles.

"You're a popular man."

Jack pushes himself up to his creaky knees, braces a hand on the bed, gets himself upright. "Who are you?"

Confident green eyes. Slim. Muscular but not huge—the build of a college wrestler. He says, "Who I am is not important at this time. All you need to know is you're safe."

"Why did you bring me here?"

Smiling, he says, "Your people are looking for you. Offered a, shall we say, hefty incentive. They reached out."

"My people?"

"People you manage, employ. Your company."

"How would anyone even know where I am?"

"Jack." The man laughs. "In this day and age, no one can

hide. You didn't show up to work. Your wife died; people became worried. So they began the search. You bought tickets, and those were traced. After that, my acquaintances and I did the tracking of your travels. You made quite the impression on the locals."

"Matías—is he okay?"

"The truck driver? Yes. My men delivered him to his home back in Chile. He is safe."

After everything Jack has been through, he has a million questions. "How do you know me? My clothing size? My shoe size?"

The man smiles. "Jack, I know everything there is to know about you. It's what people who want to succeed do. They study other successful individuals. I know that your mother struggled. Left your father. Raised you while working two or three jobs. You went to college. Married. Built a huge company. Lost a daughter to suicide. Had a son. Lost your mother. Lost your wife to cancer. And somewhere along the way, things quit making sense. And here you are in Colombia."

"Colombia?" Jack thought he was in Peru.

"Yes, Jack. Where are my manners? Welcome to Colombia." The man spread his arms. "I apologize for the way you were brought here, but I have to keep my location private. Lot of people would like to see me no longer breathing."

"Who are you?"

"Look, my identity is unimportant. You rest. I'll get some water brought in for you. Would you maybe like iced tea or a beer? Something stronger?"

"Water is good, yes, thank you."

"How about some fresh fruit?"

"That would be great. I could use that. Thank you."

"Look, I'll get Guillermo to bring those items to you; then we'll talk over supper in an hour. Does that sound sufficient?"

Did he have a choice?

ANNE

Feet meet the moving ground. Wobbling like a knock-kneed puppet, not quite falling over, one by one Anne and the others run. The train keeps rolling on, unchanged.

Following each other over the green grass in search of town, grocery store, or gas station, they find a Family Dollar. A vanilla-colored building with a red awning. Anne removes her cash upon entering the store. Cold air washes over everyone's faces. They load up on water. Chips, nuts, cookies, and candy bars. Heading to the checkout, she feels eyes judging. Anne lays the cash down. Hands take it, count it, return her change. They leave the store with their goods.

Outside on the concrete walkway, off to the side of the store, they take their packs off, dividing up what she bought, loading everything up. What they need is a place to crash. To lie low, rest up, and figure out when they'll try to hop the next train. Cinnamon tells them, "I know a place that's secluded. Plenty of space. Kinda out of the way."

"We'll follow you," Anne says.

After walking and hitching, on the far side of town, they wait until it's nearly dark to enter an abandoned property posted with No Trespassing signs. A hundred yards from the gate stands a once-splendid house that has fallen into disrepair.

"It's an old mansion," Cinnamon tells Anne.

Slipping through the rusted iron gate, they follow a road of fractured asphalt crumbling into gravel. Rank weeds and grass are hastening the process.

Standing in front of the mansion. The walls are constructed of flat rock in various colors of tan, gray, and clay red. Windows are blacked-out squares framed in white. The grass is knee high around the perimeter. Going around back, they scale a wall and drop into what was once a flower garden, its brick beds now filled with brown weeds and dried-out earth. No one is around. Canary helps the twins up and over the wall, Anne and Trot catching them. Then Canary drops down beside them. Everything is desolate. Dead. They walk to a short flight of stone steps that lead up to a broad patio where doors used to be. They go in.

Beyond the entranceway, they find themselves in a cavernous room in a state of decay and decline. A staircase leads up into shadow. Everyone wants to explore, but it's almost dark. And rest is what everyone needs.

They settle on the third and highest floor, next to a window where they can keep watch, just in case. They shed their packs and sip their water. Munch on snacks. Wanting sleep.

Cinnamon tells Anne, "We rest six or eight hours. Try to head out at first light. Head back to the tracks to, hopefully, catch out."

"Sounds good. Where you think we'll be headed?"

"Maybe Arizona or Mexico. Who knows? We'll figure it out."

"How you know about this place?"

"Crashed here a few trips. Been a while. It's really going to shit."

"Shame. All this space could be used for something important."

Cinnamon laughs. "Listen to you. Like what?"

"I don't know, someplace to help out people like us, maybe. Bad home life, nowhere to go. Need a place to stay, reconnect, figure life out."

Canary says, "I like that idea."

Trot asks Cinnamon, "What was this place?"

"Lot of rumors. Some say it belonged to a drug lord who got busted. Died in prison. Then I heard a husband and wife built their dream home. Went bankrupt, got divorced, and never completed the construction."

"I like the drug-lord version," Canary says, pulling the twins close to her.

Everyone lies nestled close together. Cinnamon and Anne lie looking out the window, watching the sky darken. Stars are blinking on in a clear sky.

Soon they all are sleeping like corpses. Warm air is their blanket. Smells of prairie. Dirt, brush, wood rot. Anne dreams of wildflowers. Acres and acres of them. Running through tall grass with Cinnamon. Picking the long stems of dandelion, blowing on them. Watching smiles float from the petals. Holding hands with Cinnamon. Until headlights flash through windows. Anne watches as cars kick up loose gravel, heading up the driveway to the mansion.

Turning to the others, hands reach, touch, and wake Cinnamon. Rustling movement. "We got company."

Trot yawns. "Shit. I was sleeping so good."

Everyone rolls up their bedding, throws everything back into their packs. Anne and Cinnamon peek down below, watching the movements. It's the cops.

Cinnamon whispers, "Someone must've seen us coming in. We gotta scoot. They'll lock all our asses up."

Below them, someone is using a crowbar to pry the front door. The sound of feet entering. Flashlights pierce the darkness below.

"We wait. See what direction they take. Then we go straight through this area here. There's a room with a patio out a window."

High ceilings jump with flashlit shadows. Canary keeps her hands over the twins' mouths. The lights move on, and Anne and the others sneak to the other room. Looking for their escape—the window that leads to the patio. They must evade the police bumping about and walking from room to room below them. Shining their lights.

"I don't see shit."

"Me neither."

"Probably someone drunk seeing shit."

"Yeah, got nothing better to do than call the fucking police."

One of the twins sneezes.

"You hear that?"

"Yeah, spoke too soon. It's upstairs."

Rustle of feet.

Young hands pull at the boards blocking exit through the window. The twins are whimpering. Canary tries to keep them silent. "It's okay," she whispers. Feet climb and the lights flash.

"They're at the top of the stairs," Trot says.

Nerves are shivers and shakes. Adrenaline. Rushing heartbeats.

Fingers, tugging frantically, finally break a board loose.

"Over there. I hear movement."

Trot has a one-by-six board in his hands. Anne has pried loose another. "Go!" she whispers to Cinnamon and Canary. "We'll be right behind you."

Cinnamon's eyes are burning with the word "No!"

Flashlight beams dance and shadows shift. A radio crackles with static, then barks in a loud voice.

"I see someone."

"Stay where you're at!" a voice demands.

Standing beside the doorway, Anne swings edgewise at the back of the cop's knees.

"Go!" She screams.

The cop drops forward. "Shit!"

Behind him comes another. Trot swings through the dark. The cop's light falls to the floor, rolls. Then Anne swings, and he takes a board to the face.

"Son of a bitch!"

Dropping their boards, Anne and Trot run to the window. They slip out behind the others. Everyone on the patio has jumped to the ground. Down below, Cinnamon, Canary, and the twins wait. Trot goes first. Then comes gunfire. Anne jumps. Hitting the ground, knees and thighs buckle. Ignoring it. Running hard. Blocking the gunshots from their minds. Anne pats her body. Feels wet all over. It's only perspiration. Off to the right, police cruisers sit, their lights strobing in the night.

Anne and the others don't stop. They keep running, harder than they've ever run before, through high grass wet with dew. No one has any idea what time it is, only that it is night. Thick line of darkness in the distance, drawing closer. It's the tree line. They dig deeper into the burn until they meet the sheltering shadows, where they duck and turn for a split second's glance. Hearts pounding, they watch the flashlight beams bouncing and circling the mansion, searching for them.

"Let's get out of here before they figure out where we are," Cinnamon says to all. There is no disagreement.

Miles away, lying in a pasture, sleep comes until the heat and a couple of horseflies wake them. Unlike at the encampment, here they have no protection from the elements. They duck under barbed wire. Wasted and weary eyed, the little troupe of vagabonds trudges along the roadside. Cinnamon leads the way over a terrain of weeds, Big Gulp cups, soda bottles, wadded corn chip bags. Candy wrappers. Beer cans. Cigarette butts.

Coming up behind them, they hear tires on asphalt. Without looking back, Cinnamon says, "Let's try to hitch."

"Where to?" Canary asks.

"Nearest train crossing or tracks. Then we can wait and catch out."

An old black Ford pickup brakes as it passes, pulls off on the side of the road. Honks the horn. The passenger's side window comes down, and an older lady—possum-colored locks pulled back, wiry strands running in odd directions, a face etched by years working in the sun—is leaning over to peer out at them. "Where y'all headed this time of morning?"

"Nearest train tracks?"

Smiling, the woman tells Cinnamon, "I can do that. Hop in the back."

Everyone loads up in the bed of the truck and sits on bark chunks and loose dirt. When everyone is situated, the woman shifts gears, steers back onto the pavement. As the wind picks up with the vehicle's speed, they all look at one another. Tired eyes with crusted corners, hundreds of miles from where they started. Anne sits taking it all in. Glances at the faces of her family members. A smile slowly takes over her face. Hand rests on Cinnamon's leg. Anne is filled with new feelings of comfort and hope.

HUNTER

Itch stayed behind. Waited on the local law while Cory held his groggy and groaning father. The run-down house was nothing more than a pill operation—real opioids gotten with stolen or fake prescriptions. At least, that was what Itch and Hunter had pieced together from speaking with Cory.

Heat rises like gas fumes from the highway. Nugget's bike eats up the long stretches of desolation—more cactus and creosote than actual trees. There isn't much in the way of other vehicles on the road. For the most part, Hunter is alone with his thoughts. He likes that. More time to reflect, to think about his father. Their camping trips. Pitching tents, fishing. Scaling fish. Cleaning them and frying them in cornmeal over an open fire. Enjoying the mouthwatering meat of fresh-caught stream fish. There were long hikes in the woods. His father was on the road five or six days a week, but when he was home, he had made time for Hunter. What Hunter hadn't realized then—or even until this trip—was how, with his father, he always saw the world through a different lens. New eyes that readjusted one's beliefs about the world and the people in it. That there was good in others—you just had to find it, to point it out. Which explained the stories. The situations his father found himself in on the road. Regardless of how grim the circumstances, his father had always seen a solution, always had an eye toward betterment. And he was a good salesman. Could sell anything.

The bike is gliding along on silky-smooth pavement, sun warming him and reflecting off the gas tank's painted flames. Hunter wonders, where did that come from? His father's penchant for understanding others, their situations. Maybe it came from his grandfather; he was an open-minded man. Or maybe it was just being on the road and seeing real life and following his gut. His natural instincts.

Riding Interstate 80 West into California, he has the same blue skies. But the soil and foothills have changed a lot since Utah, from dusty reds to tans with patches of green—a lot more green where there had been only rock and brown scrub. Everything is clean, vibrant. Rolling along, more cars are present. More bikes too. Hunter is no longer a lone soldier. Following long curving stretches, exiting onto Highway 20, cruising through the historical beauty of Nevada City, California. Hunter can see why his father and uncle chose to live here. It is pristine. Structures are well kept and colorful, and most have a breath-stealing view of verdant wooded mountainsides.

Outside town, cruising down Evergreen Drive. His dad's home is in a nice area with plenty of seclusion. Hunter hasn't visited in more than five years. Hank's house is easy to find: it is the only one with yellow police tape surrounding the stone foundation of what used to be a house. Now just two charred walls still stand with blackened beams and no roof. The freestanding garage was damaged by the fire but had not burned down. Everything is remnants—objects that Hunter can't recall. Unfamiliar.

Throttling the bike down, he wheels off the driveway. Drives around the blackened ruin, over freshly spread red cedar mulch. Rolls to a stop. Turns his bike off. His boots press into the earth as he sits studying the place. The surrounding woods are silent and peaceful. Getting off the bike. Walking around. Glancing down the driveway, across the road to where his uncle's home stands. Leaving Nugget's bike behind, Hunter walks the driveway. Crosses the road, heads toward his uncle's house of brick and wood. Green boxwood in the beds around the entrance. Manicured yard, as uniform and weedless as Astroturf. A well-kept property.

Front curtains of a bay window move. Someone is eyeing Hunter before he gets to the porch to knock.

The front door opens, and his uncle David comes walking down the concrete steps. Gray hair, handlebar mustache, he stands nearly six feet two inches. Looks as though he is still pressing the iron. Still fit for his age. Approaches Hunter with arms spread wide.

"Goddamn, you're bigger than last time I seen you, Hunter. Guess you get good red meat over there in the Carolinas?"

Taking in the warmth of his uncle's embrace, patting his back. Releasing him, Hunter laughs. "Yeah. I can't complain."

"Where's your buddies?"

"Well, one is in Colorado. I hit a fucking bison."

"Say that again?"

"Yeah, a damn *buffalo*. Son of a bitch was in the road. Nugget stayed back to get my bike patched up and meet up after. Then had another situation in Utah. But Itch shouldn't be too far behind me. He's got your address in his GPS."

"Damn it, son, trouble seems to follow you."

"What I get for being a good Samaritan—well, *pretty* good Samaritan. I'll tell you all about it later."

"Well, get your bike. Park it over here and unload your gear, whatever you got. The guest rooms are ready for some company. Then we can talk, get you to the lawyer's office, get the documents signed."

There would be no funeral, only an urn. They had been waiting for Hunter. The estate was his. Everything. The home. The land. His father's savings, which were around a quarter million. He was a penny-pincher. Had always saved and invested. Lived simply but comfortably. He had paid for his own funeral arrangements years ago. But the way things are set up, nothing can be done or processed until the next of kin, Hunter, signs off in person. And there is the oddness of Hank's death.

After getting cleaned up and having a bite, Hunter joins David on the back deck, sitting at a wooden table with cushioned matching chairs, sipping Knob Creek bourbon. A second, empty glass sits waiting next to the bottle. David pours a finger. Slides the glass across the table to Hunter. Taking a sip and leaning back on the cushions. Hunter is beat. The alcohol relaxes him. Itch arrives, having homed in by GPS, and goes inside to clean up. He got everything straight with the cops. Hunter feels bad for the kid, Cory. He has nowhere to go. No place to stay.

David explains that the police and the fire marshal are stumped. They have no idea how the fire started. It is strange. It wasn't electrical, and there was no sign of an accelerant. No fuel other than the house itself and all its contents. It is as if a portal had opened up and created a fire and then erased all trace of its actions. Hunter's father had died of smoke inhalation. His body was discovered near the front door. He had not been shot, bludgeoned, stabbed, or poisoned. Hunter tries to imagine Hank's final days. His last minutes or hours. Asks David, "What did he do every day?"

"Kept to himself. He read a lot. He walked every day. Did these three- and four-mile hikes most days. He was active."

"Who'd he run around with? Friends?"

"Other than me, he didn't really keep company with strangers. He had a whole slew of gals he passed time with. And there was a new lady he'd been seeing. I never met her. Your dad was personal about his gals. And very respectful of all women. It's how we were raised. You know how your grandfather was about your grandmother."

Hunter does. You didn't speak ill of his grandmother unless you wanted a maul upside your head.

"When was the last time you spoke?"

"Day he died. He had a date or something. Stopped by afterwards. Went home. I worked out and went to sleep. Was woke up by the fire trucks that night."

Taking a sip of his bourbon, Hunter asks, "What did you guys talk about?"

"Not much. He'd just been out with this woman. They had some wine. A good steak. He was headed home to reread Dostoevsky's *The Possessed*."

There is no reason someone would burn his father's home down with him inside. And Hunter asks, "And no one knows who this woman was?"

"The cops are trying to figure it out. They've spoke with witnesses in town that saw your dad with her. It's like she was a ghost, or some shit."

Both men finish their drinks, and David asks. "Want another?"

"Please."

David refills their glasses. Slides the glass of bourbon back to Hunter. "I got something your father left for you."

Walking back into the house, he is gone for a minute. He comes back out and lays a square wooden box on the table.

"Your dad gave this to me months ago. Said that if anything ever happened to him, to give this to you."

"What's in it?"

"No idea. Never opened it. It's yours."

Taking the box in his hands, holding it, he wonders again what his father's last moments were like. Reading a book. Hunter runs his fingers over hardwood that had been sanded smooth and stained. The hinges are tarnished brass. It looks to have been handcrafted, not store-bought. It is about the size of a shoe box for work boots. A latch on the front keeps it closed. Hunter thumbs it and opens the box.

His uncle says, "You know, there was a string of strange house fires in Sicily back in 2003. They blamed a kid but said there was no way in hell he'd started all the fires. Something like ninety-two fires logged. Breaker boxes going up in flames for no reason. It was unheard of."

"No shit?" Hunter says. Inside the box, piles of photos are stacked, separated with paper clips. Some are Polaroids, some black and white, most of them with a string of sentences on the back. Information. Dates. Years. Places. Women with kids. Young to older. With his father. Names and birth dates.

And David asks, "Not trying to be nosey, but what'd he leave you?"

"Not sure. Stacks of photos with other women and children. Birth certificates."

Thumbing through all of them. Laying them on the table. His uncle starts looking at them. And Hunter says, "Other lives. These are other lives my father had. This a past I never knew about." Pausing, he looks at David, who seems really taken aback. And Hunter asks, "You know anything about any of this? Anyone look familiar?"

"No. You know, your father was always very private about women. I don't get this. This is kinda crazy—creepy, even. I mean, he was my brother, and it's like—"

"He had another life. A separate identity from what we knew."

"Reminds me," David says. "I got a photo I wanted you to have. Come across it a while back, was gonna send it to you. It's of you and your mother. At the hospital when you were born."

Hunter continues leafing through the photos until he gets to the bottom, the last picture. Trying to take all this in. It is a picture of Blake and Annie. "Son of a bitch."

David comes back and hands Hunter the photo of a woman holding a baby. "Who's this?" Hunter asks.

Chuckling, David says, "Told you. That's you and your mother at the hospital before you went home."

Hunter is lost. The woman holding him is different from the woman he remembers from his childhood. What little he could remember is different from the photos his father had kept for him.

"You sure this is my mother?"

"Yeah, I remember them dating and getting married. I was there when you were born."

"I've never seen this lady before."

"What? Didn't your dad have wedding pictures or birth pictures?"

"Come to think of it, no. I mean, growing up, there was a woman who I was told was my mother. There were pictures of them together, but no birth pictures. And none of this woman here."

This is too much to take in. Hunter's father dying in a mysterious house fire. Dating or seeing a woman no one knew anything about. This box of pictures, and now Hunter doesn't even know who his mother was. But he has these pictures of people. People he can hunt down. Speak with. Start putting names and faces together—figure out who his father really was. What he'd been hiding all these years.

"Hunter, I'm sorry," his uncle says. "You know I was absent

for a few years out on the Louisiana fishing line. Gone for long stretches pulling in those red snappers and speckled trout. Not sure what your father was up to. This is crazy."

Later, phoning Olivia, he tells her what he's discovered and that it will be a while before he comes back home. It seems he has a bigger journey ahead of him: finding his real mother and whoever killed his father.

JACK

A man with three days of stubble and an AK-47 leads Jack from his room, down a stone-floored hallway, through a sunroom full of exotic plantings, to the courtyard he saw earlier from his window. Now he stands before a feast. A table big enough to play Ping-Pong on is laden with grilled steaks, sausage on a bed of white rice and black beans topped with fried eggs. Sliced avocados, fried plantain with sweet cream, cornmeal flatbread. A mound of buñuelos—ball-shaped fritters of cassava and white cheese. Sliced wagyu roast. Candied sweet potatoes, fresh strawberries, papaya, and cherimoya. Red wine. Everything Jack loves to eat lies spread out before him.

At the other end of the table sits the bronze-skinned man with wavy black hair who hunted him down and brought him here. A man Jack doesn't know.

"Please, help yourself, Jack. And have a seat," the man tells him. He is wearing a silky shirt and more gold rings than he has fingers.

Seeing all this excess after being among people without even the basic necessities of life, Jack is confused. Shaded by the thick canopy of a rubber tree, he takes a clay plate, forks a steak onto it, picks up the carving knife, and slices off a hunk of roast. Spoons some potatoes and rice and plantains. Fills a wooden bowl with salad, pours a glass of wine. Sitting back down, he asks himself, *How is this fair?* After seeing all he has seen. All the lives of struggle, women and children living off so little.

Jack's perception is split—one side with guilt, the other with want and hunger.

Unrolling a large burgundy cloth napkin, Jack places it on his thigh, takes the fork and knife and cuts into the steak. Blood and juice run from the meat. It is two inches thick. A real slab. Taking the chunk of beef into his mouth, he savors it. It's as good a piece of meat as he has ever tasted.

From the other end of the table, the man tells him, "Jack, you are like the drug lord without drugs. What you've built. What you came from."

"I came from a world of struggle. But somewhere, I forgot about my roots. Who I was," Jack tells him, chewing his steak, reveling in the texture and the glorious taste. Jack tells the man, "I was never introduced to you. I never got your name."

Smiling. The man's mouth forms a cold and mirthless grin. "Where are my manners? Call me Sebastián." Putting a piece of cherimoya into his mouth, he chews the creamy white fruit slowly. He tells Jack, "You know, you remind me of Pablo Escobar. The son of a farmer and a teacher. Starts out his life of crime selling fake diplomas, then making report cards. Genius, no? He came from little and created an empire worthy of the Incas."

"He also stole cars," says Jack. "Tombstones. But I never partook in any of those types of actions. Nothing even remotely similar."

"Ah, you know of his story. No, but you came from little or nothing, only relied upon hard work. Your hard early life prepared you."

Forgetting his manners, Jack speaks with his mouth full. "By the midseventies, Escobar had established an organization that would become the Medellín cartel. Are you saying his cartel was like me building my company?"

"Yes. Something similar. Different means to a similar end. He ruled the cocaine trade. Made so much coin, he used it for fire—heated his home with legal tender and still never went broke. He had planes. He had houses. He was a provider. A man before his time. The two of you share the same ethic for work and the same passion to succeed."

Tearing into the bread, Jack revels in the joy of eating. It is the first good food he has had in weeks, and his senses are on overload. He swallows and says, "But Escobar was a drug lord."

Sebastián says, "In this part of the world, you don't have many options if you want to be comfortable. You take the path that is sometimes risky."

Jack's business head, his philosophy to succeed, kicks in and he says, "A person's choices dictate their future. Create where they find themselves. What they are doing. How they'll react. And what their next choice will be." He thinks of Carlos. His family. Choosing to be a farmer. Making coca paste. The man's choices were limited by his surroundings, by those who ruled around him.

"A synergy," Sebastián says. Then he stands, holding a news-paper. He approaches Jack. "See here." Unfolding it, offering it to Jack, who wipes his hands on the napkin in his lap. Looking at the paper. On the cover, a headline: FORTUNE 500 MOGUL BUYS TICKET AND DISAPPEARS IN SOUTH AMERICA. The subhead below reads, "Friends and Company Worried, in Search."

"That's you," he says, setting the paper on the table.

Jack looks at his plate of food, ignores the paper. "I don't care," he says. "I don't want to be found."

Sebastián walks back to the other end of the table, sits back down. "Why?" he asks. "You're a very popular man. Powerful."

"I don't wish to be. I don't want it. I want to disappear."

"Why?"

"Because I have no one. Money means shit without my wife, my daughter. My mother. Without my family."

Swirling the wine around in his glass, Sebastián inhales the bouquet, then takes a drink. "Family? You could remarry. Create a new one. Shit, you could *buy* another if you wanted."

"It wouldn't be real. Wouldn't have any substance."

"Substance? Why do you need substance? You came to South America, Jack. What were you running from? Death? You're a man who has a lot of power. What more could you want?"

Jack feels a surge of anger. And he asks, "Do you know what I've been through? Where I've been? Struggling to exist in conditions I never even knew existed, let alone encountered."

His host looks amused. "You're funny, Jack," he says. "This is my country. I was born into struggle. I used to be a farmer's kid myself, much like Escobar. I looked up to him. Then, to break away from my parents, I became a delivery man. Then a *sicario*, and now a leader. A boss. I can't feel compassion for you, Jack. I can only admire what you built. Please. You're what, sixty? And never suffered like me until now. Is that it? Ha! Please. You have the business smarts, but not the savagery to survive real strife. That do-or-die mentality. I thought, with all you've done, your roots of being raised by a struggling single mother. What you built, you could be like the great cocaine baron of Colombia. Pablo Escobar, only in an alternate universe, in an educated manner."

Jack is not seeing it in that same distorted, fragmented light—words and views twisted to fit Sebastián's agenda. And Jack tells him, "All that Escobar did for his people, his family, was create grief and misery."

"Jack, how can you say that?"

"Because I know what I did for my family. My wife, my kids. I wasn't there for them. I worked all my life for money. More and more of it. And in the end, it was for nothing. Now they're gone, and I have no one. *Nada.*"

Taking a small black box from his breast pocket, Sebastián opens it and pulls out a cigarette. Lights it. Inhales and blows smoke. "Cry, cry, cry. You're swimming in self-pity, my friend. A victim mentality. Look at what you've survived in South America. We tracked you. You want companionship. You could buy all the women you want. I can introduce you to a harem of beauties. Untouched."

"That's not love."

"Love? Love only bleeds you of worth. Distorts your discipline. Your emotions. Confuses the soul. You make bad decisions when you rely upon love. Was it love that helped you build your company?"

"At first, it was—the love of wanting to succeed."

"And you did. And had you not, your family wouldn't have lived in the comfort they had. Regardless, I'm sending you back to your people, Jack. Back to *los Estados Unidos.*"

"I don't want to go back."

"Look, your economy supports my trade. Your people reached out to me. I'm returning the favor. Your people miss you. Finish your supper. Freshen up, and then I'm getting you to my contacts, who will get you to Panama to meet your people in Guatemala."

"I'm not going."

"Oh, Jack, don't make this exchange difficult."

The smoke-black Mercedes G550 4×4, covered in road dust, pushes through the crowds that spill out into the road. A chain of bodies stretching hundreds of miles. Fleeing oppression. Seeing all these migrants through the car's tinted windows, Jack decides. Freedom means not being found.

He says, "I need to piss. Really bad."

"You're gonna have to hold it," the driver says.

"I've been holding it."

The man in the front passenger seat says, "We're not moving. Let him out. We could all use to stretch our legs. Get some air."

Getting out, the driver nods toward some trees. "Over there."

Studying the area and the movement of the pedestrians, Jack nods back, heads to the left side of the road. Sweating, he works his way through the swarm of people. Gets to a tree. His heart rate picks up as he contemplates what he is about to do. He starts to piss. In his peripheral vision, he sees the driver turn away. If they catch him, will they kill him? What does it matter? It's Jack's life. His choice. He doesn't want to go back. It is now or never. He sidles around the tree, runs down an embankment.

A voice behind him yells, "Hey! Get back here!"

The driver tries to chase him. Jack runs forward and digs back up the hill and into the crowd. The driver's voice fades behind him as he loses himself amid brown men in ragged dungarees and women in blue ponchos and bowler hats. Jack blends and shuffles his way into the mass of bodies. Into the caravan. Feels their energy. Their freedom. Keeps moving and bumping through the mass of bodies. Heart beating in his throat, he smiles. Just keeps moving. Doesn't know where he'll go. All he knows is that as long as he keeps going forward, he'll be free. Have purpose. A choice.

He runs. And he doesn't look back.

ANNE

Catching out, they run from a tree line through weeds wet with early-morning dew. Eyeing the cars, calculating which one to hop up onto. Reaching and pulling themselves up, one by one, helping each other. Breathing hard. Sweating, they lie in another empty boxcar. Everyone is hungover on adrenaline. Drunk on high adventure and the freedom of not being tied to a job. To school. To abuse or authority. Trot, Canary, and the twins sit with their backs to the car's back wall, looking out at the world flitting past them.

Anne lies with her head in Cinnamon's lap. Cinnamon telling her, "Lucky. We're all lucky. Riding twice in an open car."

The sound and feel of the car bumping over the tracks. Steel on steel. The heavy clatter of working metal becomes the normal rhythm, almost pleasant. It is their lullaby and their soundtrack.

Soon, the others have dosed off. Sleeping like the dead. The smell of dirt fields outside seems to draw smiles over sleeping faces. The smiles disappear as two men shake them awake. Shadowed faces. One is younger, one older. No expressions. Traveling with them are two girls. Mascara running like painted eyes, unhappy joker faces, mimes performing outdoors in a big city. But these girls are more than unhappy joker faces.

"Abducted," Cinnamon whispers to Anne.

Before anyone knows what is happening, Trot rushes one of the men. He is a big slab of a man, like a Texas steer. He gives Trot a pounding. Brandishes a knife. Stabs him in the gut. Anne screams, "No!" Scrabbles in her backpack.

The pistol. Where is the fucking pistol?

The outside world rushes by. Eyes wild, Canary pulls the twins tight to her chest to shield their faces from what is happening. Trot lies on the hardwood floor, arms pressed to his gut. Doubled over on his side. Blood spilling and dampening everything. Himself leaking away.

The two abducted girls scream and cry. The men are beasts. Savages. Predatory and uncaring. Looking closer, she watches them morphing; their faces are now those of Anne's sisters from Tennessee. And they're crying, asking Anne, "Why did you leave us?"

The men come at Cinnamon, only to morph as well. Their features lose their shadows. One of them is Anne's father. The other is not a man; it's her brother. He is laughing. Anne keeps digging frantically in her pack. Her father and brother tower over Anne and Cinnamon now. There are no words. The entire car is a ball of violent energy. Cinnamon screams, "Smugglers! You're fucking smugglers, sex traffickers!"

"No!" Anne screams. "It's my family."

Her father slaps Cinnamon. Then he slaps Anne. She still digs. Looks up at her sisters. *Abducted.* How they look. Drugged. Half out of their minds but aware they've been kidnapped. Anne feels the cold steel. Pulls it from her pack. And her father smiles. "*There's my fucking gun,*" he says.

Her brother says, "Her thieving ass stole it. Just like she stole your money."

Suddenly, the scene starts to come apart. The train derails. Cars are coming off the track in an impossibly loud eruption of noise. Metal crashing, twisting, and exploding. Anne feels a rush of air in her lungs. Her eyes fly open. And she sits up, panting. Everyone is asleep. Everyone except Cinnamon.

"Whoa. You okay?"

"Men," she says. Looking around. "Girls. They abducted two girls. My sisters. My dad and my brother."

"Honey, you were dreaming."

Getting her bearings straight. Her breathing slows back to normal. "It felt so real."

"Dreams do that sometimes," Anne tells her. "But mostly, they're trying to tell us something about what we fear."

"My family."

"What about them?"

"It's what I fear. It's where I came from. All I ever knew. It's how I got here." Anne pauses, her mind moving a mile a minute. "I want to create a project."

"A project?"

"Yeah, I don't want any more bad things to happen to good people—no more Dredds to pull others into a slave-like existence."

"We already kinda help others," Cinnamon said. "Leaving messages and word of mouth for others we encounter."

"It's not enough. I was lucky to meet you."

"I understand what you're saying, but—"

"No. We don't break up our family. We help others create other families. Teach them to bond and to love. They don't have to be part of some dictatorship, some cult-like group. They'd be free and work together to create their own family."

Cinnamon reaches for her and kisses her.

"So young and full of want. Thirsty for community, for knowledge. We can do whatever you want."

"I'm serious."

"So am I. We can do whatever you want."

Adrenaline and endorphins pulse through Anne as she and Cinnamon sit watching the world go by outside the open boxcar door. This is her freedom, her family. And she can help others discover the same, until the day comes when she no longer can.

Frank Bill is the author of the novel *Donnybrook,* now a major motion picture; the short story collection *Crimes in Southern Indiana,* one of *GQ* magazine's favorite books of 2011 and a *Daily Beast* best debut of 2011; and *The Savage.* He lives and writes in Southern Indiana.